summer
we came to
life

Deborah Cloyed lives in Los Angeles, in Humphrey Bogart's old room with a view. As a photographer, travel writer or curious nomad, she's previously resided in London, Barcelona, Thailand, Honduras, Kenya and New York City. She's travelled to twenty other countries besides, several as a contestant—with her childhood best friend—on CBS's *The Amazing Race*. She runs a photography school for kids and is happily at work on her next book.

DEBORAH CLOYED

the summer we came to life

MIRA

MIRA is a registered trademark of Harlequin Enterprises Limited, used under licence.

Published in Great Britain 2012
MIRA Books, an imprint of Harlequin (UK) Limited,
Eton House, 18-24 Paradise Road,
Richmond, Surrey, TW9 1SR

© Deborah Cloyed 2011

ISBN 978 1 848 45101 8

54-0612

MIRA's policy is to use papers that are natural, renewable and recyclable products and made from wood grown in sustainable forests. The logging and manufacturing processes conform to the legal environmental regulations of the country of origin.

Printed and bound by
CPI Group (UK) Ltd, Croydon, CR0 4YY

To Bianca, the kind of best friend
who makes you want to write a book about best friends.

To my mother, my first editor, to all my family
(including *mi segunda madre* and my own unlikely family),
who have guided and accompanied me through
this world of love, loss, and above all, laughter.

To The West Clovernook Society and women everywhere
who laugh, dine, and empathise while going about
their way of making the world a better place.

To Fran and Emily, whose belief in me changed everything.

To Jonathan. Yes, definitely to him.

not
~~CHAPTER~~

1

BIRTH AND DEATH ARE THE TWO OCCUR-
rences in a person's life that seem to say one thing: we are
not the ones calling the shots. "The only consolations are
love and best friends." That's what Mina told me two days
before she died.

This much is true—June 25, a Friday, in the summer of
2010, we were alive—me, Kendra and Isabel—and Mina
had been gone six months.

I was renting an apartment in Tegucigalpa, Honduras,
until my "artist in residence" began at the university. It
had been planned for a year. I remember thinking I would
have to cancel it in order to spend time with Mina in her
final days. But the doctor's estimates were generous, and

her death left me instead with six months to wander or languish. I chose to wander, as per usual.

After the funeral and the long, unanchored days that followed, I took a friend up on an offer to stay with her in Paris. That's where I met Remy. Remy Badeau—Parisian bad-boy film director. I welcomed the whirlwind he provided with open arms. It distracted me from the pile of dead leaves I would have been otherwise.

Summer came faster than expected, like it always does. But for once, the surprise solstice wasn't gleeful.

For the first time since we were little girls, there would be no summer vacation with Isabel and Kendra and their mothers, Jesse and Lynette. Mina and I, both motherless, had struck a cozy balance with the mother-daughter pairs. And every summer the six of us took off for some exotic locale for a week of laughter and memory making. But now what would I be except a pathetic fifth wheel? It was bad enough going from a circle of four to a tottering triangle. Maybe if life had been sold to me as a tricycle, but I thought I'd bought an ATV. No more Mina, no more vacations. But wasn't my life like one big vacation, an escape from responsibility?

I already felt guilty enough about the laughing.

In the six months following the funeral, I was continually ashamed by my residual tendency to laugh. At the fruit stand. In the shower. On the metro. I'm the type that shares conspiratorial giggles with children. I flirt with old men. I laugh at myself when I stub my toe.

But grief hacks away at the soul, leaving only vestiges

of your self behind. So every time I chuckled with Parisian strangers, I felt guilt like a dropkick to the sternum. It created many an awkward silence when my smile snuffed out, catching them in the laugh like a Peeping Tom in a flashbulb. Sometimes they shuddered as if a chill had found its way into the smoggy city. Then they looked at me with pity. Europeans are good at spotting the haunted.

So, that's when Remy proposed, when I was practicing not to laugh anymore. He proposed on the day before I left Honduras, in a hasty manner that smelled of panic, with a ring he said he would upgrade after my return.

I said yes, because saying no was too final, and had too many immediate consequences. I said yes because I wondered if it would fill me with genuine lingering laughter. I said yes to cloak the fact that I had failed to fulfill my best friend's dying request.

Now I had to figure out if I really intended to marry him.

CHAPTER

1

SO, ON A FRIDAY, JUNE 25, I WAS ROLLER-skating around my Tegucigalpa apartment, watching the sun set beyond the sliding glass doors, watching the golden light transform the grimy city into a shiny postcard. First thing I'd done when I arrived was move all the furniture into the bedrooms along with my rolled-up canvases and camera gear. The floors were just like a high school cafeteria, providing a flat expanse to soothe my bumpy thoughts.

Roller-skating was my therapy. You had to give the body something to entertain itself with so the mind could tackle all that metaphysical, esoteric, life-decision stuff bouncing around between the ear canals.

I was almost thirty. Why is it that just before thirty the carefree blur of your life stops and you hear an unfamiliar voice you identify as your grown-up self ask: *Aren't you getting too old for this?* And I don't think the voice was just talking about the roller-skating.

Hey, I was on the track to normalcy and respectable overachievement once upon a time. I graduated from Yale in Physics. Ask me how many of my classmates were lanky redheaded females. I had both feet pointed toward graduate school when I decided to spend six months backpacking Eastern Europe instead. I took a camera. Turns out I took to the artist/gypsy life like a baby to his first taste of sugar. Or like Isabel to social causes. Or Kendra to a six-figure salary in the fashion industry. Besides, Mina was the one meant to be an academic.

I rolled to a stop, near a gold journal on the floor. When the final diagnosis was in, Mina started three journals, one for each of the girls. Mine was a team effort, an earnest plan to contact each other after her death. I moved back in with my dad in the D.C. suburb where we all grew up, and stuck to Mina like Elmer's. My job was to compile all the physics—translating everything I could find about consciousness and death into laymen's terms for Mina. Her entries came from the heart. We passed the journal back and forth between visits, and spent most every afternoon discussing, forming our plan. In this way—as the maple tree outside her window set its leaves on fire then shook them to the ground—we spent the days, the hours, and the last minutes of Mina's life like we'd spent the twenty-four years prior—laughing, crying, and together.

When she died, I read the journal over and over, obsessively trying all the ways we'd devised for me to contact her, with no results beyond excruciating sobbing fits. I felt silly and naive, totally unprepared for the weight of real grief.

In Paris, I eventually abandoned the rituals. And by Honduras, I'd begun to read the journal like the I Ching—pose a question and flip to a random page for the answer. My questions varied from day to day. Where should I go next? Is it time to give up on my dreams? Why did you have to die?

I reached down and untied the roller skates. I picked up the journal and headed out to the balcony. "Isn't Gmail more practical?" I'd chided Mina, but she wanted something tangible, something that "would last." I touched the antiqued cover and had a vision of growing old with that journal, my arthritic hands resting atop the thinning pages. It gave me the chills. One deep breath and I placed my right hand flat like a plaintiff, squeezed shut my eyes, and added my voice to the din of Tegucigalpa:

"Mina, should I really marry Remy?"

When my thumb settled on a page, I opened my eyes.

October 17
Mina

Love is not inevitable, Samantha, like you seem to believe. It is a gift. It is the thing that wraps you up like a plush bathrobe to insulate you against cold, illness, and all of life's indecencies. It is the thing that makes you less naked in the mirror of reality. It blankets you. It warms you. It saves you. No, that last part is a lie. It doesn't save you. My father loved my mother from birth and she died anyway. And now me...

Today, I planned to write about how grateful I am for the love you three have drenched me in. But I confess I am feeling sorry for myself instead.

And I am preoccupied with the question: Does love last?

Otherwise, how else would you describe what is left when a person dies and leaves you behind? Look at my father. I know you see him as cold and brittle, but that's because he hides inside himself, clinging to the embers of my mother's love.

He came into my room last night and fed me crumbs about her, tiny things really, but details I'd been begging for my whole life—how she wore her hair, how she smelled, how she laughed. And when he went off to bed, I felt a warm buzzing cloud hanging in the room, just the same as when you and I laugh hysterically and then fall silent. It's love that hangs in the air, lingers in the world around us. Love is what lasts.

But, maybe...

Maybe love is less of a gift and more of a distraction from an ugly truth: in the end we die alone. That is the truth, isn't it?

And it is the living's love for the dead that lingers, not the other way around.

So, when I die, I'm taking nothing with me, and leaving nothing behind.

Our "research" is going nowhere, right? It's all websites for crazies and desperate rich widows. I'm one of them, aren't I? Desperate to believe that somehow I can still enter a world I am unfairly being asked to exit.

P.S. Sam, I'm sorry. I'm never entirely myself after the chemo. Love is real and it's all there is. You love so much easier than the rest of us, and you're the easiest thing in the world to love. I'm sure you've got yourself a man and I'm sure he's wonderful. Don't get sidetracked by my bitter ramblings. Don't listen to Isabel's cynicism or Kendra's fairy-tale nonsense. Love isn't perfect, but it's all there is.

I snapped shut the journal and laughed—a foreign sound in my ears. I kept laughing until my eyes watered with tears. Firmly, I told myself to simmer down; forced my ears to open to the sound of the traffic, the garble of one million people going doggedly about their lives below. I leaned over the rusty railing to peer down on the city.

Structures of every kind—body shops, gasolineras, pupuserias, makeshift beauty salons—spread out and snaked around lumpy, haphazard neighborhoods. The poorest inhabitants got pushed up the sides of the mountains, where they'd built shantytowns out of scrap metal and concrete. The shantytowns now ironically occupied the choicest real estate free of charge.

I smiled, but with the bitterness of orange rinds. I saw

in the city a metaphor for much of how I'd lived my life. I saw good intentions and big dreams and spurts of real accomplishment. But I saw them all thwarted by sudden twists and setbacks, restlessness, and reckless jumps into uncharted territory.

I went inside to get my camera and tripod.

Click went the shutter, and I closed my eyes and listened to the city's soundtrack. Men cheered goals in open-air sports bars. Children played pickup games of kickball on dusty back roads. Mariachis cued up their first love songs of the night, unfazed by the harmonies of chickens and stray dogs. Click, and I opened my eyes.

My art combined photographs on canvas with drawings, oil paint and text. I'd had small shows in six major cities around the world, as I bounced about traveling, but never real, lasting success. My Artist Statement said I combined different mediums to "explore connections between nature, people and emotion—looking for meaning in synthesis." Right then My Life Statement would have branded me jumbled and disconnected.

"What if I'm losing it?" I asked the sun and the birds and the one million residents of Tegucigalpa.

And then my phone rang.

2

"NO, ISABEL, IT WOULD BE LIKE ROLLER-skating over her grave."

I glanced down at my pink roller skates and regretted the comparison. But no way were we resurrecting the vacation club.

"Samantha, I need you. I already told my work I'm taking the time off. You have over a week till the residency. I looked at flights—"

"No. I'm here anytime you need to talk to me. But I need to be alone."

There was a silence, a distinctly disapproving pause.

"Sam, what're you doing? Huh? You just disappeared on us. Paris? Honduras? And now you told a man you would marry him—a man none of us have even met? I'm coming."

I dug my nails into my palm. "I don't *want* you to come. I know that makes me a jerk. But I need to think. And I can't just sit around and laugh and drink and make everything into a vacation. Not anymore."

"It's not like that. You need us—"

"I'm sorry. I have to call you back."

I hung up my iPhone and sent it sailing across the gritty floor. Slumping down against the wall, my body slid in tandem with the tears.

I *was* losing it. And I didn't have to ask one million Hondurans to know it.

Could Isabel really not get how *abominable* it would be to vacation without Mina? It wasn't the first time we'd broached the subject. After the funeral, when I was packing for France, I assumed it a nonissue, but both Kendra and Isabel mused about a summer trip in her memory, reminiscing how Mina always loved Paris. How could they not see it as a betrayal? Why didn't they understand that without Mina, everything was irrevocably different?

But I knew why.

I ran my fingers along my scalp and looked out at the night sky over my latest hometown. The stars were mostly obscured—by smog, by lights, by all the aggregate effects of human inhabitance—just like that night in Paris, the summer before we left for college.

Isabel's mother, Jesse, found a great apartment for rent in the bohemian neighborhood of Montmartre, and we arrived in July to a charming albeit sweltering abode bearing fuzzy wallpaper.

We had a longstanding tradition for the first night, what we playfully called The Opening Ceremony. We cooked a meal together and christened our new temporary home with a night of dancing, storytelling and laughter. It was supposed to remind us that the traveling was important but the company was what really mattered.

That first night in Paris, the sweaty kitchen was already overcrowded by Isabel, Kendra and their two moms. Mina and I took off to explore the apartment complex, and stumbled upon a door that led to the roof.

The view was so breathtaking we both gripped the railing and gasped theatrically at the same time, which made us burst out laughing.

"We are some lucky bastards," I said.

Mina shook her head and chuckled. I remember exactly how she looked, lit up by the tangled string of lights dangling behind her. Her hair—that I was infinitely and eternally jealous of—dark, full and shiny, no taming or wrestling necessary. And only she could wear a cotton skirt and a T-shirt and look glamorous.

She didn't answer, I remember. She looked away and down, snagged by a sound from below. The apartment was directly beneath us. With the windows wide-open, voices drifted up lazily, without much gusto. But at that moment the crescendo of mothers and daughters roaring in laughter had rushed over us.

"Are we?" Mina said, asking the few stars that had wriggled free of the city haze as much as she was asking me. "Are we so lucky?"

I put my hand on Mina's shoulder. I'd let the stars

answer. Mina's mother died in a car accident when she was eight months' pregnant. Her whole life, Mina heard what a miracle it was she was born at all. But it's hard to hold on to gratitude for a lifetime. Especially when it feels more like loss.

It's kind of like the balls of candy wrapper foil Lynette, Kendra's mother, kept for each of us on her windowsill. Every holiday we added a layer, Lynette's version of tick marks on a doorframe. Mina was like that about her mother. She just kept adding to a ball of mismatched feelings, wrapping layers as the years passed.

My mother bailed on my dad and me. It provided an iron stratum of anger that prevented feeling much of anything else about her.

Mina always knew what I was thinking. At that moment, on a rooftop in Paris, without even a glance at my hardening face, she put her hand over mine.

"We are lucky bastards."

On a cold, hard floor in Tegucigalpa, I looked down at my empty hands lying in my lap, then up at my empty apartment in the middle of nowhere. And then I cried as loud as I wanted. There was nobody to hear.

October 27
Samantha

Our research is not "going nowhere." We'll just dig deeper.

The essential problem, Mina, is this:

Nobody knows what consciousness is or exactly how it arises and functions.

Scientists don't really have a clue what's happening at a fundamental level of reality. They have fancy equations that explain everything from particle interaction to black holes, but the "how" is linguistically and conceptually challenging, to say the least.

Light really *does* behave as both a wave and a particle. Matter and energy *are* interchangeable. Particles really *can* influence each other at opposite ends of the earth instantaneously. A single electron *does* somehow go through two holes at once to interfere with *itself*.

It is the "how" of envisioning such things, and the metaphysical implications, that are disturbing.

Or encouraging.

Mina, this is gonna work. I promise I'll find you.

Sleep tight.

—*Sam.*

CHAPTER

3

I WOKE UP THE NEXT MORNING TO THE sound of fluttering pages. I wrested my heavy head from the air mattress in pursuit of the source.

Mina's journal lay open, its pages oscillating. I watched it for a second, mesmerized, then smacked it still and dragged it over.

But then I couldn't help thumbing through the pages myself, touching Mina's elegant script and grinning sheepishly at my surplus of graphs and exclamation points. Page after page I read the words I'd read a thousand times. *Luv, Sam. Always, Mina. I'll find you. Promise me.*

In the margins were notes I'd added after her death, next to specific tasks we'd planned. I landed on a page from October, where I'd rambled on about Amit Goswami's *Physics of the Soul* and consciousness. I'd boldly listed methods of communication Goswami mentioned. The first thing on the list was automatic writing.

I closed the journal.

I lay back on the air mattress and clenched and unclenched my hands at my sides. My mind drifted to a night in my second month in Paris. I watched myself slip out of bed, leaving Remy snoring upon his Egyptian cotton sheets, and walk onto his balcony in the middle of the night. High above the rain-soaked streets, I watched my shaky hand hover over a blank page in the journal, willing every part of my soul to disband or vibrate or do whatever it was supposed to do to connect with Mina's. I envisioned her—down to the tiny scar on her cheekbone. I conjured her seven different ways of laughing. I replayed our favorite memories. Then I brushed away every sound and image like sweeping a storefront, and waited.

I didn't even realize I was sobbing until Remy appeared like a ghost on the balcony. When our eyes met, it would be hard to say who was more startled. Without a word, he took off the plush bathrobe he was wearing and wrapped it tight around my shoulders. Then, with a cooing "silly girl," he took the journal and the pen away, and led me back to bed.

The air mattress protested as I lifted my arms and hugged myself. I had no desire whatsoever to roller-skate that day.

And then my phone rang.

"ET TU, JESSE?" I QUIPPED, HOPING IT WOULD make me sound less like the puddle of misery I was that morning. Isabel's mother had absolutely no tolerance for misery.

"Samantha, get that tush o' yours out of bed this instant!" She took a loud slurp of something for emphasis, and I imagined a mocha frappuccino.

"Jesse—"

"Don't Jesse me, sister, get out your calendar and tell me if you prefer Monday or Tuesday."

"I don't get it."

"We're comin', honey. All of us."

I sat up so fast my butt smacked the floor through the air mattress. "What? Didn't you talk to Isabel?"

"You bet I did. And Kendra and her mama, too. If ever there was a need for a Honduran vacation, this is it, kiddo."

"Are you talking about *this* Monday and Tuesday?"

"Yup and yup."

"Um, no and no. And I'm done discussing it, so please don't plan on calling in any more reinforcements."

"Well," Jesse said, and slurped, "just so happens I've considered your reservations in advance and have called in *new* reinforcements to address 'em. The boys are comin', too."

The journal's cover flipped open again next to the bed, a breeze shuffling through the first few pages. "What boys?"

"What boys do you think? Cornell and Arshan."

The thought of Kendra's and Mina's fathers joining in on the already unwelcome festivities made my jaw clench in indignation.

"Sorry, Jesse." I was shaking. "I have to call you back."

I shut the journal and shoved it under the air mattress.

I paced the stuffy room until I was sure I was suffocating. My phone read noon when I hauled myself out onto the balcony. The city was in full gear, engines chugging along clogged streets, shouts of every emotion fighting to be heard. I looked at my phone. How was I going to fix this? How could I explain? Could I really tell them *I don't fit anymore? You're not my real family. My life's a mess. I don't want you to see me like this. I failed Mina just like I'm failing at everything else.*

Halfway to the railing, my foot scraped across something soft and scratchy at the same time. I froze in trepidation. *Please don't be a squished tarantula, please don't be—*

A curling red and yellow maple leaf bolted out from under my toes, so sudden I dropped my phone while bounding after it, just barely rescuing the leaf from a nosedive over the edge.

I pinched the leaf by its stem in between my thumb and forefinger and stared at it as if I'd found a diamond ring in my salad bowl. Not willing to risk the slightest breeze, I held it fast against my chest before leaning forward to peer in every direction around the balcony. Barely any trees at all, and certainly no autumn maple trees like the ones in Virginia outside Mina's window. I gripped the balcony with one hand to steady myself as I gasped aloud. Then I burst out laughing.

Holding the leaf up to the sun, I wept and laughed simultaneously like a hurricane survivor—juggling hope and grief inside a single human heart. The leaf was a labyrinth of glowing gold and amber veins. The way they were lit up, they looked like crisscrossing canals or waterways. Like the routes of ships. Or airplanes.

I picked up my phone, pressed the call button and listened to it ring.

"Tuesday will be just fine."

CHAPTER

5

SO, TWO DAYS LATER, MONDAY EVENING, after I'd done all the shopping and arranged the rental cars, and talked to my sole Honduran friend, Ana Maria, about renting her uncle's beach house, the vacation club, freshly reorganized, was packing bags in Virginia. Minus Isabel. She was already en route.

Jesse Brighton, Isabel's mother, picked up the gift—a deck of cards with a little red bow—from her nightstand. A glitter of a tear appeared at the corner of her eye. Jesse wiped it with the back of her hand, not worried about smearing her black eyeliner. It was tattooed on—a service Jesse offered at her beauty salons. She set the cards back

down and clasped her hands together, her scarlet acrylic
nails pressing into her tan skin. After all this time, she
might actually be falling for someone. *The Cranky Professor,* no less, Jesse thought and chuckled at the frowning
visage of her neighbor and bridge partner, Arshan Bahrami. Jesse put a hand to her throat and felt her fluttery
pulse. It wasn't the world's most romantic gift—the new
cards commemorated their winning streak in bridge. But
he'd said yes to coming on the trip, just as soon as she'd
asked him.

Jesse clapped her hands together and shook her butt in
her leopard pajamas. She looked back to the bed, where
her red suitcase perched like a treasure chest longing for
booty. Jesse pumped up the stereo and Michael sang his
heart out about Billie Jean. She reset herself to "packing,"
by which Jesse meant dancing around the bed, picking
up an item—lace panties, a beach cover-up, a container
of Texas RedEye Bloody Mary Mix—and tossing it into
the suitcase. She paused and looked around the room for
anything else she might be forgetting.

An itemization of Jesse Brighton's bedroom would produce a most befuddling mix of clues about a woman's
life. A picture of her daughter, Isabel, hung next to the
Don't Mess with Texas sign and an original Dali, next to
a framed poster of an eighteen-year-old Jesse on a 1975
cover of Vogue. Jesse leaped up and kissed the photo of
Isabel and then of herself, before plopping down on the
bed. She pulled a gold lamé stiletto out from under her as
she dialed Lynette's number. Lynette could decide which

swimsuits Jesse should bring now that you know who was coming. Jesse sighed. How to hide the ravages of time?

Jesse was about to hang up when Lynette picked up on the fourth ring.

"The Chanel one-piece or the Christian Dior bikini? Which one do you think makes my ass look less like a wrinkled elephant?"

"Jesse, I can't talk. I'll call you in a bit."

"Why? Ooohhh—"

"I'm hanging up."

Jesse looked at the clock. "Nookie Night! Are you doing that thing? From Cosmo? That lucky dog—"

A man's voice from the background bellowed, "She'll call you later, Jesse!"

"'Bye, Jess," Lynette said, and laughed her throaty Kathleen Turner laugh.

Lynette Jones set down the phone and looked at herself in the mirror. She smoothed down the nurse's costume that had arrived in the mail in an unmarked brown envelope. Who would've thought a size large would ever be too small on Lynette Jones? *That's why you married a black man, honey*, her husband always said when she cursed the scale. *We appreciate extra curves.* Lynette wouldn't be sorry to have a few less curves to haul around, but make no mistake, Kendra's mother would always be beautiful. Lynette smoothed her shaggy blond bob and made her mirror face—that puckered Pamela Anderson look all women make at themselves in the mirror. Then she spun around to face her husband.

"Are you ready for your exam, Mr. Jones?"

Cornell was lying on the bed in his boxer shorts and favorite argyle socks. He was tied to the bed frame with some of Lynette's pantyhose. It was number three on *Cosmo*'s most recent "Spice up Your Sex Life" list. She bought it at the grocery store when they had the Saturday special on scallops. Of course, *Cosmo* mentioned black lace thigh-highs, not the control-top hose Lynette used to hide her varicose veins. And the socks were a modification, as well. But Cornell had insisted: "You know my feet get cold, baby. Bad circulation."

Cornell answered, in an overdone baritone, "Yes, Nurse Jones," making his big belly jiggle like chocolate pudding in an earthquake. Lynette pursed her lips to stifle a giggle, and sauntered over to her husband as best a lady could manage in white patent leather.

Lynette stepped around the suitcases and perched herself on the edge of the bed. She wasn't exactly sure what to do next. She decided to use the stethoscope and creaked onto all fours atop Cornell. As she bent over, a boob flopped out of the costume. Lynette harrumphed as if gravely offended. Once upon a time, she'd had great boobs. She stuffed the breast gruffly back into the dress before she remembered *Cosmo*'s number three. Cornell confined himself to a small chuckle. She straightened up to avoid another costume malfunction.

"Ow!" Lynette yelped.

"What, honey? Your back?" Cornell moved to comfort his wife and remembered the panty hose. At the same instant, he realized his hands and feet had fallen asleep. Lordy, that was it. Cornell's laughter filled every inch of the bedroom.

Lynette took one look at her husband tied up and shaking with laughter and added her own husky laugh. Once they started, they couldn't stop. She pointed and laughed. He couldn't wipe the tears from his eyes, and his frantic blinking made her roll over and clutch her side. Something like this always happened. Lynette and Cornell spent a lot of time deepening their laugh lines together.

"My feet are aslee—" Cornell struggled to say in between snorting fits of hiccupping.

"Bad circulation!" Lynette guffawed.

She crawled over to undo Cornell's hands and feet. After Lynette finally managed to untie him, Cornell wrapped his wife up in his arms and hugged her tight.

Lynette skinny-dipped in her husband's embrace. "Well, I hope you can see how much I love you." She snuggled into his arms and planted a soft, wet kiss on Cornell's chest. "Can I make love to you now, Mr. Jones?"

"Proceed, m'dear. Proceed."

The widowed professor looked up at the silver lamp he'd carried from Tehran so his wife would have light from the home she'd never wanted to leave. His fingers moved to their position above the piano keys, but stopped to hover like an ominous cloud. With a frown, he smoothed his cardigan and trousers. Arshan believed pajamas were only appropriate in the bedroom, even now, years since Maliheh or children filled the house. Arshan felt how thin his legs were. He'd always been trim, but *after sixty, trim starts to look gaunt,* he thought. He pushed his glasses back into place over the pronounced crook of his nose. Arshan Bahrami, no matter where he was, ever looked the part of the respectable professor.

Arshan's eyes lingered on two identically framed photographs illuminated by the lamp. One showed a woman hugging a laughing teenage boy. The woman's expressive eyes, as big and dark as Brazil nuts, included the photographer in the joke. The other photo was of a teenage girl with teasing eyes not unlike the adjacent woman's.

Arshan began to play Beethoven's Ninth, his eyes still fixed on the photographs. Ghosts had been Arshan's only audience for many years. Besides bridge nights at Lynette and Cornell's, Arshan's entire outward life consisted of astrophysics—teaching and research trips to distant telescopes. Arshan slammed his fingers discordantly on the keys. He'd heard a girlish chuckle above the music. Why had he chosen that song? His daughter's favorite. He pried his eyes away from the photos.

Arshan took a breath a yogi would envy and forced himself to go upstairs. Ten minutes later, the piano watched him sneak back into the room. He plucked up the photograph of the young girl and transported it across the room to a zippered suitcase. He tucked the gold frame between two halves of perfectly folded clothing. Then, his eyes resolutely averted from the remaining picture, Arshan turned off the lamp.

Isabel was at the airport, the only one taking a red-eye flight through Miami. She was certifiably in a state of shock.

She hadn't told anyone yet, but she'd been fired. Laid off was more accurate, but it stung like "fired." She'd gone in to work instead of preparing for her trip—a testament to her job dedication—and they let her go, saying the vacation only sped up the process, budget concerns meant they'd have had to do it sooner or later, as much as they hated to see her go. She'd packed her career life into a cardboard box, come home and deposited it on the side of the couch opposite her packed suitcases. Isabel sat down between her old life and her carry-on, her cat making the only sound in the room. But Isabel wasn't experiencing silence—she was awash in a deafening waterfall of thought. It was only after her Pavlovian response to the horn of the cab and the blur of arriving at the airport that she felt the desperate need to tell someone.

She almost called me, but was understandably wary after our last conversation. Isabel tapped her perfectly manicured fingers—from her latest biweekly appointment at her mother's salon—on her BlackBerry. She knew she should call Jesse, but her mother was liable to dispense some cloying phrase like "Lemons have a way of becoming martini decorations, sweetie."

She would've called Kendra straight away, but it was

after midnight. No way Kendra would be awake. She'd be all packed and organized, asleep in her white silk nightgown, next to her perfect boyfriend, Michael, in their meticulous SoHo apartment.

Screw it. Kendra it would have to be. She couldn't imagine boarding a sleeping plane with a head full of "what the hell do I do now?" She dialed Kendra's number and listened to it ring through to voicemail. When she hung up, deflated, she couldn't repress a curse word or two, prompting a shh from a nearby mother cradling a little girl in her lap. She dialed again. Then again. What was the deal with her friends lately? When did they become so self-absorbed? Mina would've answered on a floating ice cap in Antarctica.

Kendra pressed "ignore" on her phone, for the third time, without taking her eyes off Michael. He was still pacing like an agitated tiger. He was having the exact same effect as that of an angry tiger on Kendra Jones.

Kendra was sitting very still and straight on her lavender loveseat. Work papers—million-dollar orders for dresses in five shades and sizes—had fallen to the floor, and were shocked that Kendra hadn't noticed. If the papers weren't really shocked by the negligence, they were certainly appalled by the mess. As Michael paced and ranted and lectured, he navigated a very uncharacteristic rug of chaos—slippers, discarded work clothes, a full coffee cup, and a half-empty bottle of vodka. His. Not hers.

Kendra put a nervous hand to her hair. While waiting

for Michael to arrive, she'd started to scratch between the tightly plaited rows of braids. Impulsively, she'd undone them, one by one, each careful braid untwisting into a frizzy poof of caramelized curls.

Kendra was having trouble concentrating on Michael's surreal barrage of words. She held tight to the phone in her hand, bearing Isabel's name, and looked to the ground. A picture lay where it had landed. The very first trip with the vacation club. Kendra longed to pick it up. A little raven-haired girl farthest to the left was smiling at her. She'd looked at Mina's face at least a hundred times that day. Suddenly, Michael's last words registered.

"I didn't do it on purpose," she spit out.

Michael stopped, surprised. He ran his fingers through his sandy-blond hair, like he did when he was about to reprimand an office assistant at his firm. "I'm not saying that you did, I'm just saying *if* you did—"

"But I didn't. And if you think I would, then how well do you know me, Michael? Or vice versa."

Michael rolled his eyes. He resumed pacing, nudging the framed photograph out of his path with his shoe.

Kendra watched him with widening eyes, and felt the black hole in her sternum swell, too. Kendra planned her days and future like most people would only plan Thanksgiving dinner. Down to the last detail, in full consideration of timing, with an obsessive flair for perfect presentation—that was the way of Kendra since childhood. If Michael could suddenly mistake her for the girl that tries to trap a man with—

"It's a baby, Michael. Not a death sentence."

This time Michael didn't look up, the coward. "No, it's not. It doesn't have to be. A baby. Yet." The yet was meant to be a loving concession. He looked at the picture of the four little girls. No, he needed to be firm on this. "I don't want it to be. A baby."

Now he looked at Kendra, really looked at her for the first time since the news, and felt some of the anger drain away. But as he took note of her disheveled hair and clothes, the soothing visage of his girlfriend became a stranger that filled him with fear.

"Do you? Do you want it to be, K?"

Kendra tried to think of how to answer. Of course she didn't want it to be like this. This was horrible, not at all how it was supposed to be. This was the opposite of a Thanksgiving dinner of a life—her perfect boyfriend who would be her perfect husband, who would make partner while she made V.P. Their first child, a boy, wouldn't be born until three years from now, leaving just enough time for a girl the following year, taking care of the children thing so she could return to work—

"Kendra?"

"I think you should leave."

"Ken, come on, we have to talk about this if you're leaving for freaking *Honduras* tomorrow."

Kendra felt the vibrating phone in her hand like a low rolling of thunder. She picked up Isabel's fourth call and put it to her ear.

"I'm not going to Honduras."

November 2
Samantha

This isn't how it was supposed to be.

It's not freaking fair that life gets to muck around in our plans like this.

I sound like Kendra, don't I?

But we were supposed to be friends for another fifty years. Friends that wrinkle and giggle and whine through the flagging days of youth into our eccentric golden years. I can't grow old without you. That can't be what's meant to be.

Obviously today was not a good day, seeing you like that.

Sigh. Okay. Let's move from *the world is against us* to *us against the world*.

For physicists, the Holy Grail is the *Theory of Everything*—a single mathematical theory in which the equations of the microscopic world agree with the macroscopic world we experience. A theory that would explain:

What is life? When does a soul/human being become or stop being itself? Roe v. Wade but even deeper.

Imagine a single theory that unites biology, philosophy and supernatural phenomenon.

I'm sitting here amongst a mountain of my old textbooks and new ones, so at least we know we're not the first ones to have gone this route. I'll keep you posted.

But right now I'm freaking exhausted, and I still want to go to the hospital with you tomorrow, butt crack early, as promised.

xoxo

—*Sam.*

6

THE NEXT DAY I WAS ROLLER-SKATING again, chastising myself for letting Isabel talk me into letting her take a cab. She was late and her cell phone went straight to voice mail.

And there are no addresses in Tegucigalpa. Not numerical, maplike directions anyway. Instructions to my apartment translated as "up the hill near the electronics store, past the police headquarters, before the gated neighborhood at the top." Isabel could be dead. Car accidents in Honduras were like blue skies in California. Isabel was probably dead and it was my fault.

Argh. This was the thing—I was losing my grip on my identity. The old Samantha didn't worry. She lived and breathed a world that was safe, exciting and ultimately fair. Now the two incarnations of me were at war.

A rap at the front door interrupted the battle. I stumbled out of my skates and made for the door.

A flash of dark hair and aquamarine eyes leaped into my arms. Isabel stepped back to look me over then wrapped me back up in another hug.

She put two slender, perfectly manicured hands on either side of my face. "Man, it's good to see you!"

What do you get when you mix an American supermodel with a Panamanian heartthrob? Isabel Brighton was so stunningly beautiful, you never remembered *how* beautiful and always ended up speechless. And I'd known her for over twenty years. Fresh from a filthy cab ride, Isabel looked like she'd stepped out of a magazine ad. Her tan platform sandals and her crimson toenails matched her fedora. You would never know that this girl was the archangel for the world's poor. Which was the only reason I'd let her take a cab by herself. Isabel was nobody's fool.

She swatted me with her purse. "Lemme in, I'm beat. I need to sit—" Isabel looked around the empty living room. She burst out laughing. "You are hilarious. You are aware you have four adults coming to visit, right?" I loved how we weren't considered adults most of the time. But then I frowned.

"I can't believe Kendra's not coming. You believe her about work? It doesn't make sense. I mean, *you* got off work."

Isabel frowned, too, but she didn't respond. Instead, she

beelined for the kitchen. "So whatcha got in the way of refreshments for a weary traveler?" She opened the fridge and took out two Port Royals, the local beer.

I looked at my phone. It was three o'clock. Isabel arched an eyebrow and shoved the beer further toward me. "I've got bad news."

We sat in the chairs with our feet up on the railing. Isabel had her skinny second toe crossed over her big toe. It was no party trick. That's the thing about being someone's friend that long—you know all their ticks and their warning signs, usually better than they do. The toe thing meant her mind was off wrestling an alligator. Isabel hated to complain. She also hated to mope, belabor or reveal any amount of vulnerability. I knew it would take some careful best-friend maneuvering before she told me what was wrong.

"I got canned."

Or maybe not. I studied her face for clues of what she wanted me to say. "And now you can take those tight-rope-walking lessons we always talked about?"

She giggled. The one thing that always gave no-nonsense Isabel away—her schoolgirl giggle. She sighed. "I think you had it right all along. Live free in exotic locales watching the sunset, not chained to a desk, drowning in case studies of awful things happening to people who don't deserve it."

For the first time, I could see little lines under Isabel's eyes.

"Ha. Hate to break it to ya, but I'm having a crisis in

the exact opposite direction, wondering what the hell I've done with my life."

Isabel turned to look at me, her turquoise irises narrowing. "Oh, jeez, don't ruin this for me. I'm one inch away from moving here to work in an ice-cream store."

I nudged her foot with my toes. "What happened?"

"Oh, you know, just that the economy is shit and *obviously* the first thing we should do is abandon the people that need the most help. Makes sense to cut back funding on the ones that will probably die anyway, right?"

Her compassion moved me. She wasn't worried about herself. God, all I'd been worrying about lately was myself. I felt ashamed.

"So, then you got laid off, not fired?"

"Does it matter? I'm tired of trying to change things that are never going to change, Sam. Poverty, corruption, disease. For as long as there have been human beings, there has been evil."

I'd never heard Isabel talk like that. She rubbed her temples and continued. "We all die alone anyway, don't we? Why do anything except try to be happy—bum around the world and have fun."

She wasn't trying to insult me, but it cut deep anyway. She noticed.

"No, I'm being serious. It's not only my job. Ever since Mina's death I just don't see the point of drudgery in the face of this—" She waved her hand across the balmy, admittedly beautiful skyline of Tegucigalpa. "But—"

But that would make you question every single thing about who you are, I thought.

"But then I wouldn't know who I was anymore."

I raised my beer. "Welcome to my world."

Isabel looked at me long and hard. She clinked beers, but then lifted up my left hand. "Okay, lady. Talk to me about Remy."

I looked at my finger where there would be a ring if I hadn't buried it deep in my suitcase. "He's getting me a better one anyway." But I knew Isabel didn't care about the carats. "Look, I panicked. If I'd said no, I wouldn't have had any time to think about it."

Isabel laughed, not exactly nicely. "You are one of a kind, my friend."

I stuck out my tongue.

"So you don't think maybe *he* panicked? Forty-three is getting old. And you're a little American hottie. Time to lock it down? Make some babies?"

"Hey, thanks but watch it. Yes, he might have rushed a little, in order to ask me before I left the continent. But he knows me well enough to let me travel freely. I think it's sweet."

"Or manipulative." Isabel didn't believe in marriage. She thought it was an outdated arrangement that led inevitably to female sacrifice, a lesson gleaned from her mother's devotion to the single life. Jesse was the closest thing I had to a mom, but I'd somehow managed to hang on to a belief in love.

"You haven't even met him."

Isabel whipped toward me so fast her hair boomeranged around her face and back. "Exactly."

No shy violets in our group. But she was right. I was in no real position to make this into a *me against the world* situation. I didn't know what the hell I wanted yet. "He makes me feel safe. I've never had much of a family, wasn't ever sure I wanted one of my own. But I do. And it might not be so bad to have someone to take care of me for a change."

The look on Isabel's face killed me. That wasn't what I meant at all, but now I saw what really scared her. I backtracked. "Oh, come on, you know we'll always have each other. But—"

Isabel looked like she might cry, except that Isabel never cried. She shook her head. "No, look, you're right. We will always have each other, but it's not the same as a boyfriend. Or a husband," she added begrudgingly. "Anyway—what kind of friend would I be to talk you out of marrying a rich, famous French movie director?" Isabel winked.

CHAPTER

7

WE SPENT THE WHOLE REST OF THE DAY chatting and catching up. It felt marvelous to have her there. I completely forgot not to laugh, and the sound warmed the empty apartment like a day at the beach.

Later, while Isabel showered to go meet the others at the airport, I wandered onto the balcony with Mina's journal. I didn't have a specific question; I just missed her. This was exactly what I dreaded happening, that bonding with Isabel would fill me with guilt. It was one thing when after Mina's death we sat around and talked about her nonstop, but it seemed so unforgivably unfair for our lives to go on and for us to be together and happy.

November 8
Mina

You came to visit me twice today. I can't stand seeing you afraid. Sammy, you have the worst poker face I've ever seen. Forget what the doctors say, I know how I'm doing by the look on your face when you walk in my room. But I appreciate that you never lie to me. You don't tell me that everything's okay, like Kendra. You don't sugarcoat.

So, when you get excited, I get excited because I know it's genuine. Thanks for my quantum physics "crash course" this week. Nice use of diagrams, you nerd. LOL. I don't pretend to understand it all, but it's fascinating stuff. And let's face it—otherwise, kiddo, we're stuck with Rose Eynden's "So You Want to Be a Medium." Ha-ha.

Anyway, I just wanted to say thank you, for doing this for me, and give you a little reminder to never give up. I mean, move on, be happy, but keep trying to find me. Just in case.

I'm not ready, Sam. I'm not ready to leave you guys.

I looked out across the city, and gradually up at the clouds. *Why did I stop looking, really? Why did I stop believing?* I looked back at the journal. I flipped toward the back to the page that held the drying maple leaf. Twirling the leaf by its stem, I went back to the entry.

P.S. Call Kendra. I know she hates being so far away in New York. It's ridiculous how much that girl works. But she does it to herself, now doesn't she? LOL

I wiped my nose and went to look for my cell phone. What was the deal with Kendra? I smelled a big fat decomposing rat on that one. Initially, maybe I *was* surprised that she'd agreed to come on a moment's notice, her being so easily offended by anybody's lack of planning. But Kendra worked for a clothing distribution company where the absent owner, off gallivanting, compensated her handsomely and let Kendra make all the decisions. Kendra worked seven days a week, whether she was in the office or not. She'd assured us she could still get work done in Honduras, and had even said it was good timing because a lot of her clients were on vacation, too.

Then she suddenly changed her mind, something Kendra didn't do.

I fired off a text and waited. When no response came, I sat on the balcony cradling the maple leaf in my left palm and stroking it with my right.

Just me and the city and the leaf.

CHAPTER

8

ISABEL WANDERED OFF TO FIND COFFEE while I stood near the welcome gate at the airport, one of the few gleaming new buildings in the city. I shivered in the air-conditioning and realized how excited I was for the vacation club to arrive.

Mina and I had struck out in the family department; it was our greatest bond. A mother that dies versus the one that runs away. It's hard to measure which is worse.

I was two, so I can't say if my mother left the man I know as my father, or if my father turned into that man once she left. My dad is a brilliant surgeon. Once I read about a child he miraculously saved, about how he wept at her bedside. I cut that article into fifty pieces and burned them one by one, because I never knew that side of my father at all. When he was home, which was rarely to never, he asked me about my grades and that was about it. He dismissed any discussion of my mother or her whereabouts. No photographs remained. As I got older, I postulated mental illness, love affairs, cult brainwashing. My father would pull off an amazing feat of glaring at me while looking straight through me, and say only, "Better left alone, Sam." I hoped she was dead. Otherwise, she's a monster.

In any case, that's why the vacation club was never just summer camp for me. Isabel's mother, Jesse, loved to tell how she scooped up Mina and me like two stray kittens, two lost little girls trying to be each other's parents. Of course, after Arshan Bahrami, Mina's father, became Jesse's bridge partner, it wasn't such a nice story to tell anymore. You don't call someone a bad father to his face.

"Isabel, they're here!" I pointed to a cloud of blond hair and laughter emerging from customs.

Clicking heels and a squeal, and Jesse Brighton was charging through the crowd toward us. Typical Jesse—her long ash-blond hair flowed over her leopard-print shirt tucked into skinny jeans, tucked into five-inch leather boots.

"Oh my stars! Look at those two gorgeous women! Those are my girls!" she shouted into the ears of the poor passengers she plowed over to reach us. "Hug me quick before I die of excitement!"

I fell happily into her warm embrace that always

smelled of Chanel No. 5. Jesse splattered me in lipstick kisses.

Lynette, with her carefully bobbed blond hair and her red tunic and jeans, waited a step behind before taking her turn hugging us and laughing.

The two men hovered awkwardly back a few paces. Arshan looked ready for class, with his collared shirt, pressed khakis and stern expression. Cornell's clothes were more casual, but his face was just as *manly serious.*

"Oh come here!" I hugged them both. Cornell instantly relaxed, but Arshan tensed more. I thought of Mina, trying to remember if I'd ever seen them hug.

Jesse took my hand and petted it like a Chihuahua. "Ok, my precious little angel, let's get those automobiles, shall we? Let's get this show on the road! Tradition is tradition. The Opening Ceremony begins."

The party was a huge success. Shakira blasted from speakers attached to Isabel's iPod. Isabel spilled her news and Jesse launched a campaign to get her to move home. Lynette and Cornell danced and smooched in the middle of the room. Arshan helped me in the kitchen with the drinks. I'd insisted on Johnny Walker Black with club soda, the Honduran drink of choice, and Arshan was effusively appreciative. Well, effusively for Arshan.

When Beyoncé came on, Jesse called us onto the dance floor/roller rink. We danced and shook our hips until Lynette begged me to turn on the air-conditioning and I burst out laughing. Everyone collapsed into plastic chairs to fan themselves and started gabbing again. I went out to the balcony to get some air.

I was out there less than a minute when Arshan joined me, sliding the door closed behind him.

"Hey," I said, surprised. I could count on a single hand the number of times I'd spoken one-on-one with Arshan Bahrami. Even in all our research, Mina and I hadn't included her father the astrophysicist. It was mostly at her request and I hadn't insisted; I knew how difficult it was to forgive fathers who let you down.

"Hello, Samantha. I want to thank you for inviting me on this trip. It's been very hard since Mina—"

"It wasn't my decision—" *That sounded like I didn't want him to come.* "I mean, we all thought you should come." That wasn't exactly true. Jesse didn't ask me before inviting Arshan and Cornell. *Things change,* Jesse said later. *Adjust, darling. Or sit in a corner and lament.* Sitting around lamenting was a cardinal sin in Jesse's book.

Arshan was no dummy. He knew who had invited him. He stood and looked out across the city lights. "It's beautiful, no? It reminds me a bit of Tehran, the city lights in the mountains."

I peeked at him out of the corner of my eye. I always forgot he spent half his life in Iran.

"So, you're going to become a married woman, huh, Sammy?"

I don't know what shocked me more—his question or the nickname. "They told you? Lynette and Jesse?"

Now *he* seemed surprised. "What do you think we

talk about?" He looked at me. "We talk about the four musketeers." His gaze darted away quickly. "About all you girls."

Three musketeers, not four. A pointy triangle that doesn't roll. *Oh, Mina. Why am I here and not you?*

Something cool and smooth touched my shoulder. Arshan picked it up between his fingers and stared at the maple leaf in wonder. He looked up at the sky, then behind us on the balcony. He'd raked thousands of these in his yard. The deep line between his eyebrows almost made me giggle. I took this new leaf by its stem and twirled it between my fingers.

"There are so many things Mina and I never talked about," he said as he watched the leaf.

I didn't respond and we both lapsed into thought. I remembered when Mina and I were children, how we were left to ourselves, how we played "house" for hours in the woods and made TV dinners together.

"Is he the one?"

"Excuse me?"

Arshan continued as if he was no longer talking to me. "You will give him your youth, your idealism, and your capacity for hope. He will seal or destroy your belief in fate and love. You only get one chance at these things. He will fill your life's bowl, Samantha. So is he worthy?"

I reminded myself to breathe. My heart pounded in my throat. *How dare he, of all people?* "Was Mina's mother worth it?" *Worth becoming so bitter?* I thought.

Arshan laughed so unexpectedly and so loud that I got

goosebumps. "You bet she was." He slapped the balcony railing and laughed again. I had no idea he could laugh like that.

Seemingly having surprised himself as well, Arshan cleared his throat and smoothed his slacks. He nodded his head at me, his dark eyes still crinkled from laughing. Then he turned to walk inside.

"Mr. Bahrami? Arshan?"

He turned back. I held out the maple leaf. He took it from my fingers like a long-stemmed rose and studied its colors of campfire embers in the moonlight. His face assumed a softness, like milk spilling over jagged marble. Then he opened the door and the party music flooded the balcony, rinsing away the moment.

November 10
Samantha

Okay, Mina, tell me this: What is the difference between matter and non-matter?

The craziest lesson of quantum physics is that at the most fundamental level, we don't know what the world and/or us, as human beings, are made of.

Particles are hard, substantial points in space, like electrons. Waves are spread out and immaterial, like sound. Things have to be one or the other, right?

Wrong. The most famous experiment in modern physics is The Double Slit Experiment. Electron particles are fired through a screen with two slits onto a particle detector *one at a time.* You would expect the electron to go through one of the two slits and be detected somewhere directly behind one or the other. But after you've fired thousands of electrons, you see *not* two slits of accumulated particles, but a series of thick and skinny bands—an interference pattern indicative of a wave. But how did each particle know where to end up on the wave interference pattern? The electron somehow interacts and acts both as a wave and a particle at the same time, completely defying classic notions of space, time and matter.

See, Mina, we really have no clue about "reality." At what point are we separate from everything around us? How are thoughts different from, say, your collection of maple leaves?

Scientists aren't any closer to solving the mind/body debate than the Pope of Rome.

Which is not to say that there aren't theories....

WHILE THE OPENING CEREMONY STRETCHED into the night, Kendra nestled in Michael's arm, savoring the familiarity. They always lay the same way, on their same respective sides. Kendra loved all things that had that kind of automatic comfort—cutting her banana over her bran cereal, the concierge hailing her daily cab, the TiVo bloop when she sat down on Sunday to watch all her favorite shows Michael wouldn't watch.

After the previous night's fight, Kendra and Michael hadn't discussed the issue further. Both had said what they had to say for the moment, and neither one was the type to repeat themselves for the sake of drama. Michael came over late with Chinese takeout. They'd watched ESPN and gotten into bed. They hadn't had sex, but that wasn't unusual on a weeknight.

The problem was that Michael thought he had won, and figured Kendra didn't want to discuss the details of abortion. Kendra figured Michael just needed time to adjust and might even propose soon. But this was just a fleeting whisper at the edge of her mind, because really she was happiest ignoring the whole situation.

Then Michael furrowed his eyebrows, and Kendra's world was just about to explode.

Kendra didn't see it, of course, in their usual pose, so she was stroking his arm contentedly when Michael said, "I'll go with you, baby."

Kendra knew exactly what he meant before he even finished saying it. Words are often superfluous between lovers. Skin speaks its desires; moods hang in the air; intention travels faster than words. Kendra's face crumpled halfway through "I'll go," and Michael said nothing more after that sentence because he could feel her disappointment seep into his skin.

So, with both of them finally on the same page, minus the words to confirm it, their usual pose turned into something entirely different, as Michael hugged Kendra so tight it squeezed out the sobs Kendra took immeasurable pains to contain, at which point she sprang away as if from a branding iron, and curled up on the far edge of the mattress.

Michael wanted to comfort her, but he knew that they

were back on the battlefield. He would lose his last five years of youth if he went soft on this one.

Kendra was crying because she knew exactly what he was thinking.

Later, after she was sure Michael was asleep, Kendra picked up her phone to reread my text from that afternoon. She read the words several times, pushing the star key every time the phone darkened to sleep mode.

Kendra, I know something's wrong. Call me. We all love you no matter what.

Kendra touched her hairline, which had broken out in a fine sweat. She hadn't gotten her hair redone, a fact that set off alarm bells in the secretary when Kendra came in late that morning with a hat squashed atop a tangled mass of hair.

Kendra hid in her office all day, but hardly accomplished a thing besides staring at her in-box and managing not to cry.

Remembering, Kendra got out of bed. She tiptoed into the living room and picked up the picture of the four girls. Their very first summer trip. Kendra stroked a finger over Mina's beaming face. She sat down on the couch, studying the picture like an Italian *Vogue*. Four girls and two mothers in Paris. Kendra's mother and Isabel's mom, Jesse, were already best buddies by then, soldiers in the battle against suburbia. They'd started the vacation club to *get the girls out of Conformia* every summer. Kendra smiled. She was old enough to understand that both mothers secretly loved the celebrity status afforded them by the *Conformia* of the conservative little burb outside of Washington, D.C. Jesse got to brag about being a supermodel, and flaunt her taste for leopard print. But her mother? Kendra hadn't quite figured out what made Lynette Jones so wary of the picture-perfect neighborhood, though she was sure it had to do with her father, a civil rights lawyer in D.C.

Kendra set down the picture. It wasn't fair to worry them. She grabbed her BlackBerry and sent a group text:

Swamped with work. Wish I was there.

One lie and one truth. Kendra looked back at the photo, but this time she saw her reflection in the glass of the frame, her frizzy hair and sallow skin illuminated by the streetlight seeping through the window. Kendra stood up slowly and shuffled over to a full-length mirror. She stood stiller than a sentry, a judging scowl on her face. What was she guarding?

All my sacred plans, she answered the reflection wryly. Career. Wedding. Family. In that order.

Guarding them against whom?

"Against you," she whispered at the unkempt woman in the mirror.

She stared down the imposter, eyes narrowed and chin up as though she could reshape the image by force of will.

But she couldn't. The frazzled, disheveled lady continued to glare back at her. Kendra let her nightgown slip to the floor. She saw a woman that was no longer the youngest, prettiest girl in every business meeting.

Stretch marks scurried around her nipples. Her stomach was soft and fleshy. Her waist was narrow but flared into wide dimply hips. The woman's face was a Picasso of curves and shadows, but with lips as full as marshmallows.

"Kendra?" Michael called gruffly from the bedroom.

The woman's eyes filled with tears. She put her hand out to Kendra, until their fingers touched on the surface of the glass.

CHAPTER

10

"ROAD TRIP! GET UP! COME ON, UP. UP!" JESSE stood over me, completely dressed. I sat up on the air mattress next to Isabel. She opened one eye when I poked her. Jesse kissed my forehead and then Isabel's. "Get your little butts up. We gotta hit the road, girls."

We were driving to the beach house I'd rented in Tela. It was an all-day affair and Jesse was right—if we didn't get a move on it, we'd end up driving in the dark, which was a very bad idea on a Honduran highway.

I got ready in a hurry, nudging Isabel along every step of the way. Lynette and Cornell had almost everything packed and ready. I'd never seen anything like those two. Lynette had always been our organizer, but to see her and Cornell work in tandem was a lesson in harmony.

"Arshan, you're with us." Lynette was doling out seating arrangements. "Jesse, you drive the girls."

I caught Jesse give Lynette a look. *Why wouldn't she want to drive with us? Well, fine, then.* "Jesse, you can go with Lynette, I can drive." I picked up the last bag of groceries. "Actually, I would prefer to drive."

Jesse caught herself and smiled. "Samantha, darling, good judgment comes from experience, and a lot of that comes from bad judgment."

"What in the hell does that mean?" Isabel asked.

"It means I'm drivin'. Let's go."

So, twenty minutes later, a canary-yellow Honda and a tan Ford climbed the mountainous snake-shaped highway above the congested city, en route to Tela on the eastern coast.

In the Honda, Isabel was in the back and I was up front in the passenger seat. I gave Jesse a crash course on Honduran highway driving, best summarized as follows: throw out every rule you've ever learned and drive like a madwoman in a high-speed chase.

There were two speeds on any Honduran highway: chicken truck creep along may break down any minute and speed demon passing uphill on hairpin turn. There was no in-between. In-between was deadly. In-between would get you rear-ended into a pickup truck carrying five relatives, a dog and a chicken. At all times, you watched for stray dogs, small children carrying water jugs, old men with canes or cows, sudden rains that made the edge of the mountain invisible, and potholes big enough to swallow the front end of your car.

Isabel had the best seat. It was best not to look.

I had the worst seat. A complete view with a complete lack of control.

The road climbed and twisted, each new curve revealing a cluster of fresh sights. Cement-block shacks opened to supersize hammocks strung in the main room. Vegetable stands sported men in cowboy hats with crossed arms, posing against a bull. Rickety roadside stands sold dark watery honey in dusty reused bottles with dirty screw tops.

Jesse pulled over at a produce stand to add to our cache of groceries. Our place in Tela was outside town—better to stock up in advance. We parked in the ditches and haggled over bananas and mangos. Jesse made us buy one of every fruit or vegetable we'd never seen before, which amounted to a lot of strange-looking potato-ish and pear-ish items among the plantains. And of course, we bought mango verde as a snack. Unripe mango, doused in lime, salt and chili, was a seasonal treat sold by women alongside men brandishing puppies for sale. I sucked on the sour pieces of fruit and watched the scenery.

"There it is! Stop, Jesse! Pull over, quick," I yelled when we came upon a roadside shack with a line of cars out front.

Jesse whipped the car into a dirt patch out front, nearly getting clipped by a tailgating utility truck.

"My God, Sammy, *what?*" Jesse looked unimpressed by the one-room store.

"Queso petacon!" Lucky I saw the sign. "Cheese! No trip to Honduras would be complete without it," I proclaimed like an expert, quoting Ana Maria. I hopped out of the car and spotted an outhouse around back. "If you *have* to pee, looks like there's a...*bathroom* around back. I think I'll wait for the next Texaco."

Isabel groaned and headed for the outhouse, as Jesse turned toward the road, leaning against the dusty car to smoke a cigarette.

When I came out with the cheese, I saw Jesse hadn't moved a hair, still perched against the car with three inches of ash hovering precariously at the end of her cigarette. "You didn't see the others?"

Jesse jumped like a lizard had slithered into her jeans. She took a look at her cigarette and laughed. "Did you get a closer look at that outhouse, kiddo? Nah, don't tell me. If you gotta go, you gotta go. Better to approach life without knowing what's comin'."

"Jesse?" Something about her face bothered me.

Jesse dropped the cigarette on the ground. She fiddled with her purse and then her belt. Then she stood up straight to face me. "Oh, sugar, it's just that ever since I found out about that marriage proposal of yours, I keep remembering things that ain't worth remembering."

I knew from experience that Jesse wouldn't answer probing questions about Isabel's father. But she was still looking at me expectantly, so I gave it a go. "You mean remembering things about *your* marriage?"

Jesse didn't move or say anything. Then she nodded, just once, slow as refrigerated honey. I looked behind me to see if Isabel was coming. She would want to hear this, I knew.

By the time I turned back to Jesse, the look was gone. She clapped her hands together and clasped them. "Oh, now everybody knows how I feel about the institution of marriage, Sammy girl." She looked up as we heard the door slam and Isabel curse. "About the same as that outhouse." Jesse wrinkled her nose. "I know better."

Arshan drove with both hands in perfect safety position, eyes straight ahead, back erect. He checked his three mirrors in clockwise order—rearview, right side, left side, straight ahead, and repeat. The sun paraded its late-afternoon glare, so Arshan pulled down the visor and adjusted his posture.

Lynette watched him and thought about how much Arshan had grown on her. He was still morose and dry, but he'd loosened up as their bridge nights had piled up over the years, and now Lynette realized that he provided the perfect balance to their little group.

She also knew that Jesse had fallen for him, even more than she'd hinted at. Lynette studied Arshan's severe profile and his slim frame. He was a handsome man, regal somehow, and safe. He just wasn't someone she would have ever imagined Jesse with. Jesse dated businessmen from the salon, or firemen, or attractive divorcés she met on the internet.

They had no proof that moody, serious Arshan felt the same way about Jesse, which Lynette knew must be infuriating her best friend, not to mention shaking her ample confidence. No one had been hurt more in love than Jesse, and Lynette wasn't about to push.

She peered so long that Arshan whipped sideways and caught her. Lynette was embarrassed and pretended to be looking out the window past him.

Arshan appreciated Lynette's silence. He had underestimated the feelings this trip would bring back. Ghosts swirled around him in the car and rushed past the windows, interlacing with the scenery. Mina was everywhere in this group. He caught echoes of all her favorite catch phrases. Samantha's laugh sounded strange by itself. He'd always heard it aligned with his daughter's, the mixture spilling into the hallway outside her bedroom. The way Isabel talked with her hands, the private jokes she shared with Samantha—everything was an excruciating reminder of Mina's absence.

And then he kept envisioning his wife, Maliheh. Her laughing eyes. The jasmine scent she wore. Arshan had learned to accept these fleeting glimpses of his wife, but still they startled him, like the richness of gourmet chocolate. He slipped into the past like an egg sliding into water to be poached. Arshan regularly boiled himself alive for his mistakes as a husband and a father.

He remembered every second of the day before Mina was born.

Maliheh lay on the bed, with her puffy eyes and swollen belly. They'd moved to the U.S. in a haze after losing their son in Iran. Maliheh had hardly spoken to him in the months since. Betrayal by God. That was the only way to describe the pain of losing a child. But on that day, when Maliheh had taken his hand and put it on top of the baby, they had stopped discussing.

Maliheh was always the stronger one. She told Arshan that their child could not be born into such sorrow, that he must promise her to be kind, to be open, to laugh. Arshan's heart was reborn, looking into the eyes of the only woman he'd ever loved. He promised her then and there that the three of them would be happy and safe.

But he'd failed. He'd failed them all.

Suddenly, he felt Lynette staring at him. He glanced over and she looked past him, embarrassed.

Arshan smiled, even though his skin was still scalding. He broke his driving rules to look at Cornell asleep in the backseat, drooling on a pillow.

Lynette looked at her husband and smiled, too.

I was thinking about Remy. I sipped a Coca-Cola and slipped into my new favorite fantasy: being married to Remy Badeau. I pictured an art opening with flashing paparazzi. I pictured us on the covers of French magazines. I pictured a home chef serving us dinner under a chandelier. I started to picture us in bed. Suddenly I felt a little carsick. This had happened a few times recently, as a matter of fact. I was attracted to Remy. He was ruggedly handsome. Other women obviously thought so, too. And the man certainly had skills between the sheets. So what did the spin-cycle stomach mean?

I tried thinking about him again, starting with his smile—the smile that melted me like butter on a skillet every time. Remy must've gotten away with a lot packing that smile. It was disarmingly boyish and more contagious than chicken pox.

I remembered the day he threw out my collection of trinkets. I'd been collecting them since I arrived in Paris—matchbooks, scraps of advertisements, discarded ticket stubs. The plan was to incorporate them into a new series I'd begun, have them morph into photos or get mired in paint. Yes, they looked like junk, but weren't they obviously collected in a pretty box for a reason?

Remy tossed them out along with my fashion magazines. Man, was I furious. Livid. I'd barged in on him when he was working, with my chin thrust out for a fight. When he understood what he had done, he chuckled. I checked my earlobes—yep, hotter than a newly murdered lobster. A sure sign I was as angry as I could get. He dismissed his assistant and held out his hand. I shook my head, so he laughed again, and swept his arm wide to suggest a place to sit. Dizziness was fast replacing my rage, so I sat and watched him, fuming.

Remy scratched his head for comic effect, then turned his pockets inside out. From the floor, he retrieved a matchbook and a few coins and a mint wrapper. He crawled on the carpet to the wastebasket, sniffing and wagging his butt like a puppy, and took out a magazine, scripts, and a newspaper. He shredded them with his teeth, growling, then got on his knees at my feet. When he looked up at me, presenting his peace offering of garbage, he smiled that smile of his.

We spent the rest of the afternoon in bed, naked under crisp white sheets. Remy reclined on fluffy pillows and I curled around him, my head on his chest until he said it was too hot. He twirled my curls around his fingers and teased that my skin betrayed my every emotion—from anger to desire. He kissed the top of my head and told me stories about his life, his travels, his work. Entranced, I lifted my head to kiss him and he moved smoothly to meet me halfway. We kissed slowly, Remy brushing his petal-smooth lips side to side across my mouth, flicking his tongue ever so softly to part my lips. I loved the way he touched me, knowing every muscle, every sensitive spot, as if he were reciting a manual on female pleasure. I slid my body atop his lean torso and muscled stomach, easing myself down onto him, him inside of me. We both exhaled and moaned into each other's mouths, lips hovering centimeters apart.

Isabel bumped my seat. I yelped when the ice-cold soda hit my broiling thighs.

"Shit!" I sprung my legs apart and caught myself panting.

"Sorry!" Isabel yelled overly loudly, on account of rocking out to her headphones.

Jesse looked at me closely. "Well, I have a purty good idea what *you* were thinkin' about."

Jesse kept thinking about Kendra's last-minute bailout. She couldn't put her finger on it, but something wasn't right. She remembered what Lynette had told her about the conversation. Kendra blaming her crazy boss and her incompetent assistant. Normal. Kendra letting it drop about a fancy client dinner. Normal. Kendra stressed-out and overworked and feeling guilty about spending too much on shoes. Totally normal. Worrying about missing work was Kendra since her first job. But that girl cared about this group and about her family.

Maybe Kendra and Lynette had some latent issues. Lynette had confessed only a handful of times that she wasn't sure she'd done a good job raising a mixed-race daughter. Jesse had to smile. She didn't think the problem had to do with Kendra being half-black so much as it had to do with Kendra being Kendra.

Lynette came from a conservative Southern family, but turned out a hippie actress. Jesse knew Lynette had envisioned being the understanding mom to a wild artistic daughter. But kids don't care much about a parent's plans. Kendra used to infuriate Lynette by playing businesswoman and asking her why she didn't own any pantsuits. It was during Lynette's latest incarnation of the red phase—when she was directing community theater and into wearing scarlet felt clogs and burgundy tunic sweaters over leggings.

Jesse smiled. At least Lynette and Cornell had each other. It had been hard sometimes—raising Isabel by herself and running the salon—to constantly be reminded what it would've been like to have a partner. Cornell and Lynette were sickeningly meant for each other. That might not have been so bad.

Cornell was half dreaming, half thinking about Sandra Miheso. He imagined them in court, defending the case they'd been working on together for months. He also pictured the way she laughed over Chinese takeout when they worked late in the office. Sandra Miheso was such a difficult woman—proud, stubborn, with a laugh like a queen. She wore traditional African attire, wound her hair up in scarves. Cornell loved those bright, colorful scarves.

It made him feel young to talk with Sandra. Their fiery conversations brought Cornell back to the days before he discarded his Black Panther convictions, or his vows to move to Africa.

It was slippery territory, for those were the days when he had lost Lynette for almost a decade. A long, lonely decade. What was his problem? It was just that there could not be two more different women in the world than his Lynette and Sandra Miheso.

Just then, Lynette reached out from the front seat and laid a hand on his leg. He opened his eyes slowly to look at his wife—her wrinkled, rumpled shirt, her hair slightly mussed. His Lynette, on yet another adventure with him, after all these years. Cornell smiled and patted her hand.

November 12
Samantha

Aaahhh!

I'm going to drive myself crazy reading all this stuff. I just plowed through another *New York Times* bestselling physicist autobiography. I don't know what to think. I love you; I want it to be true, but it's an awful lot to swallow, Em. On one hand, how can so many case studies and anecdotes be wrong? I'm talking about the guy at UVA who studies past lives. UVA has a whole division devoted to scientific study of the paranormal—and after-death communication. It gives me goosebumps; it gives me hope. But it also rouses my inner whispering skeptic that wonders if human desperation is not what is driving all this science. Sorry.

Most scientists are determined to peg consciousness as a side effect of brain function.

Why the rush to equate the two? Because it would discount the alternative—that we have souls that operate freely and live on after death. It makes scientists happier to kill a notion without a tangible basis in science.

It all goes back to the double slit experiment. There are different theories about what's really going on. The Copenhagen Interpretation says that the wave that travels through the two slits is not an actual wave, but a wave of probability, and that the human *act of observing* collapses the probability wave into a single outcome (i.e. an electron). That means, in a nutshell, that the human mind dictates the physical world, not the other way around.

This has kept scientists in a tizzy for the last eighty years, while spawning a landslide of New Age books on how to literally *rethink* your life. Maybe, using the power of consciousness and subconsciousness, the living can join the dead in some kind of...in-between state.

It may unnerve the scientists, but if there is a way, Mina, it has something to do with this theory.

CHAPTER

11

NOW THE HIGHWAY WAS DARK, BLACK AS vulture feathers. Only a jellybean-shaped keyhole view of the road was granted by the headlights. There were no streetlamps, no reflectors to indicate lanes, no metal railings to keep you on the road. Just a dusty snake you had to ride as it wound its way through the mountains. Jesse squinted into the night, her fingers gripping the wheel. We were stuck behind a truck piled high with bananas, going twenty-five miles per hour. I searched for soothing music on Isabel's iPod. I settled on Cowboy Junkies, but it sounded haunting in the darkness.

The Ford stayed close behind us now, Arshan still at the wheel. Lynette, Cornell and Arshan were lis-

tening to Norah Jones and discussing Kendra's marriage prospects with Michael.

"This is crazy. Screw it," Jesse said, and reached for the
gearshift. She gunned the accelerator and swung beside
the banana truck.

Arshan sprang to life. He'd been anxious to get around
the truck, too. He floored the gas, feeling exhilarated.

I gulped, didn't say anything, turned up the music, and
pretended it was exciting. Isabel wasn't even paying attention. *Man, she has the good seat.* I turned to look at the
banana truck as we came up beside it. The driver was an
old man hunched over the wheel. There was the shadow
of a child next to him. Or maybe a dog. I leaned closer to
the window to look.

"Oh shit!" Jesse yelped. I spun back around to see a
tractor trailer barreling down the mountain, around the
curve. His horn blared and the lights blinded us. Jesse
looked in the rearview mirror to check on Arshan. I
could see his surprised face lit up in the glare. No way
was he moving back fast enough. Jesse squeezed her eyes
nearly shut, floored the gas pedal and sped *into* the lights.
Isabel and I screamed at the top of our lungs.

Arshan moved his foot to the brake, then veered to
the right, barely slipping in behind the truck, which then

slammed on its brakes, trying to avoid the Honda. Arshan jerked the car to the right again without looking.

I closed my eyes. I heard the tractor trailer fly past with clanking metal, searing horn and screeching brakes. I opened my eyes to see another car appear in our head-lights. Jesse cursed again and spun off the road, wheels skidding toward the edge.

Arshan jerked the steering wheel and veered around the truck toward the edge of the mountain. In front of him, out of the dust, like a desert mirage, appeared the Honda. Cars rushed by on his left. There was nowhere to go. He slammed on the brakes and grimaced, his eyes squeezing shut.

They were going to hit.

Oh, thank God we didn't go over the edge. I was a hunch-back statue, gulping in shaky breaths like a winded Chi-huahua, a hand on my chest to both affirm and calm my racing heart. *WE, breathe in, ARE, breathe out, ALIVE, breath in—*

Bam! We were struck from behind. The seat belt karate kicked my ribs, and my palms slapped the dashboard. Isabel, the idiot not wearing a seatbelt, crashed full body into my seat, adding more sounds of crunching metal and thudding body parts to the night. Jesse let out a groan. Then silence.

Silence.
Silence in both cars.

If both of us died, Kendra would be an orphan.

So help me God, I will never look at Sandra Miheso again.

Maliheh. Reza. Mina. Almost joined you.

Jeezus H. Christ. No one else here is allowed to die. You hear me, Mister Almighty? I should have told Isabel about her father.

You take me if you're going to take anyone else. You stay away from my friends.

Mina, did you save us?

"Holy crap!" I said so I wouldn't cry. I opened my car door and nearly walked off the edge of a mountain. "Holy crap!" I said again. "Jesse, get out so I can climb across."

Jesse didn't move.

"Everybody okay?" I heard Arshan call out.

Jesse started at the sound of his voice. She whipped around and looked at Isabel.

"I'm okay," Isabel choked out and looked down at her still intact body in awe.

Arshan called out again and Jesse finally stumbled out

of the car. I climbed across and made it out just in time to see Jesse fall into Arshan's arms. Arshan stroked her hair with his eyes shut tight until Isabel jumped out of the car and Jesse hugged her fiercely. *We really did almost just die, didn't we?*

I looked quickly at the bumper of our car and the hood of the Ford. Both were banged up, but most likely they'd still run. When I got closer to the other car, I saw Cornell huddled in the back, Lynette nearly hidden in his arms. I held my breath. I could make out Cornell whispering into her hair, "I love you I love you I love you."

I stood up and took in the scene, like standing in the empty parking lot of a drive-in movie theater. I watched the dark forms of Jesse, Arshan and Isabel locked in an embrace on the side of a road on the top of a mountain in the middle of nowhere, adding shallow breaths and tears to the silent black cloak around them. Cornell and Lynette were wrapped up in a world of intimacy, each silently bargaining for an eternity more of each other.

I felt suddenly cold, seeing all those arms intertwined and holding tight. The darkness threatened to swallow me. Or abandon me to infinity. Distant, haze-dusted stars were as comfortless as a burning lighthouse. I realized I was waiting to see if anyone was going to remember I was there. The silence quickly told me that the only person who'd truly needed me was gone. I mourned Mina's absence as if she'd just tumbled over the edge of the mountain.

But instead of imaginary screams, I heard one clear,

simple question in the night air: *Now what?* The movie playing in front of me and the chill in the night air were all too clear in their message.

But another part of me bristled at this thought. The old Samantha—the fearless one—was offended. Every message has a flip side. If I never let anyone get as close as Mina, I would never feel this pain again. If I went my way alone, I could stand on the fringes and observe and laugh. I could focus on my art. Or go back to science. Achievement is like love, with less risk. It would be better that way, just me. I was tough. With my screwed-up family, I should have learned the danger of human attachment long ago. It was like what Jesse said about the outhouse. I should know better.

A truck flew by on the road, blowing dust and the scent of cattle into my face. My eyes began to penetrate the darkness. Graffiti appeared on rocks lining the highway. My arms broke out in goosebumps. That meant people lived in these mountains. Or bandits. Was that the sound of pebbles falling or scrambling feet? I suddenly felt exposed, like an action hero surrounded by invisible bad guys in the bushes.

"Everybody get back in the cars!" I said. "Now!"

Cornell's eyes found mine through the rear car window, startled. Lynette lifted her head and I saw fear scurry across their faces.

Arshan, though, looked like he didn't hear me at all. He had Jesse and Isabel wrapped up in his arms snugger than cellophane and if I didn't know better I'd say he looked almost happy. Certainly he looked like he had no intention of letting go. For the first time, I got a glimpse of what losing Mina must've been like for him. She'd left him all alone like me.

It was cruel the things that could happen to you in an instant. The way people could be ripped from your arms like mice snatched by eagles.

I felt the two Samanthas ready to argue again. There was something Mina had told me once, something she'd said.

But there wasn't time. I hurried back to the car and tapped Arshan gently on the shoulder. In a daze, we all took our seats as before.

As the cars' engines startled the silent air, I sank back into my seat and stared down the darkness. Soon, I thought. The internal civil war had to end and I had to figure out what the hell I was going to do. Stay lost or be found.

Lakehouse, Rappahannock, VA, 1991

"Want some more lemonade?" Eleven-year-old Isabel stood on the dock.

I looked up at her, the sun shining high in the sky above her head. She had a hand on her hip, waiting impatiently. "Come on, Kendra. Come with me."

Kendra looked up, embarrassed. She was drawing hearts around two initials overtop the advertisements in her *YM* magazine. I tried to see what it said, and Kendra tried to hide it unsuccessfully with her hands.

KJ + A

Only one letter for the boy. "Adam!" I laughed. The boy staying next door to the lake house Jesse was renting that summer.

Kendra glared at me, and Mina giggled. She was floating on her back in the water but could hear us apparently.

"He's cute," Isabel said, to take Kendra's side. She put out her hand with pink nail polish on her fingers.

Kendra took her hand and followed Isabel up the big hill to the house to ask for more pink lemonade.

I picked up the magazine, and flipped forward and back a few pages. Kendra had drawn, like, twenty hearts that morning.

"Hey, Sam?"

"Yeah?" I said, tracing over the amazingly symmetrical hearts.

Mina swam close to the dock, next to my knees.

"What?" I said, and raised my eyebrows.

Mina changed her mind and went back to floating. She looked up at the sky, completely crammed full of drifting fluffy clouds. I watched them, too, for a second, admiring how they arranged themselves into faces and animals and a hundred other pictures of life.

"What do you think is the point?"

"Of what, Em?"

"Any of it. All of it. Boys. School. Life."

I looked at my feet under the water, thought how delicious the coolness felt, especially when miniature waves lapped at my ankles and left spots to be tickled by the wind. "To have fun?" I suggested.

Mina splashed me.

"I don't know, Em. But we got lots of time to figure it out, right?"

Mina didn't answer. She dove under the water and disappeared. I watched in amusement, but she stayed under a long time. I scanned up and down the channel, at the green water and the trees across the way.

Mina surfaced next to my feet, yanking them hard. I almost fell in and then I let myself fall in, until I came up face-to-face with Mina, grinning. My toes squished into the mud on the bottom and I made a "yuk" face. Mina laughed the way she always did at me, benevolently amused.

"I think," she said, and waited for us both to recover from laughing. "I think the point is to find soul mates."

I looked at the magazine on the edge of the dock and grinned. "You mean boyfriends?"

Mina crinkled her eyebrows. "I guess, but I was thinking more like us. Don't you think soul mates are people who understand how you see things, maybe because they've known you so long, or maybe just because they understand all your bad parts and love you anyway? I think a soul mate makes up for everything you're missing."

"Well, then, if you put it that way—you are definitely my soul mate. So now we can just have fun?" I climbed the dock ladder and then pushed off with my feet and did a backflip into the water. I opened my eyes underwater and watched the flurry of particles dance through the green, moss-colored water.

When I came back up, Mina was laughing, but a different laugh from her repertoire, a sadder one. "But don't you think there are many soul mates, in case we ever lost each other?"

I looked up at the house and saw Kendra and Isabel walking back with the lemonades, two in each hand. Mina followed my gaze and watched them. She nodded. She lifted her hand and waved. Isabel waved in a way that made Mina laugh, and we could see Kendra scold her for spilling.

Mina touched my shoulder, so I would look over. "I'm just saying, Sam. There's a lot of people in the world. There must be lots of soul mates."

I was wounded. "But—"

"Lemonade!" Isabel interrupted us with pink frosty glasses, and Mina's face told me the discussion was over.

CHAPTER

12

IT WAS ANOTHER HOUR BEFORE WE CROSSED over the bridge into Tela, and wound our way down a dirt road to the beach house. We arrived by trial and error, going back to look for a "right at the old Coca-Cola sign," per Ana Maria's instructions, and a "left after thatched-hut bar."

Both cars pulled into a dusty driveway. The headlights showed a large but basic clapboard wood house.

And a slender, barefoot black man sitting on the front porch.

That must be the caretaker, I thought, and waved out my window. Ana Maria had told me about a watchman who lived in a cement house nearby and maintained the vacation home while her family was away. Which, I only now realized after the car accident, must be because the area was unsafe. The beach house was surrounded by the local Garifuna population, whom I was excited to photograph. Their culture blended Indian blood with that of shipwrecked slaves and had grown to inhabit the coastline of Central America. They were supposedly an easygoing and self-sufficient people, but modern world poverty allows few exemptions from discontent and rebellion.

The watchman was lanky and tall, ancient-looking yet nimble. His skin was like shiny wet pebbles in the headlights of the cars. He had his hands in his jeans pockets and stood perfectly still, watching and waiting.

I got out and went to him with my hand outstretched. "*Soy* Samantha. *Mucho gusto*," I said, it dawning on me as I did that he might only speak the local Garifuna language.

The man hesitated then smiled a perfunctory smile of yellowed ivory teeth. He held out his hand. It was smooth and warm.

"Ahari."

Ahari walked toward the Ford. Arshan got out of the driver's seat. He looked at me for assurance. I had never mentioned a caretaker.

"You guys, this is Ahari. He's the watchman."

Arshan popped the trunk in response.

Ahari grabbed two armfuls of groceries and started for the house.

The vacation club piled in on his heels. It looked like any typical beach house, sandy and worn, with mismatched chairs and tables and paperback books and board games piled along the walls. Truthfully, I had expected something far more luxurious based on Ana Maria's stories from college. I hoped nobody would feel let down.

"Sammy, I love it!" came Jesse's voice, as if in answer. "It's fabulous!"

Everybody went off to choose rooms and unpack, while Lynette threw together a salad with liberal mounds of the unidentified veggies we had bought.

The house was shaped like a horseshoe, with two private bungalows on either end, and palm trees strung with hammocks in between.

Jesse and Arshan headed straight to the opposing bungalows with doors to the outside, and Cornell and Isabel took their bags to the inside rooms. I followed Isabel.

Isabel had said barely a word since the accident. When I entered the room behind her, she spun around. Her scared eyes looked searchingly into mine.

"You okay?" I asked warily. Isabel had truly not been herself these past two days.

"I want you to promise me something." Not a hint of joking in her turquoise eyes.

I nodded, waiting.

"I just almost watched everyone I love die in a car accident."

Of course Isabel wouldn't consider that she had almost died, too.

"You have to promise me that you won't die before me."

Isabel's emotion singed my skin. "Promise."

I didn't know how to reply but she read my heart, breaking at her fear, and seemed satisfied. Isabel sank down on one of the twin beds and unzipped her backpack. She took out a book and lay down with her back to me. It took me a second to realize she was reading Mina's journal.

"Read me something."

Isabel didn't answer.

"I'll let you read mine. I don't think Mina would mind. She probably expected us to."

I could see Isabel's back moving with her breath.

"You know what I do? I ask a question and then a flip to a page for the answer. It makes me feel like I'm talking to her."

Still no answer. Oh shit, I made her feel worse. I started to apologize, but then I heard her flip to a page and take a deep breath.

"'December 15. All three of you were here today. I love you, Isabel, for pretending that you and Kendra came home early for Christmas and not because you know I'm going to die soon. I look terrible, right? But when you read this, I want you to know that I'm okay. Or that I was okay, I guess. There's a kind of peace that comes the closer I get to the end.

"'The maple tree dropped its last leaves today. Oh, they were long since shriveled and brown. But I know what it means. That tree has taught me things, Isabel.

We're all so much more connected than we know. The tree speaks to me and I don't even mean it allegorically. It's probably the cancer, or the pain meds, but what that tree whispers at night makes so much sense that I don't care where it comes from. It tells me that I'm doing fine, that death isn't the end we think it is.

"'I know the tree watches you come to visit me every day. It says that love lives. That love is really all there is and everything else is just different manifestations in different dimensions. Ask Samantha!

"'I think that means that you'll be able to feel how much I love you guys even after I'm gone. And that's good. That makes me feel so much better. Because I love you three so much I just couldn't imagine how it would disappear. And maybe if my love lingers then it can help you somehow, when you need it.

"'Love you, Belly. A penny for your precious thoughts.'"

I looked closer to see what Isabel was doing. She was stroking a shiny penny taped at the bottom of the entry.

Isabel closed the journal and lay back on the bed. She looked at me with wide eyes, a technique that dries out watering tear ducts. Thought I'd invented that technique.

I must've looked like a dead bug, still stuck in the web of Mina's words, with no reply coming to rescue me. When I finally wriggled free, I found myself still holding two very heavy bags. I dumped them on the other bed, while Isabel stared at the ceiling. She was crossing and uncrossing her toes.

"You remember Mina with those baby rabbits?"

I shuddered in the humid room. "You really wanna talk about that now?" I whispered like someone might hear us. Who?

"Mina never got over it, Sam. She told me whenever she looked at that maple tree, she thought about the bunnies."

Mina's backyard, Springfield, VA, 1993

Mina's father loved yard work. In Virginia, there's plenty of it year-round. He left Mina and me to cook ramen noodles with frozen peas so he could rake leaves. He couldn't watch our homespun dance recitals because there was grass to cut. And there was no time for algebra help as long as mulch needed to be spread around.

Sometime when we were freshmen in high school, Mina worked up the courage to ask her dad if yard work was more important than her. He only frowned in response, but he let a whole week go by without even entering the yard.

The following week, as if Mina had angels at her beck and call, a neighborhood kid knocked on the door to ask if her dad needed help with the yard.

Not just any kid. Brandon Bateman. The hottest kid in school. A junior. He had thick dark hair like Tom Cruise and tan muscles from playing football. Mina and I had a new pastime. We drank Cherry Cokes at the kitchen table and watched Brandon go back and forth with the lawnmower or dig up weeds or prune trees. With military efficiency, we took turns offering him more water or clean towels. He knew we were watching and giggling. One day he strategically took his shirt off and poured his glass of water down his muscled chest. The next Saturday, Isabel and Kendra joined us.

We passed two happy summer months, until one day Mina's father strolled out of his study and caught us at our schoolgirl peep show. He was so flustered he barely could find the words. "Out!" he managed, and we scattered like bats from sunlight.

Isabel and Kendra took the following weekend off, but I was a fixture at the Bahrami house. The next Saturday, when Mina and I rounded the corner to the kitchen, we came upon her father sitting at the table, still as a paperweight, his chin resting on his knuckles, watching Brandon work outside the window. I figured he would have fired him after the last weekend, but instead he sat staring at him with the saddest eyes I'd ever seen. Both Mina and I froze, completely unsure what to do. It felt like hours—those moments we watched her father unveiled as a complete stranger but somehow more knowable. Mina inhaled and exhaled raggedly as if she were reminding herself how to breathe.

He fired Brandon when he was done that day.

The next Saturday I planned to stay home. It made my father uncomfortable. He took his coffee to the basement as usual and mumbled about how he was off to the hospital soon and could I take out the trash and how come I wasn't at Mina's. I sighed and left for Mina's house, not knowing what to expect. Even still, I was unprepared for what happened.

A note on Mina's front door told me to come around back. In the backyard, I found Mina pushing the lawn mower. She was bent over with her arms extended above her head, pushing hard to make it up the hill around the edge of the mulch. She made it to the top and then she spotted me. She waved and rolled her eyes like, *can you believe this?* But she was visibly proud of herself, I could tell. She made a big show of vrooming the lawn mower fast across the grass. I smiled and she smiled back, not watching where she was going.

I don't know when it happened, but suddenly Mina's face turned from a happy clown into a Stephen King clown, like smearing on ghoulish face paint in a dirty backstage mirror. In slow motion, I watched her look down at her legs in horror, and shove the mower away from her with all her strength. The shut-off motor produced an abrupt silence in which I struggled to get a grip on what had happened. I ran to Mina, trying to figure out the blood on her legs, the frantic grabbing at her shins, trying to understand why she was sobbing hysterically. I thought she'd mowed her feet off. When I made it up the hill, I looked at her hands as she held them out to me.

Now, I could make out the wriggling balls of flesh and blood. I looked at Mina's face, before scanning her entire body, still thinking emergency room. Mina shook her head, unable to choke out words through her tears, and dumped the contents of her hands into mine. When I realized that the warm lumps sinking into my palms were pieces of baby rabbits, I threw them to the ground and vomited. Mina ran off.

I waited for the nausea to subside enough for me to stand, then I went inside. Mina wouldn't let me in the bathroom, so I methodically washed my hands in the kitchen sink, drying them each time before deciding to wash them again.

The whole time, I could hear her crying over the sound of the faucet.

Her father came into the kitchen, looking panicked, and caught me standing there. "What happened?"

"Mina killed some bunnies. With the lawnmower." He put his ear to the bathroom door. For the second time in all my life, I could see the raw emotions Mina's father normally concealed with blanket anger. "I think she'll be okay," I said to him.

He waited a long time before he looked at me and nodded. When he disappeared again, I sat on the floor against the bathroom door so Mina would know I was there.

When I finally heard the doorknob turn, I didn't have time to stand before she was there looking down at me. She smiled crookedly, her face a big red puffer fish. "We're having a funeral. Go call Isabel and Kendra. We'll bury the bunnies under the maple tree."

13

BY THE TIME ISABEL AND I MADE IT OUT TO the porch, the salad they'd saved for us was wilting. Even if they hadn't heard us, anybody could see I'd been crying my eyes out.

Isabel sat down next to Jesse, but I walked to the railing to look into the palm tree grove and the blackness beyond that must be the ocean. I breathed in the musty, salty night air. It was soothing—the sound of the ocean mixing with the hushed conversations behind me. Jesse had Isabel laughing quietly. I wasn't quite ready yet, though, because I was still living in the echoes of a summer tragedy.

And I wanted to mull over Mina's words Isabel read me from her journal. *Why had I failed her?* She left it to *me* to make her immortal. My journal was filled with notes Mina made about meditation, and things like white noise recording, often whole passages copied from books. She obviously hadn't put any of that in Isabel's journal. She picked me to do it. *Ask Samantha,* she'd told Isabel. Maybe she'd picked me because she thought I was the only one crazy enough to believe in it, but still she'd picked *me.* I thought of the physics tomes I'd shelved, the meditation sessions I'd attempted before leaving for Paris, and how I'd since abandoned my promise. I thought of the maple leaves. I was an asshole. I'd been reading Mina's journal like a magic eight ball for my petty problems instead of as an instruction manual of my best friend's dying wishes. The last thing Mina asked of me. I wiped at my sore eyes.

"Sammy, honey?" Jesse called out from the table. "Sammy girl, now that's enough. We've had enough tears today. We're on vacation, dammit."

After dinner, we lay under the stars on the beach, watching the black water curl and crash onto the sand. It was warm and humid, and the air was scented with the intersection of sweet vegetation and briny sea. Conversation babbled back and forth with the gentle lull of long-standing friendship.

I lay with my head in Jesse's lap and listened to the laughter float above me while she played with my hair. Ever since I was little, Jesse had tucked me in at sleepovers, tickled my back and played with my hair. I let the gentleness of it soothe my jagged edges. I was starting to understand that Mina would've been appalled (not honored) if I didn't appreciate my time here with them. It would be lemon in a paper cut, to quote one of her favorite sayings. I listened to Isabel tell some silly story about one of her admirers and I thought, *how is Kendra surviving without this?*

November 13
Samantha

If we somehow pull this off—what will it be like? Will you leave me messages, appear in my dreams, warn me of dark alleys?

Because I want more. I want you to sit next to me and laugh too loud at Rose's Café. I want to see you finish your Ph.D. I want you to hug me when life hurts. I want you to be there at every Thanksgiving, on every crazy vacation with Lynette and Jesse. I want us to make mac 'n' cheese and frozen burritos in honor of our screwed-up latchkey childhood. I want you to visit me in Honduras for the artist residency.

I want you to outlive me. That's what I want. I want you, Kendra, Isabel, everyone, to outlive me, because this…this is too horrible. Watching you die has to be worse than death.

I don't feel like talking about physics today.

—*Sam.*

14

KENDRA BROUGHT THREE THINGS HOME from work that day. One—the flowers. Two—the note that had come with the flowers. Three—the fax.

The flowers were a generic variety obviously picked out by his secretary.

The note said he would be working late.

The fax was a list of doctors and clinics that performed abortions.

For the first time in a long time, Kendra was considering the man she wanted to marry apart from his spec sheet.

She'd always thought they were a perfect match, as much because of their faults as their assets. Michael was unapologetically shallow, snobby, married to his career and materialistic to a fault. But that meant he had A-list friends, designer furniture, and regularly bought Kendra Gucci shoes to wear to exclusive parties. Michael indulged and even encouraged Kendra's vices, canceling out her mother's disapproval about her *misplaced priorities*. Her hippie mother, as Michael liked to joke.

Her mother had liked Michael actually. Because he was a charmer when he wanted to be, but also because she, too, thought he was perfectly suited to her daughter. It had never occurred to Kendra to find this insulting until now.

Michael worked late even on a holiday. He laughingly recounted business deals that were less than honest. He was mercilessly critical of anyone he thought stupid, unattractive or low class. Kendra tried to bring back happy images of fancy parties, but instead was treated to the memory of the fight they'd had about him flirting at one such recent party.

Her nausea was back. Kendra put a hand to her stomach. She closed her eyes and willed it to go away. She realized she was hoping the whole pregnancy would go away. Or more precisely, she wished it had never happened.

Something clinked onto the glass coffee table. Kendra opened one eye but saw nothing amiss. The *Wall Street Journal* was fanned atop her *W* magazines. The metal coasters were in a perfect stack.

Good, the nausea was subsiding. Kendra picked up

the magazines and knocked them against the table to straighten and refan them. The vacation club picture fell forward on the table.

Kendra saw now what had made the initial noise. A clover leaf, suspended in a plastic holder, that had stayed taped to the back of the picture ever since Mina gave it to her ages ago. The tape finally gave, and now it sat on the coffee table looking up at her. She picked it up and closed it inside her palm.

Kendra blinked slowly and her head rang with Mina's characteristic chuckle. Most little girls giggle, but Mina had chuckled, almost Buddha-like, as if she'd been through this before and found all things amusing.

Kendra remembered perfectly the day Mina had given her the clover. They were fourteen and Kendra had had her worst day of school ever.

Mina's backyard, Springfield, VA, 1994

"He said he didn't want to kiss a black girl." Kendra kicked at a fallen acorn on Mina's back deck. "He said it in front of everyone." She looked up. "I'm not black."

Mina looked at Kendra calmly but with sympathy. "Yes, you are."

Kendra wrinkled her eyebrows. "I'm not. I mean, okay, I am. But, you know, I'm not *black*. Like you're not Iranian."

"I'm not?" Mina chuckled.

Kendra rolled her eyes. "You're not helping."

"I'll be right back."

Kendra waited on the porch, watching shadows fall across the lawn. She slapped at a mosquito on her ankle. When a light turned on in Mr. Bahrami's study, she tried to see inside. *What did that man do in there all day and night?* Not that her dad was home very much lately. Working on another big discrimination case. Kendra wondered what her dad would say if she tried to talk to him about the boy. Never mind, she knew what he would say. *The struggle continues, Kendra.* Jeez, men. For the hundredth time that year, Kendra wished her mother was black instead of her father.

"Here." Mina slipped back onto the porch brandishing something shiny.

Kendra looked at the square of plastic. Inside was a bright green four-leaf clover, plucked one day in its prime and now embalmed against ever aging another day. Kendra looked at Mina curiously.

"Are we going to talk about the stupid boy?"

"Nope."

Kendra huffed. "Mina—"

Mina met her eyes. "Because that stupid boy doesn't matter." Mina again held out the clover leaf.

Kendra took it and held it up to the porch light.

"It's for good luck," Mina said with a smile. "With all the things that *will* matter."

"I don't believe in good luck."

Mina chuckled. "I know you don't."

"You have to work hard to get what you want in life.

Practice and planning. My mom's the one who believes in all that other…silliness." Kendra gave Mina her most stern, serious face.

Mina chuckled again. "I'm sure you're right, KJ. But just in case one day you find out you're wrong, I figured it couldn't hurt. Right?"

CHAPTER

15

AT THREE IN THE MORNING, I WAS AWAKENED
by a strange noise. I sat upright in bed, then lay right back
down as a wave of nausea rolled over me in the pitch-black
room. The noise came again. It was the low growl of a
pitbull and it was coming from my stomach.

I bolted barefoot to the bathroom nearest our room. I
barely had time to swish my hair out of the way before
vacating the entire contents of dinner. The force of it was
terrifying, and dropped me to my knees. Then a new
sound came from my midsection—a sloshy gurgling.

For the next seven minutes, all I could do was whimper as life passed by in excruciating intestine-twisting
pain, cursing Jesse's exotic salad, doused in amoeba water,

and my defenseless American stomach. When the first moment arrived that I could breathe, a knock came at the door.

"I'll be okay," I said weakly, sure it was Isabel. Then I realized it came from the door to Jesse's room.

"Scoot over, darling, we've obviously been poisoned."

I meant to reply, but a gagging started in my throat. I think that gave Jesse her answer.

She scurried away to throw up on the palm trees.

I slid to the floor like a deflated balloon. My cheek made it to the cool, sandy floor just in time to hear another knock at the door.

"Samantha?" Isabel's voice came through in a whisper. "Lemme in."

"I wouldn't if I were you."

"I'm sick."

I groaned. This was the vacation from hell. "Join the party."

Across the hall, Cornell was in the bathroom with his wife. He patted Lynette's back gently with one hand, while holding back her hair with the other. So far, their vomiting had been symbiotically timed. Cornell wasn't surprised. He and his wife always seemed to operate in sync.

In the weak night-light glow of the bathroom, Cornell read the pain on Lynette's face. He felt sorry for her, but only until a heaving rumble snaked through his innards.

"Trade you," he eked out, and motioned Lynette aside.

Lynette propped herself against the wall and attempted to pat her husband's back, but ended up patting his butt as he retched.

Cornell turned and gave Lynette the most priceless look. Lynette managed a measly laugh. She patted the floor beside her. "Cop a squat, dear."

When Cornell sat down beside her, they linked arms absentmindedly, and Lynette let her head drop onto his shoulder. After a minute, she said, "Aren't you worried about Kendra?"

"She's a big girl, honey. All grown-up now, our little girl."

"No, it's not right she didn't come. There's something wrong. Why doesn't she ever tell me anything?"

Cornell kissed the top of Lynette's head. "Maybe some things aren't for you to understand."

Lynette stiffened. After over thirty years of marriage, certain fights always started the same way, ingrained in the relationship just like the rituals of teasing and making coffee. She knew what Cornell was alluding to. "I'm her mother. What don't I understand?" She wasn't going to let him get away with cheap shots. She was going to make him say it.

Cornell was too weak to fight. "Let it go, Lynette. We don't know what's bothering her. Maybe it's her job. Maybe it's Michael. She'll tell us when she wants to."

"That's not what you meant. You meant that I don't understand what it's like to be a black woman, and that's why Kendra doesn't confide in me."

"Do you ever talk about it with her?"

"Do you?"

Lynette and Cornell faced off, less than six inches between their eyes. Lynette looked away first. Her flesh turned colder than the floor. "I think it's a mother-daughter thing, not a race thing. Women can't help but become a reaction to their mothers."

Cornell's lawyer mind mulled this over. The one thing he'd learned about mother-daughter relationships was that they were complicated, an impenetrable rock formation made of thin, delicate layers. "At this particular time, I concede the point," Cornell said, and pulled his wife's head back onto his shoulder.

When Arshan finally made it back from the bathroom, he heard someone out on the porch. He put a hand to his stomach and slipped on his shoes. He walked onto the covered porch just in time to see Jesse throw up over the railing—hard enough that she didn't hear his arrival. Arshan watched her ease herself to the floor. He was about to politely leave, when Jesse caught sight of him.

Jesse burped and turned her face away. She wasn't wearing any makeup and knew she probably thought she looked awful. Automatically, she freed her hair from a ponytail and smoothed her satin nightgown with sweaty palms.

Arshan knew just what she was thinking. He couldn't help but smile. "You look gorgeous," he said before he had time to think better of it.

Sarcastic, Jesse thought, but her defenses were down. Being seen without makeup was actually physically painful for Jesse in front of a man. Not a man. Arshan.

Again, Arshan read her thoughts as nakedly as a child's fear. Ten years of being a person's bridge partner teaches you a thing or two. Ever since the accident, Arshan's feelings for Jesse had crystallized and taken on a delicious urgency. He was both thrilled and terrified, two sensations he'd thought were long dead to him. The past thirty years could best be described as waiting. Waiting to die? Or waiting to live again? He sat down before she could leave.

"You must know," Arshan said, and looked to see if she did.

Jesse listened to the words and weighed their meaning but still wasn't sure. She kept her eyes on the deck floor.

"I must tell you—" He hesitated for the briefest moment, hoping she would look up. He looked at the sheen of her hair in the moonlight instead. "Jesse, I'm old and I'm damaged. On top of that, I'm haunted." Arshan felt a chill in the humid air. "And even after all this time, I'm not sure that I'm ready."

First, Jesse smiled at the old, weathered floorboards beneath them. Then she lifted her chin so that the moon could unveil every wrinkle Jesse Brighton had earned in laughter and tears and dashed hopes and dreams. She looked into Arshan's sad, crinkly eyes and said, "Welcome to the club, honey."

CHAPTER

16

WHEN I WOKE UP THE NEXT MORNING, everybody was still asleep. I tiptoed into the sunshine. I walked off the porch and through the palm grove until I arrived at a fence. I put my hand to my throat and gasped. *Stunning.* It was possibly the most perfect beach I'd ever seen. The sun was still low in its early morning splendor, casting diamonds across the waves and bathing the sand in glittery warmth. A proud palm tree posed jauntily at the beach's edge, begging to be made into a postcard. To the left, I saw the beach run along unfettered until a jutting tip of jungle and rock. From what I'd read, I knew that was the biggest settlement area of the Garifuna.

I tried to run over everything else I remembered.

Aboriginal peoples from mainland Central and South America migrated to the Antilles Islands and intermixed. Columbus "discovered" the islands, so Spain colonized and enslaved the population. So many died off from disease and mistreatment that African slaves were shipped in. Runaway slaves and shipwreck survivors were taken in by the Carib population and the new blend constituted the Garifuna. Then Britain gained the island of St. Vincent in a treaty. The Garifuna resisted valiantly, but Britain rounded them up and shipped them to the Honduran island of Roatan. More than half died at sea, but the survivors persevered and even flourished. Finally, many migrated back to the coast of Central America in places like Tela. But to this present day, the Garifuna people maintained native South American and African customs. They make casabe (yucca) bread and dance punta—a frenzied ritual expressing all the joys and sorrow of their past.

I shielded my eyes from the sun to count seven canoes along the beach, all painted in bright teal and bloodred. The Garifuna were fishermen and lived off the sea and the land. I'd seen pictures of the settlements just down the road—small thatched huts by the sea. I looked around. The area we were staying in was so isolated. I wondered what would happen with the arrival of the outside world. If it was anything like the U.S. or other places I'd seen, beachfront property always went to the wealthiest bidder who immediately turned it into private compounds of cement and plastic.

But until then…*What a place to live.* It was completely silent apart from the water and the wind in the palm trees.

I turned to watch the waves, waiting for each dramatic curl to crest and crash. It was heartbreakingly beautiful—the exuberant crush of the whitewater. I loved that sound—rushing water. Everything, in fact, that morning, was perfect.

"Mina, run!" I called aloud, and took off galloping down the sand. I spun in circles, my feet pounding the warm ground. I spun faster and faster till the blue sky blended with the ocean and swirled around me like a cyclone, until I collapsed on the sand, giggling at myself.

That's when I caught sight of Ahari, standing in the shadows by the fence, watching me. I waved, a night crab caught in a flashlight beam. Ahari continued to stare, his eyes steady. He knew I could see him but he didn't smile. It gave me the chills.

Many hours later, the entire brood had made it out to the beach, and discussed every intimate detail about a person's digestive system that should never be shared in public. Empathetic groans all around. I got heartily teased for my choice of destination—treacherous roads and instant food poisoning.

I sent Kendra quick texts to update her and hopefully make her laugh. The others went on walks, collected seashells, took pictures by the fishing boats, sunbathed and dipped in the waves.

By late afternoon, we'd all assembled back under the umbrellas.

Jesse and Isabel were drinking Bloody Marys, though I couldn't for the life of me figure out how. Jesse thought Bloody Marys settled the stomach and replenished your vitamins.

In her black designer swimsuit, Jesse stretched out like a royal feline, her face shaded by an oversize Grace Kelly hat.

I followed the line of Jesse's figure from her delicate shoulders to her tanned chest speckled with age freckles to her nearly flat belly, to her gracefully full thighs to her gleaming Corvette-red toenails. My God, I hoped I would look that good at her age.

Just then, Jesse peered over her Jackie O sunglasses at me. "Sammy, we've been discussing your decision about this Remy Badeau character. You want advice from some senior citizens? Not like we got it all figured it out—a divorcée, a widower and…well, at least Lynette and Cornell should be able to tell us a thing or two."

"You can give me advice on what not to do."

"Ouch, honey, now that really stings." Jesse lay back on the recliner. "Good advice. Bad advice. I hate to break it to you, darling, but all anyone's really got is stories."

Not a bad idea on a beach afternoon. "Does that mean you're going first then?"

Jesse's whole body tensed. I just assumed that was what she was getting at.

Isabel stuffed a finger sandwich into her mouth and

clapped her hands delightedly, obviously imagining more glitz and glam stories of Jesse's modeling days.

Jesse heard her daughter's glee and slowly rolled to face her. It was hard to read her expression due to the ridiculous sunglasses. "My precious child, this trip has made me realize a few things. For one, you girls aren't really girls so much anymore. But mostly, without our dear little Mina, I see that I might not have all the time in the world to tell you a few things I left out."

Jesse sighed and lay back once more. "Like about your father, for instance."

November 17
Samantha

The Copenhagen Interpretation was one theory, but there's another one called Many Worlds.

It says that each time the universe is faced with a choice (like an electron going through one of two slits), the universe splits into separate universes, one for each possible outcome.

A recent survey found that over half of the world's top physicists (yes, Stephen Hawking) believe in the Many Worlds Theory.

Max Tegmark at MIT and David Deutsch at Oxford routinely write on parallel universes and why we don't see the other worlds. One scientist believes we glimpse the other worlds when we dream. But Brian Greene at Columbia has my heart. In *The Fabric of the Cosmos,* he describes how you could theoretically time travel to parallel universes of other outcomes of your life.

Doesn't it mean that in one universe, Mina, everyone made all the right decisions? That there is a world where we have mothers and Isabel has a father? That it is only by chance that we're the "copy" that unfortunately ended up in this universe, with all the bad possibilities? Like cancer.

CHAPTER 17

"WE MET ON THE OPENING NIGHT OF STUDIO 54. April 26th, 1977," Jesse began, and lit a cigarette. "I was twenty-one. Now, I don't know if I've told y'all this, but I used to be famous."

Lynette groaned and everybody laughed. This part of the story we knew. Jesse reminded us at least once a month, and she always began with, "Now, I don't know if I've told y'all this—"

Jesse ignored the laughter. She was staring into the waves, looking as if she was trying to remember correctly, in a way that would be honest and complete. But how is history ever conveyed completely? It arrives in fleeting moments and images, and is recalled in just the same way.

Jesse had to go back to 1977, the year she met Panama's most eligible bachelor—Cesar Guerra.

"I was something. I was a model, yes, but also what I guess what you ladies would call an 'It Girl.' I had thick wavy hair for days, and eyes to make seasoned photographers swoon. And a body like—damn, I miss that body." Jesse laughed loudly.

"I wore this shiny little silver number—all sequins and sparkle. It was a crazy night, even for New York in the seventies." Jesse laughed again, her still thick hair shaking. "Twenty-one years old. But, of course, I'd been on my own since I was sixteen, when I was discovered." Jesse waved her cigarette in the air. "That's why I've always encouraged you girls to get out there and have a little fun. My life was decided in a bar and a disco."

At sixteen, Jesse was the prototypical wild child in Austin, Texas. She and her girlfriends snuck into bars and clubs—enchanting doormen, cowboys and businessmen alike. It was in one such bar she met Richie Gibbs, a photographer on assignment from New York City. Jesse saw her chance. The photographer never believed her fake ID for a minute, and to his credit, did no more than kiss her on the cheek on his way out. But Jesse's face was the first thing he thought of when the morning came, and still the week after, so he had her flown in to meet with the biggest modeling agency in the world. Jesse was in Paris by the next change of season, living in agency apartments spilling over with girls with giraffe legs. Jesse loved it, and rose to the top of the pack by way of her gray eyes and vibrant, erotic laugh. She graced magazine covers and catwalks, jet-setting between New York and Paris. She rarely visited her parents in Texas. Jesse Brighton had money to burn.

Suffice to say, at twenty-one, Jesse was a sensation. She was lithe and freckled, with shiny full hair and steel-colored, almond-shaped eyes. She moved through a room like a championship stallion—regal and fluid, partial to dramatic tosses of her mane. Jesse was not particularly tall for a model, but her spirit and her startling laugh allowed her to tower over anyone around her. Jesse waited in no lines. She ate lobster three times a week. She donated fifty pairs of barely used high-heel shoes to charity three times a year. Jesse could arrive at a club alone at midnight and expect one hundred people to rush at her as she entered. She knew all the celebrities. She was worshipped by all the nobodies. She'd been around the world. Twice.

Jesse shook her head again, flicked ash into the sand. "I was living the life, I think you could say. Money and famous friends were my accessories of the late seventies. I was like 50 Cent, Sammy. Like a rap star. Cristal and— what do they say? Bling."

Isabel rolled her eyes, but looked delighted, as Jesse commanded the spotlight. It was no secret she revered her mother, and gobbled up her stories of the glamorous single life.

"You know, Frank Sinatra didn't get in that night Studio 54 opened on West 54th. But me? By eleven, I was snort—" Jesse cleared her throat. "Ahem, I was smoking cigarettes in the basement with Brooke Shields and Cher. We were preparing to make our *second* grand entrance," Jesse said with a theatrical swoop of her arm.

Jesse wore a silver sequin tank dress that threatened to expose her milk-white breasts along with her lean freckled thighs that showed from dress hem to knee-high boots.

Cesar Guerra sat at a table against the wall, meeting with business associates of his father, i.e. telling off-color jokes and buying martinis. He was still unaware, as yet, of Miss Jesse Brighton.

"Your father, sweetie, he was…as handsome as nature allows," Jesse said, eliciting giggles from all the girls. Arshan and Cornell groaned. "Delicious, was the word I used to describe him to my girlfriends. Perfect, I believe, was their assessment." At this Jesse grew thoughtful. "He was Panamanian royalty, his family bigwigs in the ruling oligarchy. These Zonians, residents of the Canal Zone, had a major superiority complex. They fed their children peanut butter and jelly sandwiches and sent them off to Harvard. Looking back, studying abroad is what must've shielded Cesar from his family's decline and unsavory business interests." Jesse coughed. "Course, I didn't know anything about that at that time."

★ ★ ★

At twenty-five, Cesar Guerra had big, thick black curls and clear, fair skin. Smoldering black eyes, ringed in dense lashes, lit up with his easy laughter. He was tall, muscled, smart and charming.

His international education had afforded him class and worldliness beyond his years. He debated American politics and French poetry and wine, all with the ease of one who had nothing to lose. Unfortunately, the Zonians lost everything in the 1968 military takeover by Torrijos, who made sweeping land and wealth reforms driven by his deep-seated hatred for the elitists.

"Cesar was a mama's boy in transition. He'd lived the pretty-boy intellectual life abroad, easily escaping the political upheaval in Panama. Just before he met me, well… it was time to pay the piper. He'd been brought back to Panama to start work with his father. Poor thing, he never stood a chance at staying good." Jesse looked at Isabel pointedly. "But he was a good man, once, baby. A good kid, anyway."

Cesar, like all Latin trust-fund children, was raised almost exclusively by his mother and nanny. Señora Guerra was pretty, quiet and young. The perfect rich man's wife. She filled her days with entertaining and charity events and afternoons at the Union Club. Like the other members of the oligarchy, she believed they were *entitled* to the spoils. When the unbelievable happened, when the populists came to power, she was in unspoken agreement with her husband that they must preserve the lifestyle of the family at any cost. Arrogance, however, corrupts behavior in many ways, and it was not long before she was dutifully looking the other way at her husband's affairs, both business and pleasure. Señora Guerra wisely stopped reading the newspapers.

Cesar adored his mother, and understood the predicament of Panamanian society women from an early age. In fact, as early as ten, Cesar understood that manhood would bring him to side with his father. But Cesar felt sure he would never lose empathy for his mother and sisters. Once, a teenage Cesar home on holiday break comforted his mother when media scandals forced her into shuttered rooms in their Paitilla Point mansion. He left a daring message with the head butler at their vacation home in El Valle de Anton, where Alfredo Guerra brought all his mistresses. "Tell him that I hate him. That I will take care of my mother now, so he should never come back to Punta Paitilla."

"Do you remember your grandfather, Isabel?" Jesse asked her daughter.

Isabel shook her head. She'd always told me she only had vague impressions of her father and grandparents, of dolls and sweets in a fancy house.

"Well, he was—he was something of a character. Dashing looks, impossibly white teeth. A smile that charmed and disarmed you for reasons you couldn't explain. His presence in a room was like the arrival of the Rolling

Stones, everybody whispering and poking and tripping over themselves to serve. But I'm getting ahead of myself. Let's meet your daddy first, huh?" Jesse took a long gulp of her drink.

"Let's see. Ah, yes. All the rich and famous were smooshed down in the basement. I don't recall who rallied, probably me, but we all got ready to reemerge as a group. When we waltzed back into the club, it was like something out of a movie. People parted and then swarmed around us. It was one of those moments that stick—the ones that move in slow motion with a soaring soundtrack like *Gone with the Wind*. Your soul just spills out in every direction, soaking up the sensation. Well, naturally, that was when Cesar caught my eye. He had this look. Where do they learn that look, huh? Some Latin lover handbook somewhere, I imagine. With plenty of your father's footnotes. Anyway, could've been the drugs, the booze, the lights. But time stood still when Cesar Guerra looked at me." Jesse took another swallow and smiled to herself.

"So, of course, I pretended I hadn't noticed. I made a point of dancing through the crowd, kissing every celebrity on the lips. We played a little game that way. I showed him who he was dealing with, and he indulged me. I thought I was so smart, so clever. Forcing him to fall madly in love with me." Jesse snorted. Then she lifted her chin. "He did, though, and it was real, I think," she said to herself. Then, more firmly, she continued, "It was real. Cesar said he had never met anybody like me. And I imagine he'd done a pretty wide survey of the female species."

"Well, there *isn't* anybody like you, Mom."

"World wouldn't fit more than one," Lynette said drily.

"Why, thank you, darlings," Jesse said, blowing us kisses. "I never would have made it without the support of my fans!" Jesse laughed and I laughed, too.

"Okay, go on," I prompted. "Did you guys do it that first night, or what?"

"None of your beeswax!" Jesse protested and then laughed. "It was the seventies. Of course we did it. In his penthouse hotel suite. I didn't wear clothes for three days."

I gasped, pretending to be shocked.

"Oh hush. It wasn't just sex. He extended his stay and I postponed Paris and we just lay in bed and told each other our whole damn life stories. And—whew!"

Jesse smacked a hand to her forehead. "Our stories could not have been more different. Quickly, I became his American Dream and he my exotic prince."

Jesse chewed on her lip, pondered the thought. "On the fourth day, an angry all-Spanish phone call came from his father. Cesar left immediately. I holed myself up in the hotel and refused all calls. Cesar, with his two degrees in economics and business, had talked my ear off about saving his beloved Panama. Snapped me out of my glitz and glam bubble, I guess is what I'm sayin'."

★ ★ ★

Cesar returned home to his fuming father. At Harvard, Cesar's head had been filled with the philosophies and hopes of his professors. He dreamed of modernizing Panama's economy, and of uplifting the poor. But for the last six months, Alfredo Guerra had been orchestrating his son's initiation into the family's affairs. Alfredo had quite a different plan for Cesar. The family's finances were in shambles. His son's delusions about helping the poor would have to wait. Family came first.

"Your father wasn't naive, exactly, honey. He'd seen enough to know his father was no saint. But he didn't quite understand the level of corruption or his father's complicity. Oh, who am I protecting? Your grandfather was a snake. A charming, gorgeous snake. Now, I know I am not lacking in self-confidence myself," Jesse said, "but Alfredo Guerra had vanity, greed and sadism, with loads to spare."

Jesse slapped her thigh. "Damn," she said, "Getting ahead again. So, we had just—"

"Had wild passionate sex for four days?" Isabel prompted.

Cornell chuckled. "Yeah, I think we got it, Jesse."

Jesse looked at Isabel instead of Cornell. "Oh, honey, I told you, it was much more than sex. So much more. It was like the meeting of two blazing comets resulting in the creation of earth—"

Now Lynette made a gagging noise, but Isabel shot her

a look that said not to interrupt. Arshan, for his part, let his eyes linger on Jesse, then looked away.

"I'd never felt anything like that before," Jesse finished. She looked far off toward the sea. "I'm not sure it ever happens like that twice. Not once you know how bad it can get."

The expression on everybody's faces quickly turned serious.

CHAPTER

18

JESSE WAS BACK IN THE ENORMOUS BED IN Cesar's hotel in 1977. She lay on her stomach, her head nestled into an impossibly fluffy pillow, and smiled at Cesar. He reached out his hand and gently fingered a stray curl from Jesse's hair. He tucked it behind her ear and traced her face with his finger—her arched eyebrows, the delicate bridge of her nose. He brushed his thumb across her lips. "I'm in love with you, Jesse Brighton." Jesse blinked and giggled, started to protest. "No, wait," Cesar said, stopping her. "I've waited a long time for this feeling. If you don't share it, please don't spoil it for me." Jesse pulled the smile off her lips, and closed her eyes. She found that she had memorized his face. The number of hairs in his full brows, the diameter of his curls, and the laugh lines barely visible around his coal-black eyes. She loved that face. She loved the outrageous stories of his childhood and travels. She loved his impassioned talk of changing the world. She loved him.

"I love you, too," Jesse said as she opened her eyes.

Jesse coughed raggedly with her hand over her mouth. She snapped her fingers and Isabel tossed her the pack of cigarettes. "Yeah, so, he came back to New York two weeks later and proposed. He flew my parents in for dinner, and then I packed and moved to Panama."

"Wow, romantic!" I said.

"Your father let you go?" Cornell asked, indignant.

Jesse turned to Cornell. "I wasn't asking permission. I'd been on my own a long time, and it's not like my family had any room to give advice on marriage. My mother was the textbook definition of depression. She was in and out of hospitals my whole life. My father, he hired a nanny and—" Jesse looked away "—and had lots of affairs, I assume."

Jesse looked down and realized she hadn't lit her cigarette. She flicked the lighter. "And, anyway, they were as dazzled by Cesar Guerra as I was. As everybody was." The flame went out immediately in the ocean breeze.

I shivered and looked around. The air was thick and humid with the now familiar scent of jungle meeting saltwater. But it would cool off soon. "Should we take a break and think about food, you guys?"

The group turned to look at me, a spell broken. Isabel stretched and stood up to go inside. "Let's go change. I think it's about time I got out of this bikini. We'll have dinner on the porch?"

Lynette stood up next to her. "I'll start cooking."

I patted her shoulder. "How 'bout me and Isabel cook this time?"

While the rest of the group splintered off, Isabel and I convened in the kitchen over piles of veggies—familiar ones. We had a long-standing routine when cooking together.

"I chop. You cook?" Isabel voiced the protocol.

"Yup. Chop for chop suey."

"Nerd alert!"

"Takes one to know one," I said, and handed her the carrots and celery. "So you really don't know these stories about your dad?"

"Do *you* know about the first time your parents had sex?" The fire in her eyes fizzled as she realized however little she knew about her parents' love story, I knew less about mine. "Look, my mom always talked about my father like just another crazy thing she did in her life. Just one of her passionate love affairs. Or her one oopsie misstep into the messy world of marriage." Isabel pretended to laugh. "Can't say that anybody ever gave me a different impression."

"If you ask, Jesse would know how to find him, I bet. You could call him." It was something I'd asked my father a thousand times. He must know how to find my mother. I'd had no luck so far on the internet.

Isabel sighed. "He doesn't call *me*." Isabel held out a celery stalk. "Let's mix some more Bloody Marys, yeah?"

I slid over the mix a little too hard and fast. That was exactly it. My mother certainly could've found *me*. "What's he like now, you think?"

"Who? My dad? Probably more like the way she described my grandfather." Isabel's hands froze and she looked at me. "Look, I haven't told you much about my dad because there's just not much to tell. Listen to what my mom said. They had some crazy fling. My mom was a cokehead supermodel party girl. Cesar was rich and handsome. You do the math. Then, oops, they had me. Divorce. Move. I met you and you know the rest."

I never knew when to quit. "Well, it sounds like it might be a little bit more complicated, is all I'm saying."

"Well, it better fucking not be!" Isabel snapped, and dropped the knife, which clattered to the floor. "My mother spent my entire life treating men like accessories and extracurricular activities, and encouraging me to do the same. Jesse Brighton thinks marriage is a sham and a sexist plot. Ask her."

"Have you?"

"Fuck you," Isabel said.

Silence. Neither of us moved. The frying pan startled to sizzle.

Isabel sighed. "Damn, I'm sorry. This is just weird, okay, hearing about my family like they're strangers.

You're right. I never asked much beyond the standard-issue *funny-Jesse* answers." Isabel took a bite of celery. "Maybe I'm wrong. Maybe everything was a lie."

19

JESSE SAT ALONE ON THE BEACH. HOW strange to be so affected by all these memories from thirty years ago. A floodgate had opened, and suddenly Jesse couldn't get her head out of the late seventies. *Out of the gutter*, Jesse thought. But the thing was, as she told the stories, they kept popping into her mind and out of her mouth very differently than she intended. She wanted to help Samantha. After all of Jesse's tough talk over the years, she knew Sammy expected her to talk her out of her romantic notions of marrying Remy. Jesse sighed and pulled her beach towel around her. Was it all just talk or only some of it? The little flutters she'd been experiencing with Arshan reminded her of the girl she'd once been. When it had been possible to trust a man.

"Uh-oh," Jesse muttered. *What have I done to my Isabel?*

A twenty-three-year-old Jesse lay in a marble bathtub, a mound of soap bubbles covering her pregnant belly. She moved the bubbles back and forth over her belly button. She pushed her navel in and out with her finger. With a sudden toss of her head, she dried her hand on a towel and picked up the cigarette from the ashtray on the ledge of the tub.

Without warning, Cesar burst through the bathroom door. Jesse froze with her cigarette in mid air.

"*Amor,* I'm ho—" Cesar's smile dropped off his face. "Are you smoking in the house? My mother will kill you!"

Jesse, recovered from the shock of seeing him, took a deliberate drag of the cigarette before snubbing it out slowly in the ashtray. "What are you doing home?"

Cesar ran his hand over his hair, his curls cut short at his father's insistence, as he ascertained his wife's mood. He frowned but didn't answer.

Jesse looked away. "Business trip" was all she'd been told, as usual. The Guerra women were never told anything more.

Jesse returned to playing with the bubbles and said in an even voice, "I smoke in here because I have nowhere else to go. If I walk outside of our room, I am approached by a servant. If I walk outside of the house, I am accompanied by guards. If I want to go somewhere in town, I am escorted by a fleet of security. I am a prisoner. And so I can damn well smoke in my cell. Darling."

Cesar looked down on his wife, at her thick hair curled up in the steam, at her dainty eyelashes, her graceful hands amongst the bubbles. His look was one of sadness, the anger drained. Jesse chose not to acknowledge this, and jutted her chin out for a fight.

"I thought I prepared you for this," Cesar said gently. "I told you about my childhood. About the claustrophobia."

Jesse shook her head in fury, startling the loving look off her husband's face. "Yes, you told me about your indulgent childhood and childish rebellions. I am not a child, Cesar!" Jesse felt ready to murder him. She forced in a steadying breath. "You promised me we would move out of your parents' house."

"I know I did, *mi amor*. There hasn't been time. And with the baby, my father thinks—"

"That he owns me. Isn't that what he thinks? That I am just another piece of property of the Guerra *cartel*—"

"Oye!" Jesse had gone too far. "You be more careful, *señora*. Remember where you are, my spoiled little wife."

Tears stung Jesse's eyes. She turned to face Cesar just as they spilled down her already moist cheeks. "Cesar, why didn't you tell me how it would really be?"

Jesse had asked him this countless times in the past year. But this time, Cesar heard the full weight of sorrow behind the question. Was he remembering his beautiful wife, in all her feisty glory in New York? Could he see her broken spirit? The trampled spirit of a stallion. He was a boy raised to be a prince in a patriarchal kingdom. Had he forgotten how different it would be for his wife—a fiercely independent woman? How could he have forgotten his mother's pain?

Cesar's eyes were wet as bathwater. "Jess, you're going to have to try to adapt, find ways to be happy. Appreciate everything you have," Cesar said, gently sweeping an arm around the luxurious bathroom.

Jesse didn't look around. "I had money, Cesar. I bought whatever I wanted."

Cesar raised an eyebrow. "Not like this, *princesa*." When Jesse didn't budge, he said, "Look at my mother. She has her tea parties, and her charity work, and—"

Jesse sniffed in disdain. "I am not your mother, Cesar. We don't have the first thing in common. Is that how you expected me to be?" She lifted her gray eyes to his.

Cesar stepped toward the tub. He knelt before her and smoothed back her hair. Jesse lifted her chin again. With that simple act of defiance and dignity, Cesar's face filled with regret. "What *did* you expect, Jesse? What did you want?"

"I expected you to save Panama." *From people like your father*, Jesse thought. She met Cesar's eyes. "And all I wanted was you."

Cesar cupped Jesse's face in his hands. He kissed her forehead and then her lips. Softly and then with hard passion. Jesse resisted and then gave in. Cesar pulled on

Jesse's hands, helped her up. He kissed the enormous belly that emerged from the water, and gently toweled off her glistening body. He took his wife into his arms, and carried her off to the bedroom.

On a beach in Tela, Honduras, Jesse slumped forward and put her hands over her eyes. A second later she took in a huge breath, sat up and shook out her hair, raking her fingers along her scalp. She snatched up the pack of cigarettes on the sand. Empty. *Dadblammit*. She slapped her back against her chair and glared at the sea.

Arshan laid a hand on her shoulder.

"Shit!" Jesse yelped. She turned around and saw who it was. She grasped his hand. "You scared me."

Arshan pulled a chair close to Jesse. "You looked about a million miles away. You okay?"

Jesse stared at the sea a long time before answering. "It's unsettling to remember all these things I've been trying *not to* for so long. You know, I really thought I wasn't thinking about them," Jesse said with a weak smile. "Now I realize I may have spent my entire adult life reacting to—and thereby, *living for*—people long since gone and things long since over in my life. How crazy am I?"

Arshan took both of Jesse's hands in his. He rubbed them to warm them, tried to gauge the look on her face.

"Yes, it is pretty crazy."

CHAPTER 20

AHARI SCANNED THE BEACH LEFT AND right for anyone that might harm or bother his charges. He sniffed in satisfaction when he saw the beach empty but for the dark old man and American woman. Ahari had seen the way these two danced around each other, like children at play. Now the old man sat with the woman's hands in his. They sat stiller than palm trees in the eye of a storm. Ahari held his breath as they studied each other. He couldn't tell if they were speaking, but it appeared not. It appeared they were merely watching each other. It reminded Ahari how roosters squared off to measure each other's courage by the look in their eye. The woman dipped her head ever so slightly and Ahari knew it would happen before she did. The sad old man leaned in and kissed her, soft as the brush of a blade of grass. Soft as a warm handful of sand, Ahari thought, and wriggled his toes into the beach. They kissed without touching anywhere besides their lips, not hurrying through it like young lovers would. They didn't move at all, in fact, as if the slightest breeze would tip them over. When the woman pulled away, they resumed their rooster stares. The woman's sudden loud laugh startled Ahari and the world rushed into his awareness again. Ahari could hear the rustling of the palms, the rhythm of the sea, the sighing of the stars. The man laughed, too. A laugh that did not sound as old as the man, nor as sad as his eyes. The pair resettled into their chairs and watched the citrus colors spread across the sky. The sun set at their backs, not over the water, but the colors subtly spilled across the sea like the sheen of soap bubbles. Ahari swelled with pride, seeing them watch his waves' nightly performance. He'd made a flower garden to match the colors of his piece of sky—orange, yellow and pink. Ahari closed his eyes. He knew the procession of colors by heart and imagined them now as the man and the woman must be seeing them. He stood with both feet planted firmly in the cooling sand and hooked his thumbs in his belt loops. It was a long time before the man and the woman got up to go inside.

Dinner was festive and loud. Arshan sat next to Jesse and waited on her attentively, serving her extra chicken and refilling her cup, as Isabel and I basked in compliments on our chop suey and our rum cocktails. Everybody joked about food poisoning and plan B to ditch the raw-food fad for the duration of their trip. Time to deep-fry and fricassee, in Jesse's language.

Cornell, who always complained of one ailment or another, groaned about heartburn and indigestion and everybody teased him. "My God, Cornell, what's left? Rabies?"

"No respect, no respect I tell ya," he said to Arshan.

I watched the group and snuggled into the coziness of the evening. I kept thinking about the word *gezellig,* a word Wouter, my Dutch lover, had taught me in Argentina. A word with no English equivalent, it conveyed a mixture of homey, intimate and snug, but also described moments like this one—old friends united by good food, candlelight and laughter.

Maybe it was the food poisoning that had brought them closer. Or the car accident. Or maybe it was natural to fill the sinkhole left by Mina's death by widening our circle. I experienced the expected pang of guilt at this thought, but it was more like being poked than kicked. I had no reason to fault these people. They were the ones who had raised me, for better or worse. An unlikely family, each loving me in their own way. Shouldn't that add up to enough?

"I love you guys," I blurted out, interrupting Isabel's story about the tribulations of speed dating.

Nobody needed to ask where the sentiment came from.

They raised their plastic cups on the porch by the beach and the palm trees.

"To family," I said.

"To family, baby," Lynette agreed.

"To surviving this trip!" Cornell laughed.

Jesse rolled her eyes and said with a puff, "Boys." Then she raised her cup high. "To Mina!"

"To Mina!" we all echoed.

That made it feel all right somehow, hearing her name ring out like a mantra in a moonlit drum circle.

I sat back satisfied, and followed along with the resumption of conversation by firing off text messages to Kendra, relaying her the quotes of the night.

Text #1: Honduras is known for its butt injections that give you a J Lo booty. Seriously. I read it in UsWeekly. (Jesse)

Text #2: Oh, whatever, you wear purple underwear. (your mother to your father) (sorry, dude)

Text #3: Your father has gas.

Text #4: Your mother thinks it is inappropriate to text you about gas.

Text #5: Your father says he loves you.

Text #6: "Tell her we all love her and miss her." (direct quote from everybody, including me)

Text #7: We have all conferred and concurred that you have to talk to us about whatever is going on. No way can you be THAT busy. Call immediately.

P.S. We love you and are prepared to hate Michael or your boss or anybody you tell us to.

P.S.S. Equally prepared to forgive you for anything you could have possibly done or would ever think about doing.

P.S.S.S. Isabel says if it's your health, we can take it and it's worse not knowing.

After the plates were cleared away, bathroom breaks were taken, and another round of rum smoothies was distributed ("if it ain't broke, buster, don't fix it," said guess who), we reconvened on the porch. I brought out more candles in hurricane jars and shut off the lights. Everyone shifted to get comfortable.

"So," I said, "you gonna tell us what happened in Panama?"

All heads turned to Jesse. She blew a ring of smoke at us and smiled. A smile that made me want to check my skin for fire ants.

"If I must," she said.

"You started it," was Isabel's equally misfired attempt at

playfulness, as she brought her knees up to her chest like the frontline lifting shields.

Jesse dragged her palm across the splintered wooden table, adding to my sense of foreboding. But when she began to speak, I was surprised. It was a happy story that danced in the flickering gleam of the candles, holding the looming darkness at bay.

Jesse arrived in Panama to a big family welcome party. Cesar's much older sister and his cousins were there, along with his parents, and thirty house staffers.

The house, described by Cesar as an estate, was more like a compound. The mansion was enclosed behind massive walls and a guarded gate that opened to an arced driveway stacked with a fleet of matching black security vehicles. The enormous house towered toward the sky with its stone front, looking down on two formidable structures on either side, homes for all the servants. In back of the house there was a helicopter pad, a glass-enclosed swimming pool, and a tennis court. Inside was a succession of fancy rooms all vying to outdo each other with splendor fit for Versailles.

An exuberant Jesse swirled through each room on a tour with her new family. The men chattered excitedly, showing off. The women quietly noted Jesse's long glossy hair and short paisley dress with platform heels. Señora Guerra walked gracefully behind her husband, modestly deflecting his boasts of her decorating talents. "My wife, my little queen, she spent Cesar's inheritance!" Alfredo

Guerra exclaimed, taking Jesse onto his arm and laughing heartily. "That's why the boy has to work for me now!"

Jesse, a sucker for excess, dove headfirst into her new life as a princess. She giggled when served five-course breakfasts on silver platters at a dining room table that seated fourteen. She thought it delightful that maids turned down her beds, ran her baths, and waited outside her door in the morning to escort her to breakfast. Three Pomeranians had their very own maid. The kitchen was industrial size, with a staff of six. Jesse prompted a round of laughter when she napped through supper one night and then tried to go down later to fix herself a snack. "My dear, the kitchen staff have gone home, of course. Call Ricardo, he'll go out and get you anything you desire." Jesse waved off their suggestion and left them sipping cordials to walk to the kitchen. It was locked. She could hear them laughing at her from the other room.

There were other problems in paradise. Learning Spanish was taking far longer than Jesse had anticipated. She spent many meals staring off into space, trying not to look bored or unkind. Cesar would try to fill her in, but she found that more embarrassing.

When after two weeks Jesse still had yet to leave the mansion grounds, Cesar awkwardly explained that his father could not afford the general public knowing she was there. With a pained look, he bumbled through the revelation that his mother and sister were uncomfortable with the wedding, and disagreed about the best way to inform society with the least amount of scandal. At that time in Panama, Americans were no longer in style and were, in fact, resented and disdained for their role in the Canal Zone. Jesse was shocked. "But they've been so nice to me," she exclaimed while Cesar only smiled wryly.

The wedding finally happened the next month. The press was "persuaded" to present the union as the greatest of all romances. Jesse was presented in a designer gown chosen by Señora Guerra. Jesse tried hard not to let anything dampen her fairy-tale wedding. She danced the night away in a ballroom lit by thousands of candles. Plenty of her friends came, and her father and mother were flown in for three days, though she hardly got in one word with them. Everybody proclaimed it the most beautiful wedding they'd ever seen.

And finally Jesse was allowed to sleep in an enormous gilded poster bed with her husband.

For months after, Cesar and Jesse would meet every night in their room. After a day filled with entertaining important guests during endless meals, they reveled in their precious time alone together. They would often stay up all night, giggling and discovering each other, making love, and laughing at Jesse's wide-eyed observations of her new life. They agreed it was the happiest they'd ever been.

By the next winter, Jesse's feelings had almost completely changed. She started having anxiety attacks about being watched all the time. She hid in her room for most of the day, unable to deal with never-ending visitors or maids, or with Señora Guerra's reproving looks. After four months at home, Cesar's father sent his son off on a nonstop business schedule, introducing Cesar to all the bigwigs in every part of the country and abroad. He was gone the majority of the time. When he returned, he was always sweet and polite, but exhausted. And the rounds of fancy family meals and dinner guests never ended. Jesse was scolded whenever she suggested time alone. "In Panama, family means everything," Señor Guerra told Jesse over dinner one night when he spied her tugging at Cesar's shirtsleeve to be excused.

Cesar asked his sister to bring friends to meet Jesse, but that was a disaster. The women told stories of "friends" who had open sexual relationships, trapping Jesse into telling her own wild stories. Then the women maliciously turned on her and spread the stories far and wide through high society. Jesse was shunned from further contact. Señora Guerra was mortified—minus her husband's indiscretions, she was not carefully sheltered from hearing the gossip.

Eventually, Jesse barely recognized herself in the forlorn, timid ghost of a woman who tiptoed from room to room to avoid the servants' smiles and questions.

Then, just when the first thoughts of leaving him seeped into her mind, she found out she was pregnant. Everything changed again. She was no longer allowed to be a ghost. Her diet and health were suddenly of utmost importance to Señora Guerra. She bought Jesse a closet full of new "motherly" clothes and insisted she come to every family meal. She was sent outside every day to "get some sunshine on that yellow skin" of hers. Señora Guerra even forced a baby shower upon high society, which stopped the rumors but did not win Jesse any friends.

Six months later, Cesar came home from a supposed business trip to find his wife smoking in the bathtub.

Three months later, Isabel was born.

Jesse came alive again. She had given up on her happiness, but looking down on her tiny perfect daughter, she wondered why. Jesse, who hadn't had anyone to talk to besides Cesar in two years, poured out her heart to her infant daughter. Every misery, every humiliation, every fear, every wonderful memory, every hope and dream she'd ever had. And there, reflected in Isabel's turquoise eyes, Jesse remembered who she was and what she was worth.

"Well, look who finally decided to come to breakfast," Señora Guerra said one morning, as Jesse entered the dining room with Isabel in her arms. "There's my precious little baby, come let me hold you," she cooed to the little chocolate haired infant.

"Back off, bitch," Jesse snarled. Then she walked into the kitchen and pushed past a chef to grab a banana from the refrigerator.

Jesse walked back into the dining room where Señora Guerra waited primly with folded, shaking hands. Jesse ignored her. She sat down at the table, unpeeled her banana and slipped it erotically deep into her throat before biting off a mouthful. Then she flung the peel on the table and pulled up her shirt to offer an engorged breast to Isabel.

Señora Guerra said nothing, but even her eyeglasses shook with fury as she picked up her book and blocked Jesse from view.

The war of the queens had begun.

Jesse pulled out all the stops. She bounced around the house, singing Janis Joplin songs to Isabel. She moved a record player into her room, plugged Isabel's ears with cotton, and played The Clash and The Ramones at top volume. She befriended all the servants, and hung out in the kitchen learning how to cook Panamanian tamales wrapped in banana leaves, while Isabel cooed from her playpen.

On one of Alfredo and Cesar's rare nights home, Jesse talked the chefs into a surprise. Jesse emerged from the kitchen in an apron and served Tex-Mex burgers and beer in the bottle. This was when the war expanded to include Señor Guerra. Cesar looked back and forth between beaming Jesse and his seething mother and realized what had been happening. He put his hand over the knot in his stomach.

Alfredo Guerra slammed a fist on the table. "Afuera!" he screamed at Jesse. "Out!" Her smile faltered. She looked to her friends, the maids, who averted their eyes, terrified. Jesse snatched Isabel from her highchair and ran out of the room.

Cesar lowered his head. This was a fight Jesse couldn't win. To his credit, he tried to warn her.

"Baby?" Cesar whispered into Jesse's ear as she lay in their bed, pretending to sleep. A slight giveaway—she was shaking with anger. At them. At herself. At the world.

"Mi reina, my queen, don't do this to yourself. To me. Please. It can only end badly. Worse than you can imagine."

Jesse opened her eyes. Was that a threat? "I'm not scared of them, Cesar. Why are you? Why are you scared of your own family?"

Cesar sighed and wrapped an arm around his wife. "For reasons I hope I'll never have to tell you," he said, with a tiredness that swept into Jesse.

Jesse started to ask, but something in her told her to quit for the day. Isabel let out a cry from her crib. Jesse made to get up.

"I'll go. Rest, baby. Try and calm yourself," Cesar said as he picked up Isabel from her mound of blankets. He snuggled the baby into the crook of his arm and rocked her, her little fingers curled around his thumb.

Jesse watched them and a sob sprang to her lips. She was reminded in that instant what she had to lose.

The day after the dinner incident, Alfredo Guerra replaced most of the staff. He also bought a home in a nearby neighborhood for Jesse and Cesar that would be ready in two short months. Jesse was ecstatic. "Who said I couldn't win?" she taunted Cesar. Cesar said nothing. He'd lived in that house for too long, and knew how things worked too well.

Another seven months, and Jesse was on her knees. "Baby, please don't go. Or just take us with you. I've only been to the Valle house once. One time. What do you *do* there?"

"Business! Dios mio! Business everyday! What do you think I do?" Cesar replied, irritated.

Jesse remembered Cesar's stories of his father's mistresses. "Yeah right," she snapped.

"Dammit! Pinche!" he pointed angrily out the window where there were two guards with rifles. "What do you think is going on out there, outside of this house? Eh? Do you have any idea—"

"How would I, you asshole? How would I know? You never take us anywhere!"

"It's utter chaos! Torrijos is gone. Dead. Killed by your countrymen most likely. And now Noriega is at the helm. Things change so fast, it's all I can do to stay in the game, to carve out a piece of the pie for us. My father would like to sit back and wash clean his hands, spend the fortune I create by his methods."

"Like the Guerras will ever be poor—" Jesse said in pure spite.

Cesar looked at Jesse with eyes that would chill a bed of coals. "No, my family won't be. But only because I am making sure of that. I am protecting my family."

Jesse studied her husband. He looked ragged and mean.

His face was leaner, but he'd grown a gut. Jesse could only imagine what he'd been up to trying to maintain the family's millions. In the Guerra mansion, she'd seen suitcases filled with money. Once, Ana, her favorite maid, let slip rumors she'd heard about connections to drug cartels. She almost felt sorry for Cesar. Then she searched his face. All she could see was hardened evil.

"Don't do anything to get arrested," Jesse said finally, meeting him square in the eyes.

He tossed his head back and laughed as if Jesse had told the funniest joke in the world.

By the time Isabel's third birthday came around, Jesse knew what Cesar had known would happen all along. She had lost. She was still a prisoner, now one in solitary confinement. To staff Jesse's house, Alfredo Guerra had hired a senile old woman and a handyman/chef who only spoke Nahuatl, an Aztec language. Guards stood at the front gate, the only way out, round the clock. She had no driver and no car. She had to call for one from the Guerras, who then reported anyplace she went. Señora Guerra insisted on three days a week of visitation of her granddaughter. She came by in a car and sent a guard in to collect Isabel. Jesse was never asked to visit their house again.

The worst thing, however, was that she had lost Cesar as an ally. His father kept him always away, but even when he came into town, he would dine at his father's house. He complained of the chef and of Jesse's constant nagging.

Jesse had started fanatically reading newspapers and trash magazines she bought at the grocery store, searching for clues about Cesar and Alfredo. It wasn't long before Jesse found fuzzy pictures of Cesar carousing with a woman on a hotel balcony, and had thrown a raging fit the minute he walked in from a business trip. Cesar had picked up Isabel and walked back out the door.

"You can't do that, you asshole! You can't just fuck whoever you want and then walk out of here with my daughter!"

Jesse tore at her hair and pounded on the door after it slammed shut. Of course he could. Cesar Guerra could sleep with whomever he wanted and come and go as he pleased.

Jesse was desperate for attention. The supermarket was her only approved destination anymore, so Jesse would go in and strike up a conversation with anyone who would talk to her. She gave her phone number to the clerks and told them to call her. She didn't tell them anything, not even who she was, though of course they knew. She just asked them about their lives and told them she was lonely. But that's how Jesse found out that they monitored her phone records, when she went to the store after talking to Frederico late into the night and was told he'd been fired. The phone number he'd given her was disconnected. Cesar never said a word about it. That was when Jesse realized he no longer cared about her at all.

★ ★ ★

So, by Isabel's fourth year, Jesse had not a friend in the world. Not for the first time in her life, she wished she had a relationship with her mother. She called her father but never managed to convey the situation. There was nothing he could do and it would only give him more to worry about. She talked to him about Isabel and the house and the weather.

Now that Isabel could talk, Jesse had to even watch what she said to her daughter. All day, she sat and played with Isabel. She took baths with her and invented game after game. More and more often, however, Isabel started to whine to go to *casa abuelos*. She came home from her sleepovers with boxes of toys and gifts and candy from Abuelita.

One day, Jesse caught her playing a trick on the maid. She stole her eyeglasses and told her Tenoch, the chef, had stolen them.

Something in Jesse snapped. For some reason, it was the last straw.

"Isabel! Get over here!" she yelled at her daughter. Isabel, surprised and guilty, inched a millimeter closer. Jesse ran over and grabbed her by her pink dress. "I will not let that family turn you into a monster. You hear me? You are not going to Grandma's tonight! You're going to stay here and have dinner with Marta and Tenoch and me. Now say you're sorry," she said into Isabel's defiant face.

Isabel kicked Jesse in the shin. Jesse let go in surprise, and Isabel ran off. From the top of the stairs, Isabel called,

"Abuelita will come for me!" and stuck out her tongue. "I hate you!" she added and ran to her room.

Jesse was stunned. And then the full hopelessness of her life hit Jesse in the gut.

An hour later, a guard arrived to pick up Isabel. Jesse didn't answer the doorbell. Just as she was about to yell for him to go away, Isabel ran down the stairs as fast as she could, and Jesse heard the door open with the turn of a key. Jesse made it to the door in time to see the guard scoop up a gleeful Isabel. Jesse screamed like a madwoman, grabbing Isabel's arm and scaring her, as the guard wrenched her away and locked her in the backseat of the car.

Jesse pounded on the windows as they drove away, then ran into the house, looking around wildly. She called the Guerras until all she got was a busy signal. Finally, she went outside and walked/ran the four miles to the house. Her guards didn't chase her, but when she got to the Guerras' gate, their guard held his rifle across his chest and told her to leave. After screaming and cursing at the top of her lungs, a car appeared on the street to take Jesse home.

It was a horrible three days. Finally, Isabel was dropped off on the doorstep. Isabel was delighted to see her, having no idea about the situation, and played with her new dolls and tried to cheer up her weepy mother.

Jesse sank into a depression. She no longer showered or dressed in the mornings. She lay in bed in a stained silk nightgown and kneesocks and listened to Pink Floyd records. One time when the guard dropped off Isabel, he left behind a bottle of prescription pills. Sedatives. Jesse briefly wondered if Señora Guerra was trying to poison her. With a strange feeling of glee, Jesse took the first of many pills she would take over the next months. It was during one of those droning, listless months that Jesse's mother died. Jesse did not even ask to go to the funeral.

CHAPTER

21

BACK ON A PORCH HALFWAY BETWEEN
North America and Panama, a fifty-three-year-old Jesse
stopped talking. She put a hand to her temples, shading
her eyes. She did not want to look at anyone on the porch.

"And then you left him, Mom?" Isabel asked in barely
a whisper, as she laid a hand on Jesse's leg.

The rest of us shifted in our seats and waited respect-
fully for Jesse's answer.

"And then I left him, baby girl," Jesse said, with a tone
of sorrow I had never heard in Jesse Brighton's voice.

Isabel nodded. She sniffled and rubbed her mother's leg
reassuringly. Then she wiped her nose and looked at us,
glad for the story to be ending.

"'Course," Jesse said, stopping Isabel from speaking, "then they kidnapped you and put me in jail." Jesse patted Isabel's hand, then shifted out of her reach. Isabel's mother closed her eyes and went from the Honduran coastline back to Panama City.

"When my mother died, the first thing I felt was something like relief. Then shame. Then nothing. I didn't tell Isabel because she'd never known her. I gave some silly excuse to my father. After another season passed—" Jesse broke off, realizing how that sounded. "It took me that long to realize I was to Isabel just what my mother had been to me. I could lie doped up in bed all day and reminisce about who I'd been, but Isabel would never know. I knew that soon I would start hating her for how she saw me, and for her happiness. It was the first time I wondered who *my* mother had been, if maybe she'd only *become* that spiteful sad woman." Jesse shot a look at Isabel, who was sitting now with her chin resting atop her hands on the table.

"And *that* made me get out of bed. I called my father and said I was coming home. I don't know if he knew I meant for good. I hated asking him to send me the money, but I swore on my life I would pay him back. It took a lot of scheming and bribery and flirting to get all of Isabel's paperwork and to get around the guards." Jesse's voice rose to her more usual tone. She winked when I looked in her direction.

"I felt positively high. I was back! Cha-cha-cha. I was

going to take my baby and move back to the land of the free and the brave. I packed one of Cesar's old suitcases. I used the grocery money for a taxi and found a way to trick the guards. You were so excited!" Jesse said to Isabel, who couldn't help but brighten at her tone. "I put ribbons in your hair and we laughed and sang all the way to the airport." Jesse smiled at the memory. Then she swallowed. Gulp.

"We made it through check-in no problem. In immigration, however, we were told to stand aside. We should've run. Two men took you away screaming. Two others hauled me off to a cell in the basement level of the airport. Nobody told me a cotton-pickin' thing," Jesse said, and shook her head. "Not that anybody had to. The Guerra family didn't have to give reasons." Jesse looked around the table. I took the cigarettes off the arm of a chair and lit one to hand to Jesse. Then I lit one for myself. Isabel put out a hand and I lit another one for her. "Oh, fuck it," Lynette said, and put out her hand.

Jesse looked at us and burst out laughing. "My God, you guys look like hens in a hurricane. Obviously, I survived." She brushed a strand of hair from Isabel's face and cupped her cheek. "Obviously, we survived," she said with a soothing smile.

Then Jesse leaned back in her chair and took a long drag of smoke. "I was there for two weeks," Jesse said, not articulating the images burned into her memory—shower brawls and eyes swollen shut with blood and tears.

I interrupted Jesse's private movie of recollection with a question for Isabel. "And what happened to you?"

Isabel tried hard to think. "I don't remember the airport," she said slowly. "But it fits with the few memories of my father and my grandparents in a huge house. I always assumed it was ours." Isabel shook her head and sobbed. "I'm so sorry, Mom. How could I have traded you for toys and dolls? What kind of daughter am I?"

Jesse grabbed Isabel's hand and squeezed. "You were a little girl. And you didn't know anything that was happening."

"How did you get out?"

"I didn't. I was inexplicably discharged. Two men took me to a car with black windows. I had no idea what to expect. I thought maybe I would be killed. When we pulled up at my house, I sobbed. Equal parts hope and hopelessness." Jesse took another deep drag.

"Turns out—hopelessness it was. The men dragged me into the servants' quarters in the basement. They locked me in a windowless room with a tiny bathroom and a mat for a bed. The room had been fitted with a doggie door, so they could slide my meals through with no human conta—"

Lynette gasped. She put her hand to her mouth as tears welled up in her eyes. "Oh my God! I can't take it, Jess."

Jesse smiled weakly. "Do you want me to stop?" She was asking Isabel.

Isabel's eyes were red and puffy. In a show of false bravado, she took a theatrical drag of her cigarette and smiled. "Oh, let's just do it now. I'm not going through this again later."

"Amen, baby. Amen to that," Jesse said, and sighed. "Anyway, you get the idea. They were going to deport me, I think, but wanted to scare the shit out of me first, deter me from ever fighting back. Or maybe there *were* going to kill me or leave me there." She tried to laugh, but Jesse couldn't help it—she shuddered in the warm air.

"Then—" Jesse stopped. Hot tears erupted and gushed down her cheeks in rivulets. Jesse wiped at them with surprise, but they kept coming.

"Mom?" Isabel asked with a panicked voice. Terrified. Her mother never cried like that, ever. "Jesus, what happened?"

Arshan stood up at the table, looking fierce, ready to fight God himself. A fight he'd been begging for for years.

Jesse took in a gasping breath. "Then your daddy came."

Jesse lay on a thin carpet, facing the wall in a corner. Her hair was greasy. She had on fashionable clothes but they were wrinkled and dirty. She was tapping out the beats to Pink Floyd's "Comfortably Numb" on the wall. Her eyes were glassy. There were scratch marks on her cheeks.

Jesse started to sing the words aloud, because she was hallucinating again. It happened often. She often imagined her father appearing at the door, or imagined she heard Isabel's voice in the night. This time she thought she'd heard footsteps and voices. Jesse clasped her hands over her ears. The noises were getting louder. The door to the room started shaking. Jesse was seized by terror. She shut her eyes and pressed herself against the wall.

When Cesar burst into the room, he was in the middle of yelling, but clapped a hand to his mouth the second he caught sight of Jesse on the floor. Jesse didn't turn. She started to sing.

Cesar quickly shut the door behind him. He made a strange sound like he was choking.

Something in Jesse clicked on. She took her hands from her ears and rolled slowly toward the door. When her eyes fixed on Cesar—beautiful, handsome Cesar in a pristine suit, she covered her face with her hands and sobbed.

Cesar moved to her. He knelt down and reached out a hand.

Jesse scuttled away like a caged animal. She pressed her back into a corner and pulled her knees up in front of her. "Don't you dare," she snarled, fixing him with rabid eyes.

Cesar's face blanched. He stood up and looked down on her coldly. "I came to get you out as soon as I heard. I didn't know you were here. I was told you'd already been deported."

The way he said it—proud of himself for not being the one with the key, as if it was okay that she'd been kicked away from her child like a piece of broken glass. Jesse jumped up and ran at him, screeching. She flew at him with her fists, screamed in his face, "Look at me! Look at meeeee! Look at what you did to me, you fucking bastard! I'm Isabel's moth—"

Cesar grabbed her wrists to ward off her attack, but stumbled backward onto the floor, bringing Jesse down on top of him. When he landed, he threw Jesse off and let out a string of insults.

Jesse collapsed in a heap. To no one now, she repeated, "I'm Isabel's mother. I'm her mother. I'm her mother. I'm her mothe—"

Cesar blinked and watched Jesse start to cry again. At first, his face registered nothing but disgust. Slowly he surveyed the empty room. By the time he made it back around to look at his wife, he was almost the Cesar that Jesse met in New York. The Cesar that made his mother tea while she wept in a dark room. "I'll take care of it." He swallowed. "Of this. Come on. Get up."

Jesse didn't rise, but she raised her chin at the softer tone. Cesar averted his eyes in shame. He held out his hand. What choice did she have? Jesse slid her hand into his and stood. She put her head down as she followed him meekly out of the room.

At the door Cesar barked at the guards to back off. He ordered them to sit in the basement and do nothing, forbade them to call his father. Jesse wondered if they would obey.

Cesar led Jesse upstairs to her old bedroom. He sat her on the bed and drew a bath. Jesse didn't move from wherever he led her. When he returned, she let him undress her and walk her to the tub. Jesse's bones stuck out at every angle. When she slipped into the warm water, she let her head sink under. When Cesar had to pull her up for air, he had tears in his eyes.

Cesar washed her hair and wiped her face with a wet cloth. He wrapped her in a clean white towel and laid her on the bed while he picked out fresh clothes. Then, as Jesse watched listlessly, he packed a suitcase. When he put in Isabel's favorite doll, Jesse's heart began to beat again. Her mind realigned with the living. Jesse let out a strangled sob. Thank God. Thank God.

Cesar met her eyes.

"Thank you," Jesse managed.

At her gratitude, Cesar's face flooded with regret, like dark water breaking through a levee. He came and knelt before the bed, leveling his face with hers. "I am sorry, angelita." A nickname from a million years ago. "I never—"

"Thought we'd end up like *this*?" Jesse said. The turn of the phrase struck Jesse as suddenly funny, absurd. She let out a strange, awkward laugh. She was out of practice.

Cesar didn't laugh, he watched her—his wife, clean and shiny again, smiling that gleaming smile of hers. But everything about her seemed off-kilter, and he was like the museum director that spots the imposter Picasso the thieves left behind. But wasn't he the thief? Cesar shook his head. It was too late to say anything more. Too late in too many thousands of ways. He would never be a good husband. He would never be a good father. He had done too many horrible things to ever be forgiven by God, let alone by himself. The only gift he could give his wife and daughter was a one-way ticket away from him and everything his family stood for. Everything he had become.

Cesar stood up and finished packing.

CHAPTER

22

JESSE EXHALED AND SAT FORWARD IN HER wooden chair on the porch. She slapped her two hands flat on the table, signaling that she was done. She gave a loud, unladylike sniff and puffed out her cheeks like Dizzy Gillespie. She turned to Isabel as she exhaled. "Cesar's personal guard took me to the airport and waited in the parking lot. An hour later, you were in my arms. Hours and hours later we were in Texas. I was shell-shocked for a while. Lost. Scared. I worried something else would happen, but—no. That was the last gasp of power for Alfredo Guerra. Cesar was in charge now. Six months later, I received the divorce papers and a gigantic check in the mail. When an old friend called from D.C., we went to visit. I loved it so much, I decided to move and open my spa in the suburbs."

Jesse stood up and gave an exaggerated stretch of her arms. A ripple of movement ran through the group. Jesse shimmied her shoulders and wiggled her butt. "Cha-cha-cha. And *that* is how the story goes."

Arshan and Cornell laughed, mostly to release tension.

"Holy shit," said Lynette.

Isabel lit another cigarette. She still hadn't said anything.

Jesse spun around and pointed at me with both hands. "For two hundred points—what is the moral of the story? Tick-tock. Tick-tock—"

"That marriage sucks? Especially to someone rich, handsome, famous and powerful, like Cesar Guerra? Or Remy Badeau?"

"Eh...wrong," Jesse said, and pointed at Cornell.

"That you have to choose the right person?" he said, and gave Lynette a squeeze.

"Aww. Heh-heh. Lynette?"

"That when life gives you lemons, you make lemon vodka martinis?" Lynette said, teasing her friend with a favorite saying.

"Fifty points," Jesse said.

"That life doesn't deal in safe bets," Isabel said in a small but rising voice. "Love can turn ugly, mean and dangerous. But that doesn't mean you should hold back or run and hide. You laugh and you smile and you hope for the best. But you don't hold back—" sabel's voice cracked and I could barely take what welled inside me.

Jesse looked square at her daughter and pressed her lips together. "That's exactly right, my smart little angel." Tears sparkled in Jesse's eyelashes and then she winked. "You got it exactly right."

November 22
Samantha

I'm glad you liked your surprise. I wasn't sure if it would seem morbid ("Things to do before I go"). But I figured we needed to lighten up a little, do something besides stand around your bed and hold back tears. How funny was Kendra's reaction to the stripper gram?! I can't believe your dad didn't come in! (Grouchy and prude as ever, I see.) But, listen—stripper cops, caviar, hookah—of course, those are the kind of "never trieds" I'd come up with, but please, bebe, come up with your own, too. I'm at your service.

So, I think I've about overdosed on reading about the Copenhagen Theory and Many Worlds. Somewhere in the middle is probably the answer. The power of consciousness (ala Marlee Matlin in *What the Bleep Do We Know!?*) and the existence of alternate realities (ala Gwyneth Paltrow in *Sliding Doors*). I think what we'll do is: A) me keep an open mind and try everything we've planned (short of knocking myself unconscious) and B) you find me out there from the whatever it is.

I'm not saying I'm not gonna keep at it—our research, but...

Is it like Jesse says—time to laugh, to smile, and hope for the best?

Luvvvvv, Sam.

THE INCOMING TEXT MESSAGES BUZZED Kendra's phone inside the gym locker room.

Roller-skating might appeal to some people, but Kendra swam her way through inner turmoil. Makes sense she wouldn't like something improvisational and whimsical that shifted with the stereo tunes. Kendra loved laps. Back and forth, orderly and repetitive—that was the mature way to sort through life-changing decisions.

That night after work, she headed for the indoor pool. She had it all planned out. A lap for every angle of the decision, then choose. Kendra sat down on the rough lip of the pool, and plunged her feet into the chemically balanced water. She stared down the lanes. This was Kendra's version of a pep talk. *By the time you get out of the water, you will have decided whether to A-bomb your life or not.*

Michael was exasperated, and done discussing it. That left Kendra roiling in an isolated limbo of hesitation. And in unfamiliar territory. She made million-dollar decisions every week, by following a personally honed formula. One pro, one con, on down the list, a run-through of all pertinent information, a quick projection of consequence scenarios, and then she decided. And then she stuck to it. That's it. That's how Kendra approached everything from buying bath towels to firing interns. Practice. Plan. Execute. And no looking back. She could completely avoid regret by approaching everything this way.

With a firm nod to agree with herself, Kendra slipped into the water. The chill awakened all her senses. She felt almost elated. Routine would save her. She had made countless major decisions this way. This would be no different.

I don't believe in luck, Mina. Hard work and planning. That's what matters.

Lap one. It's what Michael wants. Michael was the only person who hated surprises more than Kendra. He would want to have a baby on his schedule, in order for him to be a good father. This was the thrust of his argument these past few days. And it made Kendra's arms slice through the water with aplomb. He wanted to have a baby with her. Just not now.

Lap two. She was too old to consider abortion. It was her mistake and the adult thing to do was to take responsibility for it. She had the means to take care of a child. Apparently just not the backbone. Kendra suddenly wondered what would happen if you had to throw up while swimming.

Lap three. Moral implications. Kendra's mother always said that the right choice was the one that made your heart pound but didn't make your stomach churn. In that case, it was time for mental imaging.

Lap four. Kendra chopped at the water with her hands as she filled her head with the first scenario. She envisioned the huge fight with Michael, the standoff that would follow, the terrifying possibility of being pregnant alone, of being pregnant at work, the whispers, dealing with the vacation club in every incarnation—pity, concern, opinion, advice. Kendra's heart began to race, sending a whale's heartbeat pulsing through the water. She pictured the agony of giving birth, the destruction of her figure, the flood of hormones and helplessness. Then she focused on the thing in her hands, a tiny wrinkled screaming mashup of herself and the man she once thought she would marry, knowing that Michael would abandon her eventually if she went against his wishes. She counted the toes, stroked the little fingers, smoothed down the damp hair.

Stop! Kendra realized she was about to go into a full-blown panic attack—her heart was pounding her ribs like an Olympic sprinter's sneakers pound track. Her right hand reached out and found the edge of the pool. Thank God.

Lap five. Deep breath and then back under the water. She saw herself on the operating table, sedated, a flurry of efficient doctors and nurses quickly removing the problem. Now she walked into the waiting room, into Michael's open arms. At home, he made her tea and microwaved the heating pad. There were roses on the table, with a handwritten card. He held her all night long. The next day she returned to work and never mentioned it to anyone, except her two best friends. Everything was exactly the same as it was. Exactly.

Ouch! Kendra smacked her head against the side of the pool. She came up sputtering, surprised and in pain. She treaded water and looked around. The echoes of the last vision bounced back to her. Hooking her arms over the edge of the pool, she gave a nod. It was clear what the better decision was. Kendra slipped out of the water. She reached up to take off her swimming cap.

Then she doubled over and projectile vomited onto the concrete. A nearby child shrieked in horror.

Two hours later, Kendra hung her keys on the ring by the door and dropped down to the couch like a goldfish flinging itself into a puddle. Chills crept along her skin as she fished her phone out of her gym bag.

She read the texts one by one, the initial smile on her mouth fading as the tears pooled in her eyes. Kendra's stomach lurched along with her heart. Dizziness swept over her and she lay back down. They were right, she knew. They could take it. It was time to tell them.

She started to hit the call button but the room began to spin like a disco ball. Kendra closed her eyes and held onto the couch. The thought of talking to the vacation club was exhausting beyond measure, the sheer number of them daunting. And she definitely did not want to speak to her mother about it, maybe ever. The thought made Kendra put a hand to her forehead, where a fine sweat beaded above her eyebrows.

More than anything, Kendra was tired, the kind of tired that clogs your veins with wool. Or lead. Kendra felt she would never be able to lift herself off the couch again.

She caught sight of her calendar on the wall. She loved nothing more than the promise of hanging a new calendar every January. But now she wrenched her eyes away, the new implications of months and days too overbearing.

She looked at her phone, ready to dial again. Instead, she hit reply and typed out a text message three lines long.

Kendra hit send and the message disappeared. She leaned forward to get a glimpse of herself in the mirror. Her hair stuck up like a holly bush from all the scalp scratching. Kendra thought briefly of shaving it all off. *Black women can pull that shit off*, she thought, and gave the mirror a smirk.

She let out a craggy cough.

"Oh, for fuck's sake, stop being such a baby," she told the mirror. At which point, the girl in the reflection curled up into the fetal position and closed her eyes.

★ ★ ★

"Kendra wrote," I told Isabel when she returned from the bathroom, ready for bed.

"Yeah? But didn't *call us*." Isabel climbed into bed and stared at the ceiling.

I looked at my phone and read the text again. I'm sorry. I'll call soon. I love you all. I rolled onto my side facing Isabel. "What do you think?"

"I think people keep too many goddamn secrets."

November 23
Samantha

Besides Ivy League physicists—there are plenty of "pseudoscientists" out there connecting physics to the paranormal. Okay, Deepak Chopra, Amit Goswami, and Fred Alan Wolf would certainly not appreciate being called pseudoscientists, nor would they agree with the term "paranormal." They are all Ph.D.'s and M.D.'s and world-renowned speakers and authors. They are, however, the ones that guest appear on Oprah specials on The Secret. Hollywood yoga moms download their books onto Kindles and devour them over skinny vanilla soy lattes.

Jeez—why am I being so harsh?

These guys are the ones we need to believe in the most. And when I'm reading them in the wee hours of the morning…I do feel like I've found what you were hoping for. They talk about dying in one parallel universe and being reborn in another. They say that in our dreams we experience glimpses of these parallel universes, and of our other lives. They say that if we believe in something strongly enough, it will happen, for better or worse.

But then I come to see you in the morning, you shrinking in your big bed. And I think they're all full of shit. My best friend is dying and there's not a damn thing I can do about it. That's when I begin to suspect that you gave me this project to distract me, because you know me better than anyone in the world, better than I know myself. You raised me, you know. I've always been like the child. Who's going to take care of me when I fall now? I always fall. I'm rash and I'm impatient and I'm bossy. You know it's all a defense. Who's going to understand me better than you? Who's going to calm me, soothe me, tell me to shut up? If I only get to see you in my dreams, I might never want to wake up. Life is going to be scary without you, Mina. I'm not ready.

CHAPTER

24

I OPENED MY EYES. DARKNESS. I LOOKED frantically left and right for what could have woken me up, since I wouldn't hear a stampeding bull over the thumping of my heart. Then the nightmare came coursing back.

Any time I faced conflict in my life, I proved adept enough at managing it during the day. Struggling with Remy, Mina, or day-to-day crises—I usually appeared pretty laissez-faire. But the hidden turmoil always surfaced in merciless nightmares.

Frightening fragments now stampeded my waking mind—combining like crashing water. I listened to my shallow breathing, interrupted by a whimper from across the room. Isabel. Now I remembered.

It started out as a happy memory. Summer at the beach. Before our vacations got steadily more exotic, Jesse and Lynette used to pack us up and drive everybody to a beach or a lake. The summer we were eight years old, we went to Atlantic City.

Jesse and Lynette were still debating the ethics of taking us into the casinos, so until they agreed, they spread us out on the sand in front of the hotel. They doled out beach bags with our names written on them in glitter paint. Each bag had a shovel, a pail, a blowup doughnut floatie, and a bag of potato chips.

Isabel and Kendra set to work huffing and puffing to blow up their floaties. Kendra pretended to pass out and we all thought that was hilarious. Isabel started to bury her in the sand until Kendra popped up like an offended cobra. "This is brand-new!" she shouted, pointing at her navy-blue swimsuit with a ruffle around the hips. Lynette looked over and told Kendra to cool it. "Guess you'd better go take a bath," Mina said, and chuckled. She pointed at the ocean. Kendra stuck out her tongue. "I will!" she shouted as she took off for the water, Isabel right on her heels.

Mina waited with me while I scarfed down my potato chips. When we hopped up to join them, Lynette grabbed my wrist. "Thirty minutes, honey. Some rules aren't made to be broken." Jesse looked over. "Not many, sugar. But some."

Mina offered to wait, but I shooed her off. Jesse braided my hair while I watched my three best friends scamper on the wet sand near the waves, splashing each other and turning cartwheels.

I smiled in my little bed in Honduras as I relived simple pleasures from simpler times. I could picture each of them so clearly. Kendra with her hair done up in pigtails and barrettes; Isabel flurrying by as a blur of wavy hair and tanned limbs. Mina circled around them with her arms to the sky, smiling with her eyes closed.

And then a shift occurred. In the real memory, Lynette had played tic-tac-toe with me until my thirty minutes were up. But now, as my head sank back into the pillow, I reexperienced how a dream can turn into a nightmare.

Jesse and Lynette stood up and walked toward the water. I pouted, annoyed at them and at myself for having to stay out of the fun. The three girls waded into the waves, ringed in Lynette and Jesse's laughter. I watched them with a reluctant grin, echoing their shiny smiles. The five of them rode up the crest of a wave like a family of ducks. When the wave broke in front of them, they all watched the shore in glee. Mina waved at me and I waved back.

That's when I noticed an odd shadow rising behind them like a Russian submarine. I put my hand to my forehead like a visor and squinted. Mina mirrored my change in expression, then turned in the water to look.

The shadow wasn't an illusion, it was a tidal wave. Not a tsunami—not an underwater wave that lifts the general level of the water. No, it was a wave like the cover of Surfer Magazine, a curling, rock-solid wall of water like the open jaws of Jonah's whale.

I jumped up and ran toward them as all five were dragged into the mouth of the wave. I was my current age again, pounding the sand with my feet, wearing my gold bikini that glinted in the sun. But as I ran, the distance between us increased. Sand flowed up from a trench between beach and sea, a widening no-man's-land. I watched helplessly, running and panting but losing ground, as they rose up the wall of the wave, screaming and clawing at the water like a brood of drowning monkeys. They were calling my name.

No!

I woke up in the stuffy room, my heart again attempting jailbreak from my ribs.

I pressed my hands together; they were hot and clammy. Suddenly I was hot all over. Too hot. I whipped the sheets off my body. There was not a breath of cool air to be had in the dank room. I had the distinct impression I was drowning.

Then I started thinking about Jesse's story. Life was insane. It was a miracle any of us survived. Danger and evil around every corner. I frowned, my mind flitting from one human depravity to another. Newspaper headlines of greed, adultery and murder flashed. I was gripped by panic—was Remy a Cesar Guerra? Was he cheating on me right now? Why *did* he think it was fine to have a month apart? God, I was so stupid. It bought him one last hurrah before settling down. He was off screwing every twenty two-year-old tottering by on stilettos.

I fumbled for my phone in the dark. It was late afternoon in Paris. Should I call him? I'd told him my phone wouldn't work in Tela, so that he wouldn't worry when I didn't answer his calls. But now I realized I hadn't wanted him to call me or expect to hear from me.

I looked at the phone. One measly bar of reception. Good, so it wasn't a total lie.

What would Remy say if I called him right now? If I told him about Isabel's father, voiced my concerns, or described the terror of the tidal wave? I tried to imagine. I pictured his creased brow as he wedged the phone between his ear and shoulder, nodding while he filed paperwork and typed an email and motioned to his assistant to bring him a cappuccino.

I frowned. That wasn't giving him the benefit of the doubt. Remy had done lots of sweet things for me, hadn't he? He was actually very supportive. That made me laugh. Who was I defending him to? Myself?

Snuggling back onto my pillow, I remembered the time Remy had brought home lavender lilies—my favorite. I'd had a bad night, hadn't slept more than a couple thirty-minute stretches. So far, I couldn't find a single job teaching English, my standby job when traveling. I was sleeping at Remy's house every night and was feeling very unselfsufficient. Maybe some women liked to drop the reins and ride in a pretty carriage, but to me it felt more like a paddy wagon.

Remy came home early from set and found me on the balcony with Mina's journal. He had the lilies in one hand and champagne in the other. I smiled at the lilies and frowned at the bubbly. I said something like, "Not everything can be fixed with booze, baby." He'd kissed my forehead and positioned himself to open the bottle. "We're celebrating, ma chérie." He got me a job as a set photographer. He was so pleased with himself, I didn't remind him that I wasn't a commercial photographer per se, I incorporated photography into my fine art. But it was money. And art, unfortunately, feeds on currency as much as on the soul.

We drank that bottle of champagne and then another and made love the rest of the afternoon, giggling and running around the house in our underwear.

I smiled to myself in the musty dark room, and noticed I could make out shapes around the edges. The sun was starting to rise. Seized by an idea, I spun around and whispered to Isabel.

"Isabel. Wakey-wakey."

Twelve minutes later, we were on a blanket on the sand in our pj's. There's no better medicine for night demons and tough decisions than a sunrise. I sported a wide smile, Isabel a resentful pout. It was easy to see who the morning person was.

We sat and watched the performance. The sun peeked

at us from just above the horizon, dribbling candy-hued light across the water. I was struck by the sun's benevolence—reaching all that distance to caress my face. I lifted my chin and dug my toes into the sand, weighing the opposite sensations of warmth and coolness. Suddenly I found myself daydreaming about a beach wedding. Life with Remy in Paris had been one big party, filled with extravagant dinners and beautiful people. Imagine what the wedding would be like! I giggled in pleasure at the electricity raising fine hairs on my arms.

My faith in goodness and beauty was restored; my natural tendency toward awe renewed.

"Isn't it miraculous, Belly?"

Isabel gave a somewhat rude sniff of a blocked nostril. She wasn't exactly moved by the miracle of nature at the moment. Isabel never suffered from nightmares. Any inner torment happened after her first cup of coffee, so mornings posed only the baby demons of sleepiness and sulkiness to overcome. This was a blessing considering what waited at the edge of her mind.

Isabel couldn't help but notice, however, that the sky was bathed in baby-blues and tulip-pink. She had to admit that it was pretty. She smiled, awakening finally from the realm of slumber.

But the more she awoke, the more she reunited with pieces of her mother's story. The more she remembered, the more shocked she became. She was appalled by the horrors her mother had revealed, but also by the love.

Long-held images of Jesse Brighton were being torn down, and new ones hastily pasted up. Her history, in the course of a day, had been completely revised. She had no idea how or where to start applying the new information.

"So, you been thinking about getting another job? You gonna stay in D.C.? How do you feel about, oh, I don't know…Paris?" I kept my eyes on the ocean.

Isabel turned to me in amazement, then shook her head with a smile. "You're crazy. Two sandwiches short of a picnic, my mom would say."

I had started to make my case when I was interrupted by a cascade of giggles and stampeding feet.

A pack of eight little girls made a mad dash for the sea in their underpants. Dumbfounded, we watched the girls run past us without so much as a glance, grab one anothers' hands and splash into the waves like baby sea turtles, new to life and without any trace of fear.

They popped up to the surface one after another like corks in a creek, sending a chorus of cachinnation along the morning breeze. Their braids stuck out like crowns above their heads. The Garifuna princesses heralded the official start of day.

"Well, what are we waiting for? When in Rome—" I said, and jumped up.

Isabel grinned. She popped up, too, and put out her hand. Pajamas flapping in the wind, we sprinted and dove into the waves. When we surfaced, the water princesses circled around us, chattering exuberantly. We couldn't understand a word, so Isabel and I just babbled back in English. No one seemed particularly concerned at the lack of common language. The sentiment was understood by all. Life is grand and full of promise. And it is fun, fun, *fun* while it lasts.

After plenty of splashing and laughing, I went inside to get my camera, triggering a massive photoshoot on the sands of Tela. The little girls posed, cartwheeled, and presented proud handfuls of sand dollars. After every click they would huddle around my camera and collapse in delight upon seeing themselves on the digital display. I clicked away, feeling joyous and full of light. I didn't have the answer of what to do with the rest of my life. But I knew we'd been sent this little fleet of angels to remind us that life is nothing more than the sum of moments, and perfect moments are not to be ignored.

After a while, the mothers stepped out of the shadows to collect their AWOL princesses. They were startled by our presence, but laughed at our crusty pajamas and the girls swarming around us. When the girls had gone, Isabel and I turned to look at each other.

That was always the thing about the four of us girls. We were all so different. But we'd shared every secret, every worry, hope and dream since we were five. Which meant that in any situation I had a pretty good idea what any one of them must be thinking.

I knew what Isabel thought about Jesse's story. I knew what she thought about me marrying Remy. And I thought she was wrong about both. But I understood why she thought what she did. I could see her lifetime of happy moments and tribulations spread out behind us, running right alongside mine.

I took her hand and we headed back to the house to change into something besides salty pj's.

BY THE TIME WE SHOWERED AND CHANGED, there was a field trip underway. Lynette stuffed us full of scrambled eggs while she filled us in on the plan. They wanted to check out the Garifuna village far down the beach. I was thrilled. Photographing the girls on the beach had given me the exact same idea.

Everybody squished into the Honda in a good mood. I sat on Isabel's lap and battled carsickness as Arshan steered us along the bumpy dirt roads.

Away from the shoreline, the roads were lined with humble concrete houses in various states of completion and upkeep. Chickens and goats wandered around as usual, but now we saw barefoot children piled atop rusty bicycles three at a time. Some houses served as makeshift grocery stores and others as impromptu beauty salons, no signs or advertising required.

Arshan pulled up to a drink stand. I got out to buy cold sodas. Kids stopped in their tracks to stare at us. A teenager fell off his bike rubbernecking. The woman selling the drinks looked at me blankly, then looked past me at the car. She called another woman from the back, apparently just to alert her to the large group of albino aliens plopped down in their midst. They both pointed and laughed, seemingly unaware that I was human and could, *hellooo*, hear them.

A little girl ran up and poked me in the arm, then sprinted away cackling back to her pals, who cheered her bravery. I was used to being the only coconut-milk-colored redhead when I traveled, so I had been dare tagged before. I smiled and waved at the proud child, causing a relapse of tittering.

Armed with semicold drinks in the searing heat, we headed off down the dusty road, carefully avoiding chickens and startled cyclists.

"Okay, supposedly we cross this bridge into a more traditional Garifuna village," I said as the houses started to thin out.

The "bridge" turned out to be a narrow sandy path with ocean on one side and a lagoon on the other. But sure enough, as soon as we crossed over, there were no more concrete houses, only round thatched huts surrounded by vegetable patches, spaced evenly along the edge of the beach.

"Wow," Lynette and Jesse said in unison.

"Prime beachfront property, would you look at that?" Cornell exclaimed. "Honey, think I could pass for Garifuna?"

"Not with me as your wife, sweetie."

"And why not?" Jesse said to Lynette. "I think any woman would do well for herself to hitch up with one of these fine homeowners." She motioned at a shirtless man, built like Michelangelo's David, hoeing his garden.

"Jesse," I said, laughing, "you live by yourself in a four-bedroom house. You telling me you would move into a stick hut no bigger than your bathroom?"

"No, baby, I'd build me a castle," Jesse said. "In fact, what's the deal, why hasn't mansion building caught on out here?"

"Well, as I understand it," I answered carefully, "the land belongs to those who can prove they've lived on it over a certain number of years, so that it remains in the hands of Garifuna. Though I'm sure there are rich evildoers trying to finagle a piece."

"Like the place we're staying at?" Isabel asked pointedly.

"Maybe." I hadn't thought of that.

"I wonder how many of them sell the land for profit," Arshan mused.

"I don't think they're allowed." I was trying to remember what I'd read. "Anyway, so far the Garifuna have held to tradition by choice and self-imposed isolation." I looked out at the fields, at clotheslines strung with Levi's. "I would assume, however, things are changing."

A pickup passed by with eight people sitting along the edge of the truck bed. It didn't look like a family, more like public transport. They passed close enough to touch.

"What an adventure," Jesse said with delight.

"You know what I wonder?" Arshan said as the car turned away from the beach. "If they knew everything about the outside world, whether they would wish they hadn't known. Is it better not to know? To be content with fishing and vegetable gardens?"

"And a lack of proper health care or education?" Isabel snapped.

"Well, yes, that's actually what I meant, a place where death is just a part of life and education is for practical application only. I'm asking—would you think that there was something missing if you had no idea what?"

"Basically what you're saying," I answered, "is that because these people appear primitive, you assume their conceptual thinking is primitive, that they don't ponder philosophical matters like purpose and meaning. I think that's ridiculous, if not downright ignorant. Of course they speculate. It is the asking that has spurred all the technologies of modern day, not the other way around." I took a quick breath. I had to calm down.

We were coming up on a larger thatched building with wooden stools, sidebars and tables. A sign said Restaurante Nany. "Look." I pointed. "Maybe we can ask them ourselves. Appears we're not the first visitors from the outside world."

A stooped old woman sat out front. Kids in tattered clothes played along the dirt roads. Around back I saw a hut backed up against a river, with a fenced-in rooster. "Come on, guys, we gotta stop."

Our group of gringos sauntered into Restaurante Nany. A teenage boy approached us. He looked us over with a wrinkled brow, then turned to Cornell and asked him in Spanish what we wanted to drink.

Cornell realized the assumption and laughed. "I only speak French and English, brother. But I'll have a *cerveza*. That word I know."

I started to jump in, but Jesse beat me to it, politely ordering six beers in flawless Spanish.

The boy laughed, like we were the funniest thing he'd seen in a long time. Children from the street came over and settled onto stools around us to watch the entertainment.

I discreetly took out my camera. I walked out to the road to photograph the restaurant. I took pictures of the carefully painted sign, the stools and tables made of sticks, the colorful dresses fluttering on a clothesline just outside the door. Through my lens, I watched Jesse tell a story that got everybody laughing. Except Cornell. I took the camera away from my eye. Cornell was sitting back in his chair, studying his surroundings. He had a look of almost sadness. Or wonder, maybe?

I looked around, too. It *was* pretty amazing, this city of huts. The houses were constructed entirely of upright rows of branches stuck in the ground, held in place by a horizontal branch, and topped with dried palm fronds. You could almost see inside them through the slits. It must be awful when it rained. Everywhere there were clotheslines strung with tattered shorts and T-shirts. Out back were canoes and fishing nets or stick pens of animals.

Restaurante Nany was a coliseum in comparison. I could hear children playing in all directions, on a backdrop of ocean waves, and a distant drumming. The boy came out with two of the children, carrying Port Royal beers. I wondered how they refrigerated them. I suspected they'd been stored in the river. I tucked my camera into its case and walked over to take my beer from a little girl in a tattered pink satin dress. She ran away giggling. The first gulp of carbonation was a little piece of heaven.

I let out a loud "Ahh" and took in a satisfied deep breath. "What a cool place, huh?"

Cornell set down his beer too hard, and foam rushed to the mouth of the bottle. "It's just incredible to me—" he said, and stopped.

"Honey," Lynette said in a manner that made me instantly nervous.

But it seemed to embolden him. "It's just amazing to me the far-reaching effects of the enslavement of the African people," Cornell said, and snatched back up his beer.

When nobody responded, Cornell acknowledged our silence with a smirk.

"You mean the spread of Africa's vibrant culture to all parts of the globe?" Jesse asked, knowing damn well that's not what he meant.

Cornell snorted. "Well, no, Jesse. I meant families being wrenched from their homes, abused and killed, and then discarded in the middle of nowhere. Left to lead impoverished lives far from their history and ancestors."

Lynette put a hand on Cornell's forearm. "Baby, I'm not sure that the Garifuna would feel that way. I was thinking how magical and lovely their lives look compared to ours."

"Yeah!" Jesse agreed, smiling. "I think *we* may have gotten the short end of the stick."

"Ah, yes, you mean the noble savage," Cornell retorted, labeling us all racist imperialists with the raise of an eyebrow. Cornell looked from face to face, the lawyer in him clearly prepared and eager. He turned back to his wife. "You're right, dear. I mean, how would they know, right? Do you think the Honduran government comes out to inform them of the injustice, happily doling out reparations?"

"They don't have to," I explained maybe a little haughtily. "The Garifuna are known for passing on their history through song and storytelling. They are very aware and proud of their heritage. The way they see it, they were never slaves. They were shipwrecked en route to slavery." Looking at Cornell, I lost a little steam. "They're not purely African descendants anyway. They intermarried with the Aboriginal islanders of St. Vincent. Their culture never would have existed without the slave trade."

Cornell looked at his wife, unsmiling. "So, if the cultures mix, then all is forgiven?"

Lynette looked stung and closed her eyes. "Not here," she pleaded in a whisper, almost inaudibly.

Cornell shifted away from her and raised his voice. "Not here, Lynette? Not in front of our friends? In front of people who wouldn't understand my anger?"

Lynette's eyes shone with anger. "Cornell, get off it. Is this the part where you stake story rights to the African-American experience?"

"Don't I? Among this group?"

Jesse, who knew about this fight between the Joneses, took careful aim at Cornell. "What can you tell me about being a single mother in the early eighties?"

I caught the drift. "Or a woman turning thirty in the twenty-first century?"

Arshan surprised me by chiming in. "Or fleeing the Iranian Revolution?"

Cornell didn't look ready to back down, but as he looked at our faces staring him down—his *friends*, he seemed to be reminding himself—he begrudgingly nodded.

"The human experience is a solo enterprise, is that what you're trying to tell me?" Cornell reached for his beer, calmer. "But then you're also admitting that one's life experience is inseparable from an individual's gender, notion of social heritage and exper—"

"Goddammit, why don't you just say it?" Lynette's voice was like the sudden screech of spinning tires. "Say it, then! You're sorry you married a white woman. You should have married a woman like Sandra Miheso, a bona fide *African*. Someone who would *understand* you, who you could show off to your civil rights colleagues." Lynette's eyes bored into her husband, but I could see she was shaking. She turned her head away as if she might cry.

For my part, I was shocked to the core.

As Cornell looked at his wife, his expression changed 180 degrees. "Is that what you think this is about?" He tried to put a hand on her arm. She moved it away. "Lynette," he said, and brought his head close to hers. As he spoke, it seemed to dawn on him that he was telling the truth. "I didn't marry a white woman. I married *you*."

Lynette lifted her chin, as Jesse and I both brought a hand to our throats.

Cornell appeared to have forgotten we were there, however. He had eyes only for his wife. "Honey, listen to me now. There *are* a lot of things I'm still angry about. Things I wish I could let go of. And there are certain things that may always be difficult for us to relate to each other about. I think, I hope, and I pray it will be different for the next generation, for our daughter and our daughter's children. But no matter how much I preach about being misunderstood, I promise you right here and now that I do not regret spending my life with you. Or having my only child with you. Quite the opposite. You are the love of my life. And it has been an incredible, magnificent ride."

Lynette's eyes glistened like the sparkling ocean beyond. She leaned over and planted a kiss on Cornell's cheek. Then she nodded, just once, but it was a nod that held a thousand words, a lifetime of their memories together in good times and bad. She turned back to the group, swiped at her nose and held up her beer.

"Jeez, you guys, no secrets amongst friends, huh? Cheers?"

Teary laughter rippled around the circle. We let out a collective sigh of relief and raised our bottles.

"Cheers!"

Lynette snuggled into Cornell's arms and the rest of us watched, satisfied that the balance of the universe had been restored. Kendra's parents' marriage set my bar for happy relationships. They were the dogeared photograph in my back pocket that I could hold up as proof that love works. Seeing them fight was akin to watching the Sphinx in an earthquake. An interracial couple in the sixties, in Virginia. I started to wonder what it must have been like for them. It *would* have been a bit like building a monument in the desert.

I noticed then the ancient woman was watching us somberly, but with a definite glint of amusement in her eyes. I pointed discreetly.

"Do you think that's Nany?" I smiled at the woman, and she smiled back.

"Se llama Nany, señora?" I called.

The woman nodded her head yes. Even in a faded housedress draped over a sagging body, she exuded an aura of wisdom. An even older man, with a bushy white beard, came up behind her. He said something loud in a language I didn't understand, then cackled in laughter. Nany gave an appreciative chuckle. The old man reminded me of a leprechaun, such was his agility. He looked to be about a hundred years old, but his step was as light and bouncy as if he walked on rainbows.

Jesse watched them with mischief in her eyes. "Hey, what was that dance you told us about? Punta! I bet grandpa could teach us a thing or two."

The old man heard Jesse say punta. He grinned, showing off his one, two, *three* teeth. Jesse waved him over and asked in Spanish if he could show us the dance. The man let out a healthy belly laugh and motioned Jesse into a sandy spot in the middle of the restaurant. Nany shook her head and grinned. The children jumped to their feet, giggling.

"Come on, guys. Up!" Jesse called to the rest of us. Lynette joined her first. Then Isabel and I. The old man cracked a joke about dancing with all the ladies. He called out to the boy who'd brought the beer.

The lanky boy obediently took a seat and flipped over a plastic bucket in his lap. He started to drum.

I gave a little Shakira shake of my hips and the old man whistled appreciatively before laughing along with everybody else. He brought the little girl in the pink dress into the circle. She looked up at us shyly as the old man clapped his hands in encouragement. The girl broke out in a flurry of dance, shaking her little hips furiously in wide arcs, her arms splayed out sideways. Jesse let out a whistle and clapped. I tried my best to imitate, causing the little girl to collapse to the sand in giggles.

Without warning, the old man began to sing in a low and haunting voice, slow as lava in comparison to the drumming. As he sang, he started to dance. He took my hand into his rough leathery palm. His voice was ethereal, hypnotic. I jimmied along to the beat, scuffling my feet forward and back like the old man. The hop from one foot to the other was so fast it looked almost like it was off rhythm. But that illusion soon vanished. The old man was perfectly on beat, the larger sum of his movements singing the soul of the drum.

Lynette beckoned her husband. As Cornell entered the circle, Isabel went and took Arshan's hand. Arshan gave one shake of his skinny butt in his khaki pants. Isabel and I almost died laughing.

"Whoo—hoo!" shouted Jesse.

Cornell playfully shoved Arshan aside and started to shake it. He emulated the old man's movements perfectly, making the frenzied motions of his hips seem smooth and fluid. Lynette clapped blissfully and blew her husband kisses. I took out my phone to record a video to send to Kendra.

For a good hour, we took turns in the circle, alongside

the children, dancing to the sound of the old man's voice and the drums, in a hut halfway between the sea and the river, with a rustling jungle beyond.

CHAPTER

26

BY THE TIME WE GOT BACK TO THE HOUSE, after stopping several times so I could take pictures, it was an hour till sundown.

I offered to make pizzas for dinner. "We've got a can of artichokes. Might make them a little classier."

"Whatever you want as long as you're cooking!" Jesse said.

"Do you *ever* cook?" I teased.

"Only in the face of starvation, honey. But don't I make the most fabulous party hors d'oeuvres?" She took note of Isabel's judgmental expression. "Hey, listen, you two—I cooked enough when I was a kid, for an ungrateful mother." She waved a finger in Isabel's direction. "And I cooked for you, didn't I?"

Isabel rolled her eyes. "If ordering takeout counts."

I laughed but Jesse got visibly upset.

"Hey, I was a working mother!"

"Yeah!" Lynette said, moving next to Jesse with a hand on her hip.

I knew better than to take them both on. Jesse laughed. "Okay, I hate cooking. What is so great about it? What century are we living in? Huh? What did Gloria Steinem and all our NOW sisters fight for?"

"The right to order *takeout!*" Isabel shouted, with a fist raised like Nelson Mandela.

"Yes, my smart-ass darling daughter. Takeout. Women have better things to do than spend hours a day cooking for kids and husbands."

"Yeah," Lynette said again.

I cocked an eyebrow at them. "Why don't you two—oh ye divine Creators of Feminism—go wash up and we'll handle supper in this uncivilized land with no take-out?"

"These kids have no respect," Lynette said to Jesse as she took her arm to leave. "No idea what we fought for. For *them*."

"Ungrateful little brats," Jesse agreed.

"Whatever, Mom," Isabel said as they sauntered off. Under her breath, she added, "You made money off a billionaire ex-husband, apparently."

Jesse stopped dead and spun around. "You kiddin' me, young lady? I raised you by myself *and* ran a business. And Lynette—you don't know a thing if you think Lynette isn't worth a hearty *thank you, ma'am,* for what she did for your generation. You think it was easy for the homecoming queen to date a Negro in Virginia?"

Isabel and I stared at Jesse, speechless.

Jesse looked back and forth between the two of us, her eyebrows raised damn near to her hairline.

"Mmm-hmm," she said, her head bobbing about like a pigeon. She linked arms with Lynette again. "My God, what do they teach these children in school?"

Lynette gave a little harrumph and stalked off with Jesse. "They don't know shit, do they?"

WHEN ISABEL AND I CAME OUT OF THE house with steaming pizzas, the parents were camped out on the beach, entrenched in a heated discussion.

As we approached the blanket, the talk stopped and all eyes turned to us.

"What?" Isabel and I said in unison.

"Oh, we were just talking about your rather limited understanding of history, girls," Cornell answered. "A lot of heavy changes happened. Things we've decided you take for granted."

Isabel rolled her eyes again—she was beginning to look like a rebellious teenager. "Ooh, the sixties. The decade that changed everything. But you don't think our time is crazy? Nine-eleven. The war in Afghanistan. The Israeli-Arab conflict, Iran, and North Korea? Are you sure it's not just because there's so damn many of you baby boomers that the sixties don't just *seem* like the most important decade?"

"I have failed as a mother," Jesse said, only half joking.

Cornell thrust a hand to his heart as if he'd been stabbed.

"The sixties changed this country and the world forever. Or at least showed that you *can* change the world," Lynette said.

"Oh come on, what really changed? Everybody still runs around killing each other over race, religion, money and power," I said as I doled out pizza slices.

"She's right," Isabel said. "What difference does it really make? Government everywhere is and always has been corrupt. Hellooo, Nixon. You guys fought for equal rights, world peace and free love." She picked an artichoke off her pizza and popped it in her mouth. "What did we get but Britney Spears, the War on Terrorism, and AIDS?"

I hated this new incarnation of Isabel, but I had to agree with her. What was the true legacy of the sixties?

The four baby boomers simply stared at her.

Lynette broke the silence. "You know what? That's not only painful to hear, it's wrong. Civil rights, the feminist movement—changes have happened throughout history, and they have happened most often through the protests and actions of young people. Such as yourselves. We have a black president. Do you have any idea what that means to someone like me? Do you think that would have been possible without everything we went through?"

She sounded almost teary. I was moved. "Ok, so, why don't you tell us what it was like? Kendra hasn't told me all that much."

"Really?" Lynette said, and frowned. "Well, that's because she never wants to know that much."

"That's not fair, honey," Cornell said. "We obviously should have been talking whether she asked us or not."

"So, then tell us the story of how you guys met," I prodded.

"Now there's a lesson in ancient history. Whaddaya say, dear? Want to revisit the glory days of our youth?" Cornell asked his wife. When she didn't answer, Cornell frowned. "They weren't all happy times. Is that it?"

"That, and I wish Kendra was here," Lynette answered.

"Should we call her on speaker phone so she can hear the story?" I asked, consciously ignoring the fact that Kendra hadn't answered our phone calls in days.

Isabel smirked at me, but then she jumped up and smiled. "If I get my iPod, we can record it!"

Before anyone could protest, Isabel dashed off for the house.

I shrugged. "It's a good idea," I said, and looked down at the plates of pizza. "Eat! What is the matter with you people? I've had three pieces."

Cornell picked up a piece of pizza and flicked off the artichokes, which Lynette hated. He handed it to her like a peace offering or an assurance of love. Whichever it was, Lynette took the pizza and smiled.

Isabel skipped back to the blanket with her pink iPod. "Okaaaaaay—"She plopped down and put a pillow in Lynette's lap. She nestled the iPod on top. "For posterity. Go," she said, and pushed Record.

CHAPTER

28

(Transcript of conversation)

LYNETTE: We met when we were fifteen.

CORNELL: Dates, sweetie. Must've been 1962 about?

LYNETTE: Hmm, 1962–63. We were sophomores.

CORNELL: I integrated into her high school that year. That's how we met.

SAMANTHA: But Brown versus Board of Education was in, like, the fifties, wasn't it?

CORNELL: That's right. But Virginia wasn't in any hurry, I can tell you that. They were still betting their Massive Resistance Campaign would pan out and that the whole civil rights thing would blow over. They tried a hundred different ways to resist integration. Further south, one Virginian county closed all the public schools for four years rather than have black kids go to class with white kids. They paid for the white kids to go to private schools.

SAMANTHA: That is so—…strange. I never thought about the fact that you guys were around for segregated schools, and in the same town where I went to school.

ISABEL: But if African-American children were technically allowed to go to desegregated schools, why didn't more go?

CORNELL: Well, one way the Virginia school system skirted the issue was to set it up as a choice, not a mandate, guessing correctly that the races would segregate themselves. Black folk weren't in such a hurry to put their kids in schools where they weren't wanted, even if the black schools were pitiful shacks in comparison.

SAMANTHA: So, why were you the one to do it? To integrate?

CORNELL: My family wasn't your average black folk. My father was high up in the Virginia NAACP. My mother ran Sunday school and taught adults to read out of our house. They were everyday heroes. My father planned the integration for my sophomore year and prepared me for the worst. Or so he thought.

ISABEL: Why? It was worse?

CORNELL: It's almost indescribable how bad it was. I'm ashamed to say, I begged to quit. The KKK shot up our house in the middle of the night. People cursed me with names I'd never even heard before, way more descriptive than the N-word. They tripped me in the hallway, left excrement and nooses in my locker. I never went on a single date with any girl in that school. I was never once invited to any white student's house for dinner.

SAMANTHA: That's awful. But then what about Lynette?

LYNETTE: Well, I was certainly aware of him. Segregation was a big deal to all the parents, like Cornell said. My parents didn't tell me they disapproved in so many words. They were big churchgoers and preached the golden rule five times a day. (Pause.) There's something you have to understand. It's an embarrassing reality, but those times were totally different for white kids and black kids. Everything was so segregated I wasn't aware of the really bad stuff. My friends and family didn't have any black friends, but we didn't do any of those horrible things. I spent all my time thinking about cheerleading and math class and dress patterns. It's not an excuse, but—

SAMANTHA: But now I can see how the Holocaust happened right under people's noses.

ISABEL: Sammy!

LYNETTE: Actually, that's just what I was getting at. For you guys, it'll be gay rights, global warming, and Sudan, when your kids ask—how could you not have known?

CORNELL: Sudan? Come on, now. I think I'd better point out it wasn't all bad all the time for us black kids. I had plenty of good times growing up. I was a quiet kid that didn't like to rock the boat. A disappointment to my father. Before high school, I didn't much care about Colored Days at the park because I didn't want to be around white folks anyway. It's like this— at church, at home, with my friends—I wasn't black. I wasn't an oddity or intrinsically offensive. I was just my mama's son. My best buddy's pal. It was only around white people I stuck out like a fluorescent yellow beetle. (Pause.) That's why I was drawn to Lynette. She was just nice to me, in a real way. Not mean and not uncomfortable nice. Just nice.

SAMANTHA: What was Lynette like in high school?

CORNELL: Gorgeous. Sassy. She was the most popular girl in school. Could do no wrong in that town's eyes.

ISABEL: I can see that.

CORNELL: She was a cheerleader. Homecoming Queen. Lead actress in all the plays. Top grades. Those were pretty big deals in small-town Virginia. Did I mention she was gorgeous?

LYNETTE: Now stop it. I was preppy, naive, and spoiled. My parents treated me like a baby doll. Thank God I met this man.

SAMANTHA: What do you mean?

LYNETTE: The day I met him was the day I woke up and realized there was a whole world I hadn't even looked for.

ARSHAN: Bravo.

JESSE: So, you are listening.

ARSHAN: Of course. Fascinating to someone that still wasn't an American citizen at that time. So, who fell in love with whom first?

LYNETTE: Well, it wasn't that simple. Not back then.

ISABEL: Meaning Cornell liked you first! Who didn't have a crush on Miss Homecoming Queen?

CORNELL: Touché. However, what I think my wife means is that it was still Virginia in 1963. Sit-ins had made some progress in lunch counters and buses, and technically, blacks and whites could be friends, even publicly. Technically. But dating was not in the realm of possibility. Not that I didn't get a certain tingling down in—

LYNETTE: Cornell!

CORNELL: (Laughter.) In my belly, Lynette. Butterflies in my belly, my love. Anyway, I'm serious. Interracial dating just wasn't done. Not even thought about. Okay, maybe we *thought* about it, but Lynette and I, we saw each other at school and that was it. There was the March on Washington that summer. I heard Dr. King's speech in front of all those hundreds of thousands of Afro-Americans. It changed my life. Changed a lot of people's lives. I went back to school armored with a sense of what I was a part of.

SAMANTHA: Did you go to the march, Lynette?

LYNETTE: Are you kidding? My mother would've had my hide. And back then, I hadn't yet thought about disobeying.

CORNELL: So, the next school year we picked up where we left off. That November, Kennedy was shot. The whole world tilted off-kilter.

SAMANTHA: Like nine-eleven. Point of no return. (Pause.) And you guys still weren't dating.

CORNELL: No way. We would find time to talk during school. Eventually, we started finding ways to walk together before or after school. But it wasn't easy and we certainly didn't voice any feelings beyond *I like you*.

LYNETTE: (Laughter.) Yeah. I remember. I sure do *like*

you, Cornell. I am in deep *like* of you. However, I think they're looking for something a little more titillating, dear. Let's move on to the last summer.

CORNELL: Okay, okay. Skip over another summer when we hardly saw each other. Freedom Summer 1964. Johnson got Kennedy's Civil Rights Act passed—outlawing segregation in public places. Not like it changed overnight, but at least with young people, attitudes were changing fast. So, senior year, Lynette and I were special friends and everybody knew it.

LYNETTE: You see, a very pretty classmate of mine started flirting with Cornell. It, uh, alerted me to new possibilities.

JESSE: Ah, yes. Jealousy works on us girls every time. Good thinkin', Cornell.

CORNELL: (Laughter.) Lynette remembers that girl more than I do. I remember my daydreams being occupied by a certain cheerleader in her cheerleading skirt. Not to mention *every* boy was hung up on a lot of other awful shit going down, like the Vietnam War. The first big protest was in D.C. that April, just after Malcolm X was killed. My father wasn't a fan, being such a devotee of Dr. King. But Malcolm's death was a huge deal. Even if I wasn't in much of a position to take on all the blue-eyed devils, being one of nineteen black kids in a white school. Plus, there was this one blue-eyed devil—

LYNETTE: That summer was our first kiss. Just once, in my father's car. Well, I don't mean just one kiss—just one night. We kissed and kissed and cried that night. He was off to Howard and I was bound for The College of William and Mary. It was the end of something that never had a chance to get started, we figured.

CORNELL: Little did we know.

LYNETTE: I wanted to be an actress, though I'd barely dared mention that fact to anyone but Cornell. William and Mary was a family tradition. I hadn't even thought of rebelling against it. The rebellious gene was slow to kick in with me.

CORNELL: Though once she caught on—hell, I was glad to help.

LYNETTE: Hardy ha. So, obviously we kept in touch. With some pretty intense love letters.

CORNELL: Now, I'd been involved in the struggle my whole life because of my daddy's commitment to the movement. But nothing could have prepared me for Howard University. I came in right after a year of massive student protests. All of sudden black boys had a voice! Howard snapped me right out of any lingering "don't rock the boat" tendencies. Of course, it's easier to fight aboard a battleship full of compatriots than alone in enemy territory.

LYNETTE: He's right. It was a whole new time. The baby boomers came of age all at once. Surprised the hell out of the old folks. I convinced my dad to buy me a car and I drove down to D.C. or Cornell took the bus to see me every weekend. I couldn't have 'gentlemen callers' yet, of course. Feminism hadn't touched down at William and Mary. But now Cornell and I could at least hold hands and dare people to say anything.

CORNELL: What a rush. Our relationship was more about agitating others than about each other.

LYNETTE: Cornell, that's not very nice. Do you believe that?

CORNELL: You don't? I'm not trying to be mean, honey. I just meant that they were empowering times. Everything was about the cause. The antiwar movement. Civil rights. Flower power.

LYNETTE: I don't think most people felt that way at William and Mary. Some girls watched the protest coverage on TV, but most were more concerned about the Beach Boys and Wham-O than the cause. I can't even remember any black classmates at all, come to think of it. It was my trips to Howard that made me aware how dangerous it was to just be seen together.

CORNELL: Summer after freshman year we were inseparable. I had a tiny apartment in the city with some friends. We went to protests and organized marches in Southern cities. We drank and smoked and partied. At first, dating Lynette gave me bragging rights. We were the ultimate symbol of victory.

SAMANTHA: And then?

LYNETTE: And then the summer was over, and everything changed again.

CORNELL: Stokely Carmichael made a speech about Black Power. It changed the rules of the game. Black boys were dying every day in Vietnam. All my friends not in college were freaking out—either trying to dodge the draft or about to ship off. Plenty had already come home in flag-covered boxes. Only white kids got deferments. So, my first year at Howard, we protested mandatory ROTC. We'd had enough of the Uncle Toms in the administration. And we were losing faith that blacks and whites could ever live peacefully side by side. Or that they should. We were talking total revolution.

LYNETTE: So, needless to say, the next year, we wrote lots of letters but we saw less of each other. He didn't fill me in very much on his developing views.

CORNELL: It was something I had to work out for myself, baby, but you were a huge wrench in my thinking, you can be sure. You remember those letters?

LYNETTE: My God, you'll make me blush. We were inspired by the Haight Ashbury phenomenon, you could say. Summer of Love was coming up. Everything was happening at the same time. The free-love hippie stuff along with the war and Black Power. The rest of '66, start of '67 is a blur. I remember Janis Joplin.

Truman Capote's book. Star Trek. That movie, *Faster, Pussycat! Kill! Kill!*

SAMANTHA: It was the same at Howard, Cornell?

CORNELL: It was mayhem. More intense and serious, maybe, but fantastic! I was growing an Afro and reading all about Third World politics and history.

LYNETTE: I was a flower child, with hair down to my waist.

CORNELL: We came home for another summer. June of 1967. Loving versus Virginia.

ISABEL: What was that one again?

LYNETTE: It made interracial marriage legal in Virginia and everywhere. Even still, Cornell and I had to sneak around behind our parents' backs.

SAMANTHA: You hadn't told your parents yet?!

JESSE: Lettin' the cat outta the bag is a whole lot easier than puttin' it back in, Sammy girl.

CORNELL: Well put, Jess. Next came the riots. And the war was still a bastard thing to have to think about every day you woke up. At home, my dad and I had clearly diverged in our views again. Lynette and I started to grow apart, too.

LYNETTE: By the end of the summer, yes. (Sigh.)

CORNELL: (Pause.) When I went back to school, my

classmates had committed whole hog to Black Power. The time had come for liberation and payback. We were young and angry and fed up. But there were some wonderful, positive things, too. Black is Beautiful. The Black Arts movement. It was the first time we'd ever felt so proud of being black, proud of our African history and our looks. It wasn't something I could exactly share with Lynette.

LYNETTE: We lapsed into totally different, separate lives again. Ironic, after all we'd fought for. I went down in the fall of '67 for the Stop the Draft Week March on the Pentagon. The difference was plain. His friends were cold to me. I saw Cornell being pulled in two directions and I knew I was losing. The march turned ugly. It was a terrible day for everybody.

CORNELL: It was a tough Christmas, too. My father and I fought like wolves and it broke my mama's heart to watch. He sided with the older members of the movement who viewed the Black Panthers as thugs and criminals. Way he saw it, they were about to erode everything he'd fought for his whole life. And as for Lynette and me, we just—

LYNETTE: Talked and cried and made out passionately, freezing our butts off in Cornell's old clunker.

SAMANTHA: It's sad. Why does love have to be so hard?

LYNETTE: Sometimes you have to choose sides. Sometimes people choose your side for you. Cornell and I were through. I went back to school with a broken heart.

CORNELL: Me, too, you can believe that. But I wasn't about to admit it to my brothers at Howard. Right away, my buddies and I started planning revolts against the administration. In March, well, you know.

ISABEL: What happened in March?

CORNELL: Damn, you guys don't know anything. In March, Howard students closed down the school with an armed sit-in and forced the administration to install African and Eastern World History courses. We were damn proud of ourselves until—

JESSE: Martin Luther King.

ISABEL: The assassination.

LYNETTE: Yes. In April. On my dorm television, I watched Cornell's neighborhood burn. I watched the National Guard go in with guns and tanks. I couldn't reach him at his place and his family hadn't heard from him either. He didn't call me for weeks.

SAMANTHA: Why didn't you call?

CORNELL: (Pause. Sigh.) You can't imagine what it was like. Washington burned, Sam. Looters took everything. I got sucked into the horror and the rush of it.

Young, angry, proud black men set loose in a vacuum of chaos. We poured all our anger, all our frustration into one big cauldron, and then we kicked it over. We were unchained dragons. It's scary for any man to learn what he's capable of. Afterward, you feel like there's no turning back. In the course of a day, Lynette became a happy dream from my childhood.

(Long pause.)

SAMANTHA: What about your family?

CORNELL: I felt as if had a new family, a family of brothers and sisters and warriors that understood what I was going through—the good, the bad, and the ugly.

SAMANTHA: What about summer break? Did you guys get back together then?

LYNETTE: Nope. I stayed with my parents. Cornell stayed in D.C. I didn't see him once, and I wouldn't let anyone mention his name.

ISABEL: Yikes. And then what?

LYNETTE: Well, then it was our senior year. There was a guy at William and Mary who had pursued me for years. I went out on a few dates with him, just to pretend I was over Cornell. All he talked about was moving to California and going to med school. He was a hippie wannabe. You know, tie-dyed T-shirts with a designer label. I didn't care. All I heard was Hollywood. So I married him.

ISABEL: Whoa. That's right. I forgot you were married before. Cornell, did you try and stop it?

CORNELL: No, I went to law school.

LYNETTE: God, it seems so long ago.

CORNELL: It was, honey. Ages and ages ago. But talking about it makes it seem like yesterday, doesn't it?

ISABEL: Hey, you guys wanna stop for a bit? I need a cocktail.

SAMANTHA: You're drinking too much.

ISABEL: It's genetic. Rum or vodka, mother?

SAMANTHA: Belly, I'm serious.

ISABEL: Lay off, Sam. I'm on vacation, six months after our best friend died. Four days after I lost my job. And the day after I found out my father was a drug lord. I'm at maximum capacity here for catastrophe.

CORNELL: Okay, you two. Enough. I wouldn't mind a stiff one, myself. If that's okay with Samantha. And I don't believe this is a discussion for posterity, do you? Isabel, how do I turn this thing off?

ISABEL: Oh. Right. Gimme the iPod. I just have to push—

29

(Not in the Transcript)

October 21, 1967, Stop the Draft Week March on the Pentagon. Lynette wore a red tunic over red pants. She stood at the edge of the reflecting pool in front of the Lincoln Memorial, a few steps apart from Cornell and his two friends from Howard—Joyce and Teddy. People milled about around them now that the speeches had ended. They were about to march across the Memorial Bridge to the Pentagon. Lynette took Cornell's hand while he joked about happenings from school, all stories she didn't know. Lynette kept trying to peek at Joyce, at her impossibly perfect Afro, her cool earrings, and her striking cheekbones. But each time she sneaked a glance, Joyce, without so much as taking a breath from her flirty banter with the boys, flicked her eyes over to Lynette's and sent a jolt of ferocity straight down to Lynette's boots.

Though not a single identifiable harsh word had been spoken to Lynette, she knew they hated her. Cornell only reinforced this impression by not including her. Lynette looked around to distract herself. There weren't many other Afro-Americans, she noticed. This was explained two seconds later when Cornell apologized for insisting on this rally instead of others close to Howard. Joyce and Teddy looked around, too. They were wired and fidgety.

"Whatever, man. You know? How else you gonna storm the goddamned Pentagon, man, and not get shot by the pigs, but with a bunch of white people, right?" Teddy said with a thin laugh like greasy water.

Cornell laughed. "You know it, brother." But when his eyes caught Lynette's, they held an apology and something else Lynette hesitated to identify. Sadness? Lynette started to dread the next time they would be alone.

"So, then let's go, my brothers," Joyce said, and snapped her fingers. She strutted off in front of them, wagging her perfect ass. Lynette was definitely jealous. And Lynette Allison had had few occasions for female jealousy in her past. And she certainly hadn't ever been the shy, quiet type. What was her problem? Why was she so intimidated?

It took them over an hour to walk the two miles across the bridge and down the service road to the Pentagon.

The whole time, Lynette tried desperately to relate to Joyce, to the point that she could tell Cornell was embarrassed. Lynette almost wanted to cry. Why was it so freaking difficult? It seemed like everything that came out of her mouth was wrong. Somehow colonial or imperialistic or typical or just plain naive. And Joyce was smart as hell, witty and armed at the teeth. Cornell walked silently beside Lynette and squeezed her hand behind their backs in support. Or warning. She couldn't tell. She found it distracting, though, as she tried to follow Joyce's discursive comments about oppression in Third World countries. All the other people around them, mostly young teenagers and college students, were in a festive, charged mood. Multicolored signs for peace bobbed above their heads like a fruit basket spilled down a river. People bumped into them from every side, but few tried to talk to them. One look at the foursome could ascertain the vibe, Lynette decided.

Just as Lynette felt a third blister form on her heel, they reached the Pentagon. They weren't at the front of the pack, so they pushed along with the accelerating herd past the parking lot entrance to the front of the building.

Then, from one second to the next, it was chaos. People pushed and shoved and shouted in every direction.

"Watch it!" Joyce snapped at anyone who would listen.

Lynette was dumbfounded. For a second, she tried to take it all in—the noise, the heat of the bodies, the faces blurring past.

"Lynette," Cornell said in her ear. "Lynette, hold on to me."

Lynette looked back. Cornell caught her eye and smiled, licked his lips like he always did when he was nervous. He tugged on her hand and guided her past two guys arguing about how to best break through the ropes and ranks of soldiers. Then Lynette heard panicked screams and curses fly through the air. Kids were trying to scramble past the soldiers standing guard. She looked around frantically for Joyce and Teddy but couldn't see past the wall of immediate faces. She was getting pushed from every direction. Then a hippie guy with bushy side-burns ran past Lynette on her left, knocking her hand out of Cornell's grip. She fell backward onto a guy who said, "Keep going. You can do it, doll," and shoved her forward. She struggled to stay upright and jumped up to see if she could spot Cornell. She saw him being swept away into a section of people trying to storm a side door. Lynette screamed his name so loud the girl next to her said "Ouch!" and cupped her ear. Lynette's eyes burned so bad she could barely keep them open (was that tear gas? My God), as she continued to push against the current of bodies. People trampled over her feet and Lynette tripped and went down again. A kid in a poncho pulled her to her feet. Lynette could make out a new sound now—a dull thumping sound, followed by cries of pain. The police were beating people. Their victims screamed and cursed and whimpered. Somebody started singing, "'O Beautiful for spacious skies—'"

Dammit, Lynette realized, *this is not working*. She thrust her arms in front of her and started screaming. "Move! Get out of my way. Fuck off!" She plowed into the crowd sideways and worked her way to the front lines. It was like walking into an anthill. As an ant. Teeming masses of frantic people clutched at Lynette's clothes and hair.

"Cornell. Cornell!" she screamed again and again. Many people fell to the ground after being beaten back. As Lynette tried to see over the shoulders of the guys in front of her, something lunged at her shins from the ground.

Cornell crawled out from the forest of legs and collapsed on Lynette's shoes. His head was bleeding. Red rivulets ran down his face and onto the ground.

"Oh my God!" Lynette yelped and bent over, nearly getting plowed down in the process. "Cornell, stand up! Get up. Come on, baby. Now!" Cornell was in a daze. He couldn't make eye contact. Lynette was afraid he had a concussion or worse. She pulled on his shirt. He didn't move, just wrapped his arms tighter around her legs while people trampled over his body.

"Help me!" Lynette said to the biggest guy nearby. "Help me get him up!"

The guy turned and looked down on Cornell. He sported a buzz cut and a skeptical look. "Whatcha 'spect me to do, ma'am?"

Oh shit, Lynette thought, *a Southern Marine*. "He's my friend. Just a friend. But we gotta help him, right?"

The guy looked into Lynette's eyes and smiled as he

strong-armed a clear circle around Cornell. He hoisted him onto his shoulder and carried him through the crowd away from the Pentagon. He dumped Cornell on the outskirts of the mob and saluted Lynette. Then he disappeared.

Cornell seemed to be coming around. He touched his hand to his head and then looked at it. She thought he might pass out. Lynette almost smiled. Cornell was such a baby about blood. It was why his dad had settled for his son becoming a lawyer instead of a doctor. Lynette sat down behind Cornell to prop him up in her arms, and reached into his pants' pocket for the handkerchief he always carried.

As she raised the cloth to his head, he caught her wrist. "You know why they hit me, right?"

Lynette looked into his eyes. They were perfectly clear now, shimmering like fireballs. "Shh, baby, rest a second and then we're going to the hospital," Lynette said, and pressed the cloth to his wound.

Cornell winced. Then he caught her eyes again. "They hit me because I'm colored." A tear very slowly wound its way down Cornell's bloody cheek. "I wasn't trying to do nothing bad. They hit me because of my skin."

Long before the tear reached his chin, two twin tears sprang up in Lynette's sky-blue eyes. She didn't say anything. She didn't know if it was true. She didn't know what to say if it was true. What she did know was that her best friend, the man she loved, believed that it was. Lynette kissed Cornell three times along the trail of his tear. She tasted the blood on her lips, which made her tears run stronger. Sweat, blood and tears. *We're made of exactly the same stuff*, Lynette thought. *Why does it have to be this hard?* She put her arms securely around Cornell's shoulders and pulled him into her chest. His head rested on her collarbone and she put her chin on the back of his head, careful not to get too close to the wound.

"At least you always wear red," Cornell said as he lifted his head up to show her the blood on her tunic.

"Yuck," Lynette said, but she laughed gratefully. He put his head back on her chest and Lynette looked at the people and police milling about. Most of the protesters were crossing back over the bridge, retreating.

"I love you, Cornell. For the rest of my life. Summers, winters, chaos or calm. I'll love you no matter what this crazy world thinks. Or does. I will love you no matter what's ahead of us."

30

"I THINK I NEED TO HEAR THE HAPPILY-EVER-after part," I said when we reconvened on the sand with tiki torches and Mai Tais.

"Okay," Lynette said with a wry smile, "happily ever after started with an ugly divorce. No surprise the marriage to the doctor didn't work out. And obviously I never quite achieved Hollywood stardom."

"What was so bad about the guy?" Isabel said.

"He was a womanizer. And an asshole. I thought things would change once he had his own practice. Then I swore I'd leave him once I got famous. But after a time, I was stuck. All those years protesting for women's rights, and I couldn't imagine being on my own." Lynette laughed

painfully. "I started begging him for a child, but he insisted we wait. Luckily before I won that argument, I
caught him with a woman in our bed, and it gave me the
guts to leave him. I went back home to my folks in Virginia. I went to graduate school and worked as a waitress.
My plan was to become a drama professor. Then one day
I saw Cornell's name on a flyer at my university. A panel
discussion on the legacy of Pan-Africanism." Lynette put
both hands over her heart and smiled. "I couldn't take my
eyes off him the whole time. To hear his voice again—"

"Though I can't imagine I said anything remotely in-
telligent. I recognized Lynette the second she walked into
the auditorium," Cornell said with a chuckle.

"Oh hush. He was eloquent and powerful. Poetic. And
handsome, of course."

"We went out for coffee," Cornell said, putting an arm
around Lynette's shoulders.

"And got married four months later. We had Kendra
within the year."

"Hap—"

"Happily ever after," Isabel and I finished in unison.

What a story. I loved it—the struggle, the fight for
love. It was like Remy and I—two different worlds colliding, everyone against us, trying to stop our love

"Anyone want to play Pictionary?" Arshan blurted out.
I tried to see his face in the dark. His voice sounded odd.
Pinched.

"I don't know why you want to play, Arshan. You

know I'm going to kick your butt again. Embarrass you in front of all your friends," Cornell shot back.

"Yeah right, Black Panther Man. You think you and your boys were tough. You should've seen Iran in those days."

I held my breath. It was one thing for Cornell to critique the Black Panthers.

"Oh, you feelin' feisty, huh? Draw your sword, little man!" Cornell said, getting to his feet. "Oh, sorry, that's right. You can't draw nothin'!"

I burst out laughing.

Cornell offered his hand to help Arshan up. Arshan made a gallant display of refusing. But as he rose to his feet, he put a hand to his back and groaned.

"Pride goeth before the fall, my friend," Cornell said as he patted Arshan's shoulder on the walk back to the porch.

The watchman made his nightly circle around the property. He walked silently over the stubby crab grass by the parked cars. He ran his fingers along the wood boards and walked to the fence running along the beach. He leaned against a palm tree and scanned the darkness like a comic-strip villain. He crept slowly through the palm grove, listening intently to the rise and fall of voices on the porch. He paused at the fence, where he had a clear view of the vacationers.

Ahari heard the black man's rumbling laugh. The man grabbed the chubby woman's cheeks and noisily kissed her lips. Next to them, the fire-haired girl clapped and cheered. Across the table, the loud woman, the old man and the pretty girl all booed in protest. They were fighting. But then they laughed, too.

Ahari sat down on an overturned fishing canoe, where he could still see them clearly. He folded his arms against his chest and settled in to watch the game. It was a game of moving on and moving forward, a game of getting old and growing up. It was a game Ahari knew like the progression of a sunset—the game of learning it's okay to laugh again.

I WOKE UP AND NEARLY BOUNCED OUT OF bed. A smile reached across my face so wide it made my jaw hurt. I felt like a balloon pumped full of helium. I gave a little Jesse cha-cha-cha wiggle of my butt that shook loose a giggle.

Isabel opened one eye and caught me smiling with my hands cupped to my cheeks. She promptly closed the eye.

I couldn't get the Lynette-Cornell story out of my head. It had reignited all my Remy daydreams. *I'm gonna marry that man, world be damned.* The thought triggered an avalanche of giddiness. I wanted to call Remy and set the date right then and there. What was I waiting for? I put a hand at my hip and got a flash of his strong hands sliding up my waist. I put a hand to my lips and was nearly knocked over by a vision of Remy leaning in to kiss me. Then I thought of the fifty other things I liked about him—his friends, his nice clothes, his smile—

"You're in a good mood," Isabel said in a tone like pickle brine. There was a smile waiting in the wings, though. I could tell.

"What was so bad about marrying Remy again?" I said, and laughed.

"Oh, come on." The smile would not be making an appearance after all. I stopped smiling, too.

Isabel waited for a response. Then she understood. "Ah, you've been inspired by Lynette's story of true love."

"Well, it just goes to show that when two people are meant to be together, they can overcome anything." I folded my arms across my chest.

"No, I think the story means you should avoid years of wasting your life with the wrong man—the rich guy who cheats on you—then having to divorce him and live with your parents till you find the right one," Isabel said, and rolled away from me.

I stood and looked at Isabel's back.

"What? Didn't hear that part?" Isabel rolled back over. She propped her head up on one hand and looked at me. She must have seen the drop in my demeanor because now she looked sorry.

I sat down on a chair, utterly deflated. "Maybe Remy and I would be happy. He's so stable. He could jump-start my photography. He's famous—"

"Oh, sweet pea. I love you. I adore you. But you are the worst picker of men."

"Look who's talking."

"Okay, I'll give you that one. You are the best at picking men as adventures, as lovers, as life lessons, and stories for when we're old and gray. The professional skydiver? A Dutch DJ in Argentina? I admire your flair. I do businessmen and bankers, you do kite surfers and famous French directors. But hon, I know how you love to daydream. I suspect you think of marrying Remy as a ready-made adventure, as the answer to turning thirty." Isabel paused to take a breath. "But I think you're in over your head."

"So, then it doesn't work out. So what? It's a fifty-fifty shot."

"Yeah, so what, Sam, so then you'll be divorced and *forty*."

I looked at her in surprise. "I thought you were the one that didn't care about getting older—"

"I *do* do a good job of putting on that show, don't I?"

We looked at each other and said nothing.

Finally, I ventured a grin. "So, feminism dies at thirty? We'll have to break the bad news to your mom and Lynette."

"Ha!" Isabel snorted. "We'll blame the hormones. Suddenly all babies start looking cute. Puppies and babies. We're genetically programmed. It isn't fair."

"Isabel, whatamIgonnado?" I said quietly.

"Well, *we* are going to go swimming with the Garifuna princesses. And remember that everything's going to be just fine and you'll make the right decision. But either way, you'll remember—" Isabel snapped her finger so I looked at her and stopped staring off into space "—you'll remember that at least we'll always have each other. Me, you, Kendra. And Mina." She pointed at Mina's journal on the nightstand.

Then she lumbered off to the bathroom.

I resumed staring off into space. Something she'd said...

"Puppies and babies," Remy said, and tweaked my nose.

"Excuse me?" Remy and I were walking down the boulevard, licking ice-cream cones. We were the consummate couple in love, out for a stroll on a windy afternoon.

"Your friend. She can't help it. All women think about are puppies and babies."

I nearly spit out my mouthful of hazelnut ice cream. "That's what you got out of my explanation of Kendra's argument with Michael? Kendra is the VP of sales. She manages a dozen multimillion-dollar accounts. I tell you that she wishes her boyfriend would appreciate her more and make a little more effort at romance, and all you can say is *puppies and babies?*"

Remy chuckled and made a motion with his thumb.

"Tweak my nose one more time, mister—"

"Okay, oui. Yes. The boyfriend should be more romantic. Silly Americans with their work ethic. They should learn from the French man. Woo the woman and she will stop worrying about mistresses and babies. For a little while."

I stopped strolling. "That is your view of relationships? After all the strong women in my life I've told you about? Lynette, Jesse, Isabel and Kendra. They all have successful careers and somehow still make time for their family and for love and romance. You can't be serious—"

Remy had taken two steps without me. Now he looked back. And cocked his concealed weapon—that sexy, laughing smile of his. A weapon without a permit this time. But then he ceremoniously dropped his ice-cream cone into a trash bin and swept me up in his arms.

"I was teasing, ma chérie. Teasing. You shouldn't be so cute when you're mad if you don't want men to tease you."

He kissed me, but I resisted valiantly. It was so hard to stay mad, with the warmth of his body coursing into mine and his arms encircling me in a sepia-toned postcard of Parisian romance. With our foreheads touching, we heard a whimper. Around the corner bounded a golden retriever puppy with its female owner. The woman called after the scampering puppy but only laughed when the leash jerked her hand. On her hip, she bounced a rosy-cheeked toddler.

Remy turned back to meet my eyes and to his credit did nothing but raise one eyebrow.

I burst out laughing and kissed him hard on the lips.

The consummate couple in love on a windy afternoon.

* * *

Gulp. I reached for Mina's journal and took out the leaf. As I lifted it, dried brown pieces flittered onto the pages. The leaf was no longer soft and velvety, just lifeless.

There was no magic in the leaf.

There was just a lost soul who had no idea what to do without the advice of her best friend.

December 5
Samantha

We're losing you. Today you didn't seem "there." I know it's the medication. I know it's the pain. I'd be the biggest whiner, I bet, in your shoes. But not you. You're too good, too patient. Your pain tolerance for life is admirable, my friend, but baffling. Why aren't you angry? Mina, none of this makes any sense. Of all the people in the world, you're in the top tier. These are the days that a just God seems like an absurd notion.

Dammit! I cannot cry anymore today.

Let's keep on keeping on, shall we?

Locality: it means that if you want to communicate with or affect anybody or anything, you have to do something to the distance between you and it, whether by sound waves, by throwing something, by a laser of light, whatever. It's based on the idea that "I" am separate from everything else.

Einstein treasured the idea of locality, and tried to prove it true. In the end, locality was proven wrong. Turns out "Spooky action at a distance" (Einstein's words) does happen. Spirit mediums and Buddhists were right all along.

There is theoretically no reason why you can't communicate with me from anywhere. But it might be up to you. Maybe we don't hear from the deceased because they don't want to hear from us. So get angry, Mina. Don't disconnect. Don't accept. Don't go quietly. Don't forget about me.

THE GARIFUNA GIRLS WERE NOWHERE TO be seen when Isabel and I walked onto the sand. But Jesse was there, set up in her chair with a magazine. Next to her Arshan pored over a science journal with a Hi-Liter. Cornell and Lynette stood by the edge of the water.

"Whoa, you guys are up early," I said, and sat down in the shade of the umbrella.

"Well, it's our last day, isn't it? No breakfast yet, though, girls," Jesse said without looking up from her *Vogue*.

"I'm not hungry." Isabel threw her fuchsia towel on the blanket.

"The wonders never cease," Jesse said.

"It's probably only because I'm still full of your famous Mai Tais, Mother. Ready, Sammy?"

I was looking back at the palm grove. Ahari was in his usual position. Watching me. This time he raised a hand. First he held it out toward us, like signaling to stop. Then he turned his hand around, almost as if beckoning me to him.

"Sam?"

I glanced at Isabel and when I looked back at the spot where Ahari stood, his hands hung motionless by his side. He continued to stare.

"It's creepy the way he watches us," Isabel whispered. "You ready to go in the water?"

I shook off the eerie feeling. "Ready, Freddy."

"Dork," Isabel said.

"Nerd."

Jesse shook her head as we headed for the ocean. We passed Lynette and Cornell on their way back to the blanket.

"The waves are much bigger today. Don't go out too far," Lynette advised.

I looked past her. She was right. They looked like waves from a surf magazine. Hawaii Five-O. "Don't worry, we're just going to get wet enough to cool off."

Isabel grabbed my elbow. "My feet are burning off. Let's go!"

We took off running, my metallic gold swimsuit glittering in the sun.

I let out a loud laugh, happy to release the tension from

my conversation with Isabel. She held tight to my hand as we charged into the water and dove in unison under a wave. We came up sputtering and laughing.

"Why don't you move back to D.C.?" Isabel asked with a salty smile. "Everything is better when we live in the same city."

I dipped my head backward into the water to smooth my hair out.

"Watch out," Isabel said.

"Huh?" I couldn't hear with my ears underwater and got pummeled. I came out of the whitewash coughing.

"Blech. I just swallowed a crap-load of water. That can *not* be good, considering the first night's fiasco."

Isabel laughed and swam over. "Did you hear what I said?"

Juxtaposed with the Honduran sea and palm trees, I had a vision of ultraconservative Washington, a million yuppies running around in business suits. "I can't move back to D.C., Belly. I'd fit in there now like Laffy Taffy in a dentist's office. Now that you're laid off, why don't we go somewhere like Indonesia? Well, unless I marry Remy, I guess."

So misleading, Isabel's delicate hands. I knew what was coming, as I watched her swish her dainty fingers across the surface of the water. I squinted past her across the shimmering ocean, felt the undertow tug me off balance, when I knew I should get ready to stand my ground.

On cue, Isabel flipped her hair over her shoulder and

glared at me. "Sam, he asked you to marry him spur of the moment, with a two-bit ring."

I braced my feet in the shifting sand. Each side of my split personality had an entirely different life plan, and it was getting exhausting defending them both. "Like I said, I thought it was romantic.".

Isabel pursed her lips. "Or arrogant. Let's see." She counted on her manicured fingers. "Forty-three. Bachelor. Playboy. Domineering. And suspiciously good in bed." She held out her palm, five fingers splayed. "Do these sound like good qualities in a husband?"

I smacked her hand and laughed. I couldn't help myself. "Doesn't sound so bad to me."

Isabel rolled her eyes but quickly turned serious. "Ok, but what about your life? Your dreams became my own, you know."

I never thought about it that way. But, yes, somewhere along the way, four little girls had aligned their hopes, invested in one another's plans. "But dreams age and wrinkle, too. At what point does a starving artist just become a failure?"

I hid my welling eyes by looking away at an oncoming wave. It looked monstrous from our vantage point, hungry.

As I turned back again, Isabel adopted a soothing tone. "Don't give up. It just takes time. Less time if you'd stop running away."

She was right. But if Remy wanted to hand me a perfect new life on a silver platter—"Wouldn't marrying someone like Remy be faster?"

"Duck."

"What?" I said before getting smacked in the head by a wave and dragged into a thirty-second washing machine of water. A laugh waited at my lips right up until the instant I realized I couldn't touch bottom.

Jesse looked up the moment Isabel and I went under the wave. "Should we call them in?" she asked Arshan.

"Eh?" Arshan grunted, absorbed in his research journal.

Jesse looked at Lynette, who didn't look the least bit concerned. Well, Jesse Brighton wasn't about to start worrying if nobody else was worrying.

She pushed her sunglasses back up her nose and flipped a page in her gossip magazine. Blue fingernail polish was back in. "Even with women Demi Moore's age." *Ha! What happens after Demi Moore's age? You decide cracked old toenails are hot?* Jesse craned her neck to see Lynette's toenails. Gleaming fire-engine red. *Thatta girl.*

"What?" Lynette said, catching her.

"Nothing."

Lynette looked out at the ocean. *I told them not to go so far out.* She looked back at Jesse, who was absorbed in her magazine and didn't seem worried. *They'll be fine.*

At last I made it to the surface. I groped for sand with my toes, feeling only a vortex trying to suck me back under. So I treaded water, exhausted, and whipped my head side to side looking for Isabel. There was nothing to see but water and clouds, and flashes of me somewhere in between.

A new wave had me in its talons. Panic reigned as I tried to swim forward only to watch the beach slip farther away. Defeated, I ducked under the wave and let it barrel over me, let it yank me back two yards by my heels. Then I decided to fight. I scissor kicked my legs and dug my hands into the water as though I was clawing my way out of an avalanche. It took about a millisecond to realize I had not a smidgen of control over my locomotion.

When I was sure I wouldn't last another second, I inexplicably shot to the surface again. The instant my face emerged from the sea, I opened my mouth, gagged on acid water, and screamed, "Isabel—"

Jesse and Lynette heard the scream at the same time. Jesse jumped up and knocked her drink onto Cornell.

"Damn, Jesse. What the—"

Lynette and Jesse were already running for the water. Arshan jumped up and ran after them. Cornell caught up to them at the water's edge.

"What happened? Where'd they go?" Cornell bellowed, grabbing Jesse's arm.

"They're out there!" Jesse wailed, wrenching her arm free and splashing into the water up to her waist.

Arshan rushed into the sea past her. He collided with the first wall of waves.

Jesse yelled for him to stop and pointed. They watched my head bobbing on the surface a long way out. Arshan plunged awkwardly in my direction.

Jesse said, "Wait. They're too far out. You won't make it." She scanned the beach for assistance but saw no one. Then she thought she saw a shadow in the palm trees that might be Ahari, standing, watching. She squinted her eyes and swore she could make out—

"There!" Lynette spotted Isabel burst from the white-wash only to land in the path of the next gobbling wave.

The water was torrential. They stood anchored in fear, a row of bronze soldiers affixed to a slab. Jesse pointed as my red hair started to cut sideways through the white-wash.

All four of them watched in shock as I swam into the wave for Isabel and we joined hands for a fleeting second before being dashed into the grave beneath the shimmering surface.

We're really going to drown.

My assessment was not a scream. At first, when we crashed back under the water and I lost hold of Isabel's hand, I'd shrieked inside my skull and thrashed about like a reeling centipede. Now, the realization of real impending death was more of an incredulous observation. With the new stillness of thought, I listened to myself drown. I experienced my underwater undulations like a dance.

In a world without water, my body would be perform-

ing an exquisite ballet in zero gravity. My arms flailed and
arced, my fingers grasped at nothing. I executed somer-
saults in four directions, an elegant marionette on bouncing strings. My body flowed left and right in graceful
suspension.

Mina, are you watching?

"Isabel!" Jesse's bloodcurdling scream scurried across
the sea. She ran deeper into the water and Arshan lunged
after her.

A wave overtook them both. When they came up, Jesse
was choking, sobbing. Arshan moved to comfort her, but
another wave took aim at their heads. As the wave curled
closer, Isabel's body appeared at its rim.

"My God," Jesse gasped, and raised her hands.

The sea dumped Isabel into her mother's arms and all
three tumbled into the surf and disappeared from sight.

Lynette screeched and sobbed, jumping up and down
and clawing at Cornell's arm, inwardly bargaining with
the sea, with the world, with God, with fate. *Please.*
When Arshan came up with Isabel's limp body in his
arms and they began wading toward her, Lynette ran. She
ran smack into them and hugged them so hard they all fell
back into the water again. Isabel came to and coughed.

"You're okay baby," Jesse said, pulling her daughter to
her feet in the shallows. "You're okay. See? Stand up now,
sugar."

Isabel let out a strangled laugh as though shocked to be
alive. Everything was surreal, happening in slow motion.

Jesse grabbed her cheeks and kissed her on the lips. Isabel was so weak, she slipped through Jesse's embrace and fell to her knees. Arshan gripped her shoulders and, with Jesse's help, they carried her half-conscious to the beach.

Lynette turned from them, and let out a low wail. She waded back into the water to look for me.

Cornell stood by her side, ready to catch his wife in his arms whenever she realized I was gone.

Under the water, I was sad. *So, we were wrong, Em? In the end we all go alone?* I always hated being wrong. Pretty flashes of light appeared in the TV-screen static behind my eyelids. I thought about everyone on the beach, overcome by guilt. It wasn't fair to put them through more death. *Forgive me*, I thought, over and over.

But where was Mina? As the water tossed me to and fro, I pictured Mina's gaunt face the morning of her death. I remembered how calm she was, making jokes to soothe us, whispering in my ear to remember our plan. I held her hand until the last second and everyone said she looked at peace.

I didn't feel peace. I was angry. All that worrying over the rest of my life. How foolish that it was all for naught. But the fact that I was going into the unknown alone felt like betrayal. Every time I'd tried to contact Mina— every silly experiment we'd devised—came back to taunt me. How stupid we were. And the maple leaves? Wishful thinking. *This* was reality. This was where the path reached the cliff. Again, I envisioned Mina the morning she died, her skeleton hands, her collarbone like dried-up fish. The end was pain, injustice, loneliness—

"Come here, Sammy."

The memory vanished and I heard Mina's voice strikingly clear, with none of the echo of recollection.

"Samantha," she said, as her dark eyes appeared in the rushing gray of the sea.

I felt that I was falling, tipping forward into Mina's ink-black eyes. Inside those eyes was everything. And nothing. The ocean's roar finally stopped.

December 20
Samantha

Thank you, Mina Bahrami, for being my best friend. Thank you for every respite of laughter, every gift of comfort. The world will never be as fun, as whole, as alive or as joyous without you. You made me who I am—for better or worse, perhaps—but certainly the better for knowing you. Even now, I can't imagine a world where I can't search your eyes for approval or solace, can't hear your careful, Samantha-tailored opinions, can't grab a hold of your chuckling to snap me out of myself. I only wish I could help you more, do more for you in these days of sorrow. I don't know what lies ahead, Mina. Every book, every philosopher, every religion, every physicist says something different. The only thing I could find in common was talk of light, of a field of light encompassing "everything that is," deconstructed into the pieces we experience as reality during life.

The Higgs Field. Everything, they say, has really only ever been *one* thing: light, or a sea, or a being—however you want to envision it—dancing with itself.

Now that doesn't sound so bad, does it, my beloved friend?

All I know is that I will miss you every day. Every single day.

CHAPTER

33

"SAMANTHA."

"Mina? What's happening? Mina."

"Samantha, find me."

Mina.

Minaminaminaminamina. I can't see her. Mina as a little girl. Mina's face. Why can't I picture it?

"Mina, I can't see anything. There's only light. Can you see it?"

It doesn't matter where I look, the light fills my entire body. But I can't feel my body, I don't have any edges, I think I am the light. I can hear my thoughts. There is only thought and light.

And panic. Panic with no heartbeat, no vise around

my chest. I feel panic only in the fluttering tempo of my thoughts. The light is painful. I think I'm being erased. My thoughts are getting quieter, smothered under a pillow.

Mina. Please. I think I died.

34

"SAMANTHA. YOU HAVE TO FIND ME. I THINK you have to—You have to create me."

Mina. I can hear you. Please keep talking. Don't leave me.

"I'm not leaving you. I will tell you what I did. I was trying to comfort myself, so I built a world. But I want us to be in the same one, so I'm going to describe it. Okay?"

You're getting softer again. Muffled. The light is shimmering.

"Shimmering is good. That's what I saw, too. Samantha, listen. I'm sitting by the lake. The house that Jesse rented that summer. When Kendra was in love with Adam. You remember. I'm sitting on the dock with my feet in the water. The water is mold colored, but we love it because it's warm. The dock is warm, too, underneath my knees. I'm wearing my favorite sundress, the one with the sunflowers. We were eleven that summer, but it's easier to stay your same age, so picture me as you saw me last. Well, before I got sick. Can you see me yet?"

The water. I think I see the water. The light's changing colors, sparkling like the diamond glints on waves.

"I'm sitting here splashing my feet, waiting for you. I haven't made the trees, yet, or the house. The water goes off in infinity in front of me, but it isn't scary. It's beautiful. Behind me is the grass, green but scratchy because it's summer. The sky is the exact color of Isabel's eyes. The clouds don't move, but I can feel the sun, warming my knees and my shoulders and the top of my head. My hair is long, down to the middle of my back. I'm just sitting here waiting for you, Samantha. Listening to the water."

CHAPTER

35

"HOLY CRAP!"

I can't help but laugh at Mina's words and the sound echoes like an empty silo. I'm in a house of mirrors, piecing together slivers of landscape materializing out of the light. The water does stretch into eternity—a windowpane mirage of water and clouds.

I turn to see the grass and revel in surprise at the return of my body. It feels like goosebumps from a lover's touch—every inch of my skin springs back into being and sings in the sun. I surrender to an avalanche of sensation; I celebrate it—the air coursing down every alleyway of my insides. It feels so good I start to cry. When the hot tears traverse my cheeks, they are like drops of sunlight dripping off the tip of my nose.

And the dripping sunshine brings me face-to-face with Mina.

Seeing her is a spark of static shock, as all the details of her face rush over me at once. Her smooth, clear skin. The tiny scar above her left eyebrow, her thick hair always swinging from behind her ears, that tremble of her lips when she's about to smile—

"Hey," I say.

"Hey."

I reach out like she is a soap bubble that might vanish at any moment, but the shock of raven hair between my fingers is coarse and soft at the same time, in any case tangible.

"I tried to find you."

Mina smiles. "I know."

I hug her. Blasts of memory superimpose over the warmth of her skin, the grip of her fingers. I'm bowled over by the sensation of existence, and by the contradictory feeling of surreal familiarity. She pulls back and winks.

"This isn't exactly what I had in mind," she says.

And then we burst out laughing, like the day we rode a roller coaster seventeen times, like the time we ice-skated in the middle of the night, or gorged on pancakes after prom, like all the thousands of times we shared a perfect moment of happiness in life.

Except that none of them felt like this.

Our laughter is a thousand flashlights clicking on at once. Happiness bubbles between us like warm, oozing honey. She is every good thing that ever happened in my life, and the reason that all the bad turned out okay. Memories stream from her and rise around me like a warm bath after a long day. Listening to us laugh, I am five years old; I am seven. I am nineteen.

And everything is okay. Everything is alive. I still exist. The lake laughs with us. The sky is smiling. The clouds chuckle. I feel like I might burst of glee. It feels a little bit like falling, like a stream of water arcing toward the earth. I am a balloon filling with water. No, wait.

Light. I'm filling up with light.

The expression on Mina's face changes and then everything is obliterated by white blinding light.

"What happened?"

"I don't know, Sam. Where are you?" She sounds scared.

Green. Everything is greenish-brown. I think I'm in the lake.

Tinkling laughter. "Figures."

The water starts to swirl around me, rushing like a river, no, like an ocean. A dark, menacing ocean. I don't love the water anymore. I don't know how to swim anymore. I am a bronzed version of my former self, like baby shoes. And I am sinking.

"Sam, what's wrong?"

I'm drowning. I'm sinking at lightning speed into a

black void beneath the surface. Everything swirls gray and blue, and cold like the dead dust of the moon. Dark. The water is so loud. And angry.

"Samantha, stop it. I should have warned you. I'm sorry. I'll find you. Just listen to me. Like before. I will always find you."

Your eyes. I can see your eyes.

"There you are, silly girl. Come to the surface now. Come on."

I rise through the placid water and break through the surface. I can see the sky, blue and clear, the clouds anchored in place, like I could pull myself up by them. I look at the dock. Mina waves, trying not to laugh.

"Don't make fun of me!" *Wow. When I shout, it's really loud.*

"Yes, it is. Come sit with me."

I swim to her and climb the wooden ladder to the dock. I sling a dripping arm across Mina's shoulders and smack a wet kiss on her cheek. "Okay, Lucy, you got some 'splainin' to do. Where the hell are we?"

Mina's face falls a little, softens. "I'm not exactly Dante's Beatrice, kiddo. I didn't know you were going to die."

My stomach lurches into my throat. I'd been so focused on feeling alive that I'd bounded past the truth. In a flash I remember swimming purposefully into a gigantic wave, up, up, and reaching her, gripping her freezing cold hand—

"Isabel! Is she alive?"

Mina nods silently. Thank God.

But that means I didn't make it, doesn't it? I put a hand to my chest, try to keep my thundering heart from being ripped out. But— "But I have a body. I'm breathing." I look at Mina's chest rising and falling. "You're breathing."

Mina smiles sadly. "I think it's a projection." She brings a hand up in front of her face and then waves it across the horizon surrounding us like a snow globe. "Alternate worlds, Sam, like you said. Alternate possibilities. I created this one. From memory." She fingers the frayed edge of my sundress, an old favorite stitched up in three places. "Including us. Apparently, I can't imagine a world where we don't breathe."

So of course I have to try to stop breathing. But there's no way to stop without holding your breath, making me hyperaware of my lungs, the air pushing against them, and the fact that I'm about to pass out.

Mina snorts in laughter. "Nice try, Einstein."

I deflate noisily, but I don't feel like laughing anymore. "You've been here the whole time. Locked up here by yourself." My head is a bag of Jiffy Pop, kernels of questions about to explode like a machine gun.

"Not exactly."

I look around at the eerily tranquil summer day, my skin prickling like I'm being watched. "I don't get it. An alternate world? You just—poof—landed on a dock?"

Mina frowns. "Well, that's the thing. When I went, I heard a different voice—my mother's, I think. She was guiding me, helping me to create a space where I could join her. Same as how I got you here. But I kept thinking about you, about our plans, our research. And the light scared me, so I conjured a favorite memory—this place. Then I ended up here all alone."

I study Mina's face, sadness draped over it like a funeral veil. And, I realize now, she's trying not to show me she's afraid. Her mother's voice, she said she heard, like all those stories of near-death experiences. My next words I whisper. "But why do you think it's an alternate world, Em? And not just—" I shiver in the sun "—death?"

"Well—" Mina's face turns purposefully mischievous, a twinkling in her black eyes I know all too well "—I'll show you." She takes my hand, pressing my fingers together hard. Her eyes catch mine and hold, like now I'm the soap bubble hovering on a breeze. "I have no idea if you're ready." She scoots forward on the dock, pulling me along. "We'll find out."

I resist her tugging. The last thing I want to do is go for a dip. "What do you want me to do?"

"Jump."

Mina yanks me into the water and everything goes black. I scream like a fish hooked through the eyeball must scream inside its head.

"SAMANTHA, STOP SCREAMING."

A house. The beach house. I'm on the beach, and there's the gate splayed open to the rustling palm grove and the empty patio beyond.

"Are you here?"

I ignore the disembodied voice. I'm back! I'm alive! The dock was a dream. Isabel must be waiting for me in the house. We'll swap horror stories about the near drowning. Jesse will laugh and Lynette and Cornell will hug me tight. I look down at my feet, ready to take off running.

No! Dammit. No feet. No legs. No hands. I freeze my racing thoughts and wait, trying not to panic.

No heartbeat. No breathing. Terror without a body is difficult to describe. As is despair. I have nothing. I feel nothing, like trying to caress a hologram.

Unable to make sense of things, I focus my attention back on the house. This time as I try to make out the outlines of the hammock in the palm grove—Whoa! I'm *at* the hammock. Wherever I look, my vantage point moves, my mind positioning itself at will. I look down.

Isabel. Oh my God.

She's lying oddly still with her eyes open. Her body is sunk into the hammock at an unnatural angle, her arm hanging listlessly over the side. Isabel's eyes are so red and swollen I can't see the whites. But somehow that makes their blue more piercing than ever. *Oh, Belly.* A whimper emits ever so softly from Isabel's lips, but no words that I can understand.

"Samantha, please. Are you here?"

Isabel. Why can't she see me? I want her to.

"Samantha, answer me."

"Well, then what do you mean, *am I here?* I'm *not* here. I died, Mina." The truth stings. The truth is a homicidal jellyfish.

"I know." Mina's voice is the saddest thing I've ever heard. It ripples the air around me, a kaleidoscope of colors. "So you see her, right?"

I look down at the hammock. Isabel is crying. She doesn't move to wipe the tears, they simply run their course down into her nose and over her lips. Her hair is matted and stuck to her forehead. She begins to move her head right and left, making the hammock cut into her skin.

"Come on, Sam. Come with me inside."

I turn in the direction of the invisible voice and in an instant I'm at the kitchen table inside the house.

Arshan and Cornell are playing cards in slow motion without speaking. They're not making eye contact either. They look old, like gloomy daguerreotypes of defeated generals. Between them is a bottle of rum. Cornell picks it up and splashes sloppy helpings into each of their glasses. Big glasses considering the clock says 11:00 a.m.

"Jesse and Lynette must be in the back."

Even before Mina's voice fades, I'm inside Jesse's bedroom.

Lynette sits on the bed, while Jesse paces the room— scraping her sandals angrily across the weathered boards. They're not speaking either. Jesse keeps licking her lips and bringing her fingers to the side of her mouth like she's about to speak, but then stops. Lynette watches her, with a look that is both concerned and chary. Jesse stops in her tracks, picks up a coffee cup from the nightstand and chucks it at the wall. As the cup becomes jagged pieces oozing murky coffee over the plaster, she snarls like a cornered Rottweiler. "Goddammit, Lynette. Goddammit all to hell!"

"Mina, I want to go back to the dock."

"Okay. But I have to do something first. Go back to Isabel."

I'm at the hammock. Isabel's in the same painful position, but now there is a tomato-red scratch on her cheek from slicing it against the coarse netting. I see a shimmer on the wooden boards beneath the hammock—a shiny American penny. *A penny for your precious thoughts*, Mina always said to Isabel and all of her big save-the-world ideas. Isabel blinks.

"How did you do that?"

"I'm not sure, really."

"So, you've been doing it to Isabel, too."

"Of course. And Kendra. Didn't they tell you?"

CHAPTER

37

WE'RE BACK ON THE DOCK. I DROP MY HEAD into Mina's lap and sobs pour from my mouth like lava. Everything everywhere hurts. We've seesawed back to this strange world where I can feel my body, but now the downpour of sensation only makes me nauseous and raw. Crying here hurts worse than anything when I was alive. It hurts worse than dying. I think it will never stop. I think it will never stop hurting.

"No, it won't, Sammy. Not as far as I can tell, anyway."

The cries turn to whimpers in my throat. As Mina strokes my hair, the heaving feeling slowly passes. When I sit up, I curl my knees to my chest to anchor myself somehow. I force myself to feel the warmth of the sun, to be still like the glassy water. "So you go anytime you want?"

The look in Mina's eyes is as old as time. "What do you think I've been doing?"

"It's torture. Why do it to yourself?"

Mina looks wounded. "It's the only way to be with them."

Her response trips me into a dirty puddle, muddling my thoughts. *But I don't want to visit. I don't want to watch. I want...*

"What, Sam? What do you want?"

"I want to go back."

"Let's go. This is the most time I've spent here yet! I'm worried about Isabel—"

"That's not what I meant. I mean I want to go back to before."

"You mean you wish you hadn't died." Mina tries her best to look comforting. But she frowns. "You wish you never ended up here, with me."

The look on my best friend's face is a poisoned arrow, infecting me with shame. If I hadn't died, wouldn't Mina have been forced to watch us for eternity, a fish in an invisible fishbowl? "Of course I'm glad to be with you." I poke her shoulder. Then her leg. I poke her repeatedly until she smiles. A thought strikes me finally. "Does Kendra know about me? Does Remy?"

"Kendra, yes. Isabel emailed Remy and left a voicemail. He hasn't responded."

"Why not? What is he doing?"

Mina looks away. "I don't know. I visited you two when you were alive and with him. But I can't go now."

"Why not?"

"I don't know, Sam."

"Can I go?"

"I would think so. Do you want to try?"

I look out across the green water. "Let's go see Kendra first."

"Where are we?" Blue. Blue everywhere. And the smell of chlorine.

"Kendra's swimming."

There she is. Third lane from the right. Swimming hard, like the devil's chasing her.

"Yeah, she's upset. But, Sam, there's something else… something you don't know."

Kendra finishes her lap. She yanks herself out of the pool, and stomps a path toward the changing room. She checks the clock.

I'm in the changing room when she comes in the door. She sits down on a bench, unlocks her locker and takes out a towel. Still dripping wet, she covers her face with the terry cloth. Then she leans forward and bangs her head on the locker five times. When she stops, she tips her head back, eyes wide-open. It startles me. I can count on one hand the number of times I've seen Kendra Jones cry. She stops as soon as she starts. She wipes her nose and sniffs hard. Tough girl Kendra. Never a big fan of naked emotion. She opens the locker again. She slips quickly out of her swimsuit and into a dress, conspicuously averting her eyes from her body. She dumps everything in her bag and leans hard against the locker. Her face is all angles and shadows. Then it starts to shimmer. Everywhere.

"Mina?"

"We have to go, Sam."

I can barely make out Kendra heading for the exit. But then she turns sharply and looks back. I can see her clearly now and I follow her gaze. On the floor is a single green clover leaf.

"YOU DID THAT. HOW?"

"I don't know."

The dock is just as before—the sun shining, the clouds still unmoving but perfect. It's like a scrapbook picture of my childhood. Mina's as still as the clouds, as if she's part of the photograph, too. I touch her shoulder.

"Why did we have to leave?"

"We can only go when they're thinking about us."

"Mina, how many times have you seen Kendra cry? Of course she was thinking about us."

Mina kicks her feet in the water, rippling the photograph. "She was at first. But then she was thinking about something else." Mina hugs herself like she's cold. "Tomorrow is her appointment."

"For what?"

Mina looks up and frowns. "Kendra's going to have an abortion."

I think of Kendra's voice in our last phone call. "Why didn't she tell me?"

"I think she's ashamed."

"Of getting pregnant?"

"Of being more concerned about ruining her perfect life than creating a new one."

"Michael doesn't know?" How could Kendra not tell him? And not tell us? She must have been going crazy.

Mina looks at the water. "It's what he wants."

The water suddenly appears to boil around her feet. Mina yanks her feet out of the water and looks at me curiously.

"How can she be with such an asshole?"

Mina laughs uneasily. "Ye who live in glass houses—"

I cock my head. "Remy? You don't like him?"

Mina's answer is surprisingly soft. "Did you?"

I want to shoot her an angry look but it fizzles. The news about Kendra is overwhelming, but now Remy moves through my mind in countless flittering memories. "Should I go see him? Do you have to go with me?"

Mina pats my hand. "I'll wait here. Just think about him as hard as you can. You can do it."

Remy. Remy. Remy getting out the shower, singing a silly French song with my name in it. Remy in bed, snoring like a bear. Remy's smile with his gleaming teeth. Remy's hand on my waist, possessive but so reassuringly confident.

Wow, he looks great.

Remy is in front of a fancy crowd, making a toast. He is obviously drunk, but carrying it well, dressed impeccably in a tux.

Not exactly what I expected. He's at a party? But if I'm here, he must be thinking about me—

"Merci! Merci beaucoup. Ce prix me signifie le monde."

People applaud as Remy clutches an award in his hands and thanks them profusely. The ballroom is filled with tables covered in white linen tablecloths and towering flower arrangements. Photographers wind amongst the guests, setting off firefly blasts of light. Camera crews zoom in on Remy walking down from the stage, a trophy in hand. Beautiful women in ball gowns stand clapping and wiping fake tears, beside their cheering, handsome dates.

A busty blonde in a slinky black cocktail dress breaks off from the crowd and makes her way towards Remy, shifting her hips as she glides through the adoring spectators.

"Tu le mérites," she croons into his ear with a disgusting familiarity. She lingers a second longer to exhale onto his neck.

Remy closes his eyes and does not respond to her passionate praise. When he opens them, he looks ill. "Excusez-moi," he mumbles, and claws his way through the smiling people.

When he gets to the bathroom, a distinguished gentleman is just about to step inside. He stops when he catches sight of Remy and smiles. "Ah, Monsieur Badeau—"

Remy puts his hand on the doorknob and averts his eyes. "Pardonez-moi," he says as he slips past the startled congratulator.

Inside, Remy barely makes it to the toilet in time to vomit. His face is splotchy and dripping sweat. He flushes the toilet and wipes the seat with a wad of seat covers. He clenches a fist and punches the metal wall. He smoothes back his hair as if trying to calm himself down, but then he kicks a gilded trashcan and it careens to the floor clattering like armor. The kick sends Remy staggering until he slumps down on the toilet seat in his tux. With the growl of a grizzly, he drops his head into his hands and sobs.

It's heartrending to see. I long to touch him, comfort him. And I need to be held, feel his strong arms wrap around me and confirm my existence. But there is no me here. Here I am, a freshly completed last chapter. And a source of pain.

Helplessly watching Remy cry is the ultimate confirmation of my death. There is nothing to separate us, none of the usual barriers between lovers. No skin, no eyes staring into another's, no discordant heartbeats to denote the boundary between us. I am not him, I am not here. I am an observer of a world where I no longer swim. I'm a visitor to the aquarium.

CHAPTER

39

"HE'S NOT AN ASSHOLE." THE SOLIDITY OF the wood dock soothes me, moors me to a world where at least I *feel* alive.

Mina's floating on her back in the lake. She looks over, surprised, but then her face sinks into dullness, her eyes gunmetal gray.

"Well, I suppose it doesn't matter anymore, does it, Sammy?"

It's like she punched me in the stomach. But she's right. "Will this go on forever?"

Mina sighs and looks up at the sky. "I don't know."

"Will it stop when they stop thinking about us?" The tranquility of our snow globe is beginning to irritate me.

"I don't know."

The smooth water reminds me of the swimming pool. "Is Kendra going to go through with it?"

"I don't know, Sammy."

Anger hisses up from my stomach like vapors from a tomb. "Why don't you know?"

Mina looks me flat in the eye. "I. Don't. Know."

I want to slap her. The clarity of that thought scares me. She challenges me with her obsidian eyes. *You can hear what I'm thinking.* She nods her head. We stare each other down like rival tigers. The water is so still it makes Mina look like a bust on a mirrored platter. "Does it ever rain, Mina? Does it change? A dock. A lake."

Curiously, the lake begins to tremble. Mina notices when waves start to lap at her chest. But I can't slow down. My anger is a hurricane barreling through my ribs. "Billions of people arguing about God, and this is it? An unfinished memory. A sliver of puberty. This is what we get? Why did you stick me here?"

"Samantha, stop."

It's too late to stop. "What if you'd listened to your mother? Maybe you broke the rules and now we're cut off from whatever was supposed to happen! What if now I'm stuck here for eternity? While everyone in the world slowly forgets I ever existed—"

My blood runs cold at the thought of such a fate. In tandem, my skin chills, like that instant when the sun dips behind the clouds. I cover my face with my hands and drop to my knees with a thud. It's impossible to make out

Mina's reply over the sound of my tears and the rushing sound of rain.

Rain? My eyes spring open as the first drops hit my shoulders. The rain begins to hammer, much like the tempo of my heart, striking my cold skin the temperature of warm tears. Black clouds swarm in the sky, churning like the outrage in my belly. In the distance, lightning crackles in fury.

"Stop!" Mina's trying to ride a lake turned into a dark roiling ocean.

The water is rising. I jump to my feet but it rises to my waist and then to my chin and I have to tread water. We're swimming in a hurricane from hell—no dock, no land, no grass. Just an infinity of storm.

A swell rises behind Mina, like the tidal wave from my nightmare. She's screaming something at me, but I can barely understand over the roar of thunder and water. She points at me, then at the sky. "You. You're—" Her words are swallowed again by the wind. The glinting wave curls above me and I raise my arms to shield myself. Mina puts out her arms. "Your emotions! Sam—"

The sea dumps Mina on top of me and we go under. But Mina's hands find me in the darkness, hooking under my arms, and drag me to the surface. Her face is twisted in remorse, lit up in flashes of lightning, as she struggles to keep us afloat. "I'm sorry! I'm so sorry!"

I try to consider what she said. My emotions command the water and clouds?

"I'm sorry I didn't spend more time on it," Mina sobs. "I—I spent all my time with you."

With those words, the wind of the world is snuffed out. The waves drop and the water stills. Mina watches in awe as we find ourselves standing on the dock with the water draining to our knees, our feet, and then gurgling through the wood boards to settle into its prior level.

I reach out and put a hand to Mina's cheek, already drying in the sun. "I thought about you every day, didn't I?"

Mina nods. "I was horrified when you and Isabel got trapped in the water, terrified when I realized you might die. But then…then I was just so amazed that it worked, that I got you here. I knew, though. I knew that you'd have a million questions. You're Samantha the scientist. You always have a million questions. I didn't want to mislead you into thinking I had all the answers." She sits down on the dock. "But that's not to say I haven't come up with some theories."

I sit next to her.

"I think there's a reason I ended up here." Mina's hand lingers at her throat; she's thinking. "I think we were on to something with our research. Everything you taught me about thought, intention, belief. We must have been at least partly right. It gave me the power to hold on, and the power to create from my mind." Mina looks up and realizes the clouds move now, drifting lazily across the sky. She grins at me. "And it kept us connected. The first time you tried to reach me, that's the first time I learned

I could go watch." Mina's smile widens. "And now you're *here*."

My heart is as calm as the lake. "Love lasts."

"What?"

"The journal. What you wrote. Love lasts." I clasp my hands together like Jesse always does when she gets a neon lightbulb of an idea. "Mina."

"Yeah?"

"I know why *I'm* here." I smile so big Mina can't help but imitate me. "To bring you back."

40

"WE CAN CHANGE THINGS." I FEEL LIKE myself again. Bright as the sun and ready for a fight. I wave my arms across the sky and a flock of Canada geese squawk overhead. Mina laughs appreciatively. "But not just in this world. I mean in the other one."

Mina is amused. She cocks her eyebrow. *Oh yeah?*

"I'm serious. You left all those maple leaves. The penny, the clover leaf. If we can manifest things, we can figure out how to materialize. I don't know whether we'll be ghosts or what, but we can definitely appear in some form, like that research on quantum bodies. That Gos-wami guy. Then we can just hang out with them forever. Well, maybe not with Remy forever." *Uh-oh, I see the glitch.* "That wouldn't be very nice, would it? For either of us."

Mina looks sad. "That's what I've been wrestling with."

The itchy feeling of disappointment spreads across my cheeks. "So how did you do it? The leaves? And pennies and clover leafs?"

Mina scratches her neck, a nervous habit. "I just do it. I thought about all that stuff you told me about belief. I... sort of...sweep away all doubt, and just *believe* that the leaf is there." She looks up. "Like you had to make yourself believe this place existed."

There is a stirring like robins' wings in my chest. And then a lightbulb. "But, Mina, when you put the leaves there, I *saw* them. Meaning you changed what *would* have happened, in the living world."

"I never thought about it that way."

Belief. Belief and consciousness. The thorn in physicists' sides is consciousness. What is it exactly? What are its boundaries and limitations? What are its powers?

Mina nods, excited. *Go on.*

Okay, how much do you remember about the electron slit experiment? When you set up an experiment to see where an electron or light particle is, the mathematics tell us it is spread out in many places at once, a wave of possibilities, not a particle. But when we, human beings, do something to measure it, there it is in just one place. Why? Because it is brought into a specific existence by the human consciousness? i.e. The Copenhagen Interpretation. But then there's Many Worlds Theory, an infinity of different worlds where we exist in each one, living out each pos-

sible outcome. Two different theories that say completely opposing things. One where we have divine control, one where we are just copied into infinity. But if there was a way to combine them, a way to control which world we are in, and what happens—

I stop. I look at Mina. She's not saying a word. Now she purses her lips.

"What?"

Mina has a look of exasperation. "It doesn't make sense. When we go watch, it's always the same one. And we're both dead. Where are all the other universes? And besides that, we don't know what is happening until we go to them, so it can't be our consciousness creating the outcome."

Very good points indeed. I tap my fingers on the dock. Nervous habit. "Well, I suppose if there are universes where we're alive we can't see them because we're living them and then we couldn't be here to go watch." My coherency of thought evaporates. "Shit, you're right. It's hopeless."

Mina smacks my shoulder. "Don't give up so easy. I was just playing devil's advocate to help."

I lie back on the dock, feel the stretch in my stomach muscles. *Go with your gut.* My eternal advice to myself and my friends. I sit up fast and smile at Mina. "You used the word *believe*. You believed the leaf was there. Well, everybody believes that we are dead. Including us. What if we can believe ourselves back to life?"

Mina has her hands on her hips, a spitting image of the little girl that used to scold me. "What do you propose?"

"For now, research. Let's go see if we can shake things up."

CHAPTER 41

"I HARDLY KNOW WHERE TO BEGIN," ARSHAN says from his chair on the sand.

The vacation club is on the beach. It's afternoon, but the sun's starting to falter. Isabel's lying curled up with her head in her mother's lap, Jesse looking down and softly playing with her daughter's hair. Cornell is in his designated chair with Lynette sitting on the blanket between his knees. He has his hands on her shoulders. Everybody's eyes are rimmed in red.

Arshan looks out at the waters that stole me from them. He looks at Isabel. *The world takes so much away, when you have so much to lose*, he thinks sadly. He's imagining my father alone with the news of a daughter's death. *That man will never see the sea the same again. And I shall never return to Iran without seeing my Reza everywhere.*

"Start like David Copperfield, my man," Cornell says. "You know—I was born on a Friday."

Arshan coughs as he struggles to recall Dickens's opening lines. "As for whether I'm the hero of my own life…I won't fare very well by those standards, I'm afraid."

Nobody knows what to say, so Arshan begins like Dickens.

"I was born in Tehran, in the house next to Maliheh's family. We were born six days apart. I came first, earlier than expected. That was our joke. That I was older, but I wasn't ripe yet. She came second, fully formed and wiser."

"Mina?"

"Shh, Sam, don't do anything. Please. I waited my whole life to hear this story."

"What was she like?" Cornell asks kindly.

"Maliheh was the very definition of beauty. Hair black as crow feathers. Eyes that were always laughing at you. Like Mina's, but Maliheh's eyes had tiny flecks of gold. She had eyelashes like reeds on a riverbank. Her eyes turned to obsidian when she was angry, but that was very, very rare." Arshan breaks off to smile. "Oh—and she was tiny, like a little Yoda. Childlike but somehow ancient. If I hadn't known her my entire life, she would have intimidated me, like she did the other boys. But I spoke to her every day of her life, and we always knew it would be that way."

"Oh, Mina, wow."
"I know. Shh."

"Wasn't that type of interaction taboo in Muslim society?" Cornell asks.

"Ah, well, Tehran was very different when we were growing up, and I suppose on top of that, our families were somewhat unusual. In the forties and fifties, the Shah and then his son were in power, and the drive was towards modernization, some would say Westernization. Things were much more liberal than you might imagine. My family was especially secular, and was becoming rich in the new economy. Maliheh's family was stricter in their faith, but our parents were best friends and jokingly matched us up as infants, so we enjoyed a special leeway."

"What was good 'ol Tehran like back then?" Jesse asks.

Arshan doesn't seem to hear her. He looks like he just remembered a private joke. "You couldn't have invented two more different people. I was rash and opinionated. Stubborn as a donkey. Maliheh was a winding creek, easily adaptable and forgiving. Those eyes, so mocking, but so full of love. She taught me to laugh at myself. It was the worst thing I lost by losing her. One must remember to laugh at oneself, don't you think?"

The group settles in for the long haul. This is not an

interactive story. It is a story written and revised and re-
hearsed. Waiting all these years to be delivered.

Arshan shakes his head free of invisible cobwebs. "The
Tehran of my childhood remains only as sugarcoated
slivers of memories—our house with the stone tiles,
the fountains, our enchanting garden, swimming pool,
city palaces and public baths. We shopped in the winding labyrinth of the Bazaar, licking ice-cream cones. We
vacationed on the Caspian Sea, took trips to the snowy
mountains. Our houses overflowed with family, laughter and discussion. My father was a businessman, but his
real passion was literature. My mother loved to sing, and
always played music in the house. Vigen Derderian sang
the soundtrack to my childhood."

"We'll have to look that one up on Google, Arshan,"
Jesse says, and everyone except Isabel chuckles quietly.

Arshan nods in all earnestness. "Well, look up Goo-
goosh on Google, too."

"That's funny! Mina, your dad is actually funny."

"I told you. Now shut up. You're so much louder than
them."

"At the end of every schoolday," Arshan continues,
"Maliheh and I met back at my house. We played and ate
Zulbia—like funnel cake—while our mothers whispered
and laughed over boiling stew and doogh."

"Well, now that *does* sound like heaven," Jesse says, and

lights up a cigarette. "Except maybe the doogh. I've had it—a fermented, carbonated yogurt drink. It's...peculiar."

"Says the woman who eats pickled cactus from the can," Lynette points out.

"We are all a product of nostalgia," Cornell says. "By this age, who's to say what is preference and what is habit?"

"Cornell, you will never convince me I don't miss Maliheh's pomegranate chicken on merit alone." Arshan's view again fills with Maliheh's laughing eyes. Talking about her aloud is such a strange sensation for him. For the most part, Maliheh is a dusty book in Arshan's library, recited by heart for comfort. Describing her to strangers causes fresh details to rush back at him. Maliheh shockingly appears before him in the twilight as a vibrant, living being. It is delicious and excruciating.

"Mina, I can see her. I can see your mother through his eyes. Mina, can you see her?"

Mina is weeping.

"We were happy children. And we took it for granted, just like all happy people. Our life was composed mainly of laughter—beneath the juniper trees that lined our courtyard. Of course, when we became teenagers, the world grew more complicated."

"What year we in now?" Cornell asks.

"I turned 18 in 1960. Inside the courtyard was still a happy world, but—" Arshan sighs. He looks around at the women's faces and ends on Cornell's. "It is not an easy thing to explain—a religious revolution. I think it's like you trying to explain the legacy of African slavery to me. It's slippery and complicated. And uncomfortable. I feel ridiculous posing as a representative of Iran."

Cornell doesn't say anything for a moment and then he puts one of his big hands on Arshan's narrow shoulder. "I think we just talk to each other. Tell our stories. One generation at a time. Go on. Please."

"I left to study physics in the U.S. at 18. Maliheh's family would've sent her abroad if she wanted. It was somewhat fashionable for girls then. But she said she'd never leave Tehran. Why would she? The trees would miss her, she said. So I went off to the hated and revered world of America. It is hard to explain Iran's feelings toward America. For most Iranians, both fundamentalist and secular, America is the symbol of hypocrisy, corruption, imperialism and sin." Arshan avoids their eyes to look out over the ocean, still roaring. "My family, being middle class and intellectual, benefited from relations with the West, from the economic reforms, and they saved their rials for Western-style clothes and products. Later, they rejoiced in reforms like women's rights, for example. But they resented America's actions toward Iran and other countries like Israel, of course. So cocky, so intrusive—"

"All the things that we are," Lynette says with an encouraging smile.

"True. Nobody likes to be forced to do anything. The

veil was outlawed. The government shoved Westernization down the country's throat. So, at the same time that
we enjoyed certain freedoms of American culture, others
saw a threat to Iran's way of life. This was complicated
by the actions of Reza Shah and how he was viewed
as pandering to Western leaders. Eventually both sides,
secular and Muslim, turned against him. And SAVAK,
the Persian CIA, interrogated, imprisoned and executed
thousands of people from the middle class—intellectuals,
leftists—anyone they felt was a threat to the government.
Oh, but wait. In 1960, I was at Georgetown University,
before all that, writing letters to Maliheh and trying to
sort out my feelings about my new host country. But by
the second year, I decided I would never feel at home in
America. I wrote to our parents and began preparations
to return to Iran and marry upon graduation. Maliheh
was pleased, but in her usual fashion, looked like she had
known my entire reaction in advance."

Arshan picks up a bottle of wine and pours the remain-
der into a plastic cup. He takes a sip.

"Summer break, after my second year, we were married. Our son Reza was born nine months later while I
was away. Then Maliheh's letters started telling me the
horrible things about SAVAK. My uncle and then my
cousin were jailed. Friends were picked off the street in
vans and never heard from again. A lot of it I wasn't told
until visits on holidays. These were things people only
whispered about behind closed doors. Reza Shah was
building up to his White Revolution and wanted no de-

tractors. There were good things—education, industrial-ization, healthcare, jobs. But it wasn't enough. The divide between rich and poor was too great. It is very danger-ous to make promises to desperate people. The role of a savior is not easily filled. Only promises have the power to inspire. Reality rarely satisfies. The Shah's land reforms brought chaos to the farmers and factories. Jobless, angry young men crowded the cities. Even more dangerous, the reforms took land profits away from the clergy at the same time that they eroded their power and influence in government. This was an arrogant move for the Shah and the clergy responded as should have been expected. I came home to a strange mix of celebrations and parades, demonstrations and unrest. One man, a lowly clergy at the time, Khomeini, protested the Shah. He was impris-oned, then exiled. But the damage was done."

"Our buddy Khomeini. Knew he was about to show up." Cornell sits forward in his chair.

Lynette stirs, too. "But wait, Arshan, tell us more about your marriage, your home life. Tell us about your son."

Arshan watches the baby while Maliheh gets dressed for dinner. Reza is not yet two, and chubbier than a su-per-size cherub. His black hair is so thick and straight it sticks up no matter how Arshan tries to smooth it down. Every time Arshan licks his fingers and tries, Reza kisses his hand. This makes Arshan laugh so now it is a game they play as he walks his son around the dinner table. The sofreh is piled with steaming dishes. In the middle,

Maliheh has set out kebabs of barbecued beef skewered with onions and peppers. Nearby lies Arshan's favorite—Khoresht Anaar Aveej—chicken with pomegranate juice and herbs. Arshan points out other dishes to a giggling Reza—Khoresht Aaloo, Morasah Polow, Khoresht Loobia-Sabz. Arshan's stomach starts to rumble. He walks back in on Maliheh doing her makeup. She is dressed in a fashionable empire-waist sleeveless dress printed with green and gold flowers. She is plumper after having Reza, but Arshan thinks it makes her appear more womanly. Even his little wife moves about like a child, unhurried and playful. She is humming. Arshan smiles until he remembers the argument that drove him out of the room. About Khomeini's exile. A fire ignites in his belly.

"I can't believe you think—"

"Shh, Agha." She instantly knows what he is thinking. Maliheh always knows her husband's thoughts, moving with or against her own. "Let's not discuss this now. He is gone, let that make you happy if it does. All I said is that his message will continue to ring true to many good Muslims. Now, give me my little Reza. Reza. Reeez-zaaa."

Arshan smiles. His wife is such a good mother. "Like you. You mean the message speaks truth for a good Muslim like you, as opposed to me—the scientist. But I am not happy with the Shah's methods either. It is a violation of human rights, I agree. But this madman, Maliheh. His way of speaking. It will ignite the wrong kind of change. The wrong kind of following."

Maliheh sets down her lipstick gently. She turns around slowly, rocking Reza, and gives Arshan a look he hardly ever sees, naked disappointment. "My husband. My best friend the scientist. Are you scared of your fellow Muslims? Of seeing more faith infused in our lives? Khomeini is silenced. Exiled for saying something I agree with— that perhaps our government should have asked before turning my beloved Iran into a garish, bargain imitation of the West. Maybe some women here do not want to be like the women in America."

"Oh, so you'd like to take off that makeup and cover your new dress in a chador? You'd prefer that I *want* to hide your beauty?" He steals Reza back from his beautiful wife. He fingers her silky hair with a free hand. "How could I hide this hair from the world?"

"My beauty is for you. If you wanted only you to see it, why would that bother me?" Her response is firm, but Maliheh's eyes glitter. She is teasing him. Before Arshan can answer, Maliheh snatches Reza from his arms and swings him up in the air. Reza jiggles with giggles, delighted to be so loved by both his parents. "Let's go wait for the family, shall we?"

Arshan takes another sip of wine, thinks of the long list of things that are now forbidden in Iran. "Of course, that wasn't the end of Khomeini."

He clears his throat. "I got a position teaching science at the University of Tehran. My students represented the sliding scale of all the factions of society—from the socialists to the religious right. Everybody wanted change for one reason or another and took up the cry for revolution. The fervor swept over us all. By the seventies, the call for revolution in Iran had spread outside the universities. People crowded into teahouses and cafés. Over carrot ice-cream floats and lemonade, young men argued about the course of the New Iran. Tapes of Khomeini's rants were distributed like candy, traded like baseball cards. Reza was a teenager by then, and just starting to find himself. He identified with the rebellion, like any teenager would. Demonstrations became a veritable job for the whole community. They took to the streets like a block party. Everybody expected all the injustices of their existence to be righted by the revolution. I knew enough to know better. Napoleon. Mao. One African dictator after another. Revolutionaries always claim they aren't in it for the glory or the power, only to be exposed as slaves to those very same demons."

Arshan tips his cup only to realize that it is empty. He picks up the bottle and sees that it is empty, too. "I think I'm going to need a steady supply tonight."

He leaves the others on the beach to get another bottle and hit the restroom.

"I'm going after him." Mina's voice is a whisper, a whisper that is both childlike and wise.

As Arhsan washes his hands, he looks in the mirror. He rarely looks anymore. *Imagine if Maliheh could see this face.* He smoothes his beard with his hands. *But you would be old, too, my darling.* Imagining Maliheh anything but smooth and nimble was harder than imagining heaven. *That is one thing about dying, huh, my love? You will be forever young and pretty. And mine.* Inevitably, he thinks of Mina and me.

"Mina, now."

"What?"

"Do something."

Arshan covers his face with his hands. His mind is awash in pain and nostalgia, the bittersweet mixture of love and loss. When he opens his eyes, he flicks off the light and turns to leave. But out of the corner of his eye, he spies a gold journal sitting on the corner of the sink. When he opens the journal, his eyes widen and then fill with tears.

Arshan appears on the sand in a rush, the journal clutched tight in his hand. "Who put this in the bathroom?"

Everybody looks confused.

"What is it?" Jesse asks.

Isabel doesn't raise her head but her eyes focus outside of herself for the first time that evening. "It's Mina's journal. To Samantha. I have one, too. So does Kendra."

There is a silence of disbelief. Arshan doesn't know if

he is hurt or happy or angry. But he *is* confused. "Why did you put it there, Isabel?"

Isabel rubs her eyes like she's being rudely awoken. "I didn't. But you can have mine, too, if you want." When nobody says anything, she finally looks at Arshan. The pain emanating from her is palpable to all. But especially to me.

"Samantha," she says at last, "told me to read it like a crystal ball. To use it as a way to talk to Mina. But it doesn't work. Mina's gone and now Sam's gone, too. I can't talk to them ever again. I should have died, too. It has to hurt less than this."

"Mina, I can't take it. It's breaking my heart. Come back to the dock."

CHAPTER

42

"YOU OKAY?"

I can't answer. I feel that I'll explode if I so much as breathe. Isabel's sorrow is physically painful for me. It's like the needles of a cactus, carving every inch of my skin.

At the first boom of thunder, I open my eyes. The rain falls timidly upon us. I look at Mina, but she nods and gently smiles. "Go on, it's okay. Just don't overdo it, yeah?"

So I laugh until I cry. The rain absorbs my tears and sends them back down, plastering my hair to my face. I close my eyes but lift my chin up to the sky. It feels so much different from anything when I was alive. This world cries with me, for me, for everyone I loved.

I feel so sorry for myself I can hardly bear the weight of it. I feel sorry for Kendra and Isabel, for my father, and for Jesse, Lynette, Cornell and Arshan. I feel sorry for Mina most of all. Where was the light taking us before we ended up here? To me, the light felt like obliteration, but Mina said she heard her mother. Now I beg the light to come back. To tell me the secrets of this world and the next, to guide me and teach me. It will take away the pain of dying and the pain of remembering. I wait for it, for the white light that erases everything in its path as effortlessly as water carves stone.

But it doesn't come.

The rain eases and I can hear myself breathing. The sun breaks through the clouds as I let out a shuddery sigh.

I'm alone on the dock.

I blink in the sunshine. Then I hear a voice skim across the lake like water spiders.

"I'm listening to my father, Sam. He's continuing the story."

Silence.

The sun, the gently drifting clouds, the barely lapping water. And silence. Funny how silence can be the loudest sound.

Without Mina's presence, I study the landscape with a new intensity. Time to experiment. I put out my palm and a beetle scurries across it. I close my eyes and open them to a mosquito buzzing in front of my nose. I chuckle and jump to my feet on the dock. With my arms spread wide, I twirl in a slow circle. A fish jumps out of the lake, is snared in an eagle's talons, and dropped through a cloud of bees into grizzly bear's mouth. The bear looks at me and then ambles off on the plain of grass, making me smile like a new mother at her firstborn.

Wildflowers spring up, the dock is freshly painted, flip-flops and a magazine flutter in the breeze. An idea forms in my head, clear as koi swimming to the surface.

It's up to me.

This is my job.

I won't tell Mina until I figure it out. But there is a way back. There is a way to bring us both back, and I'm going to find it.

"Samantha, are you coming or not?"

"I'm coming."

43

ARSHAN SITS IN SILENCE, SWIRLING HIS WINE in his cup. The next part he has never spoken about to more than a handful of people. All of them in Iran.

"Reza and I began to argue frequently. He idolized Khomeini, saw him as the answer to every evil in his young life. He had my temper, but no angel like Maliheh to buffer it. He saw me as too secular, too intellectual, too Westernized. He also loved me fiercely, and the conflict was overpowering him. He poured all his anger into the movement. I, unfortunately, was distracted by other problems.

Maliheh and I had been trying to conceive again since Reza's childhood. She'd had five miscarriages over the course of fifteen years, and each one locked a piece of my wife away from me. I begged her to desist from trying, but then in 1978, Maliheh became pregnant. I braced myself for the horror of another miscarriage. But another month and Maliheh was still nauseous in the mornings and rounder. I felt hope stirring in my heart. I let it color the atmosphere around me. Maybe there could be a whole new start, I thought. Khomeini spoke of equality and justice. Of returning the pride of Iran."

The wine turns to vinegar in Arshan's mouth. "Another three months, and I knew my first instinct had been right. The demonstrations turned violent, the rhetoric fanatical. I saw what the revolution would mean to men like me. And my family."

Maliheh, Arshan and a teenage Reza sit around the dinner table. Arshan is yelling, Reza is fuming, and Maliheh is disgusted with them both.

Reza's appearance sums up his crisis of allegiance. He's wearing a shiny new green athletic jacket, but doing his best to grow a respectable Muslim beard. He scratches at the patchy hair and pointedly averts his eyes from his father.

In the center of the table is a pile of cassette tapes.

Arshan picks up a tape and waves it in the air as he yells at his son. "Stalin, Hitler, Lenin, Chiang Kai-shek—I did not raise my one and only son to be an idiot, a sheep, a mindless martyr!"

Arshan is quaking, his tie quivering as he tries to control his rage.

"How can you not see that Khomeini is no different? How can you not see if you do not open your eyes, my young son?"

Arshan moves his face inches away from Reza's. Reza's so upset that tears spring to his eyes, the very thing he's trying to forestall. He jerks his head away so his father won't see.

Maliheh leans closer to her son, the scarf over her hair falling from her furrowed forehead.

Reza jumps up and leaves the table. Arshan watches him go, then tosses the cassette back onto the pile. He kicks the leg of the table. Maliheh only shakes her head slowly in response.

On the beach in Tela, Arshan says, "Maliheh had carefully instilled our son with patriotism and faith. I countered with sordid history, science and skepticism.

The combination turned out to be a mistake. We handed our son his own private war."

Arshan rubs his eyebrows, as if he can blot out the memories, stop what's coming.

"By the end of summer, Maliheh and I had opposite objectives. She wanted to set up a nursery for the baby. I wanted to move to Washington with my cousin before she gave birth. She wouldn't hear of it. Reza wouldn't even respond to the prospect of moving. And then the calendar brought September eighth, just like any other day." Arshan sighs raggedly.

"It was becoming impossible to maintain my classes at the university amidst the constant protests. I'd seen Reza's friends in the parades. They moved like a herd of cows, chanting in unison. *Death to the Shah. Death to America. Death to Zionists.* Chanting makes it easy to forget the meaning of words, a pack of teenagers drunk on the feeling of unity, as addictive as any drug. And so the students planned another major demonstration. That morning, Reza was excited. I forbade him to go. 'How long do you think the government will tolerate this rebellion?' I asked him. Reza made some statement about the glory of martyrs, and I lost my temper. I told him he was a fool, more or less. I told him I had failed as a father if he intended to kill himself for an imaginary harem of virgins in heaven. I mocked him and his precious revolution. Basically I did everything I could to drive a sixteen-year-old straight into the streets—" Arshan stops again to rub his temples. Thirty years later, he can feel the same drum roll of doom he felt that morning. The same panic that comes with a glimpse of one's powerlessness.

The people around him on the beach experience the same sense of foreboding.

Now I know how Mina's brother will die, but I can't stop the story any more than you can stop a memory from finding you in the dark. I look at Cornell. He is somewhere else. He's hearing the sound of a sea of marchers.

An orgy of youthful energy and powerful emotions—love, egoism, urgency, righteousness, the bliss of belonging. Now Cornell hears the thud of batons, the scurrying of scuffle, firecracker gunfire, and the kinds of screams that haunt you the rest of your life.

"They called it Black Friday," Arshan says. "The name Americans give the biggest shopping day of the year. I went to work and sat in my empty classroom. After a while, I left. I ran into a worried neighbor. He asked if Reza had come home yet. As the words came out of my mouth explaining he was at school, I understood that my son was at the march. Still, I went home first. It didn't seem possible that—"

Maliheh's eyes—cold. Searching Arshan's face with her metallic eyes. A stranger's eyes. Where is my son? Where is he? Her inflated belly between them as she leans in close to his face. Go back. Go get Reza. Go get my son.

Arshan puts his hands over his eyes. Flashes of running, falling in with the hundreds headed for the demonstration. Coming up against of a sea of thousands. Bobbing signs with the face of Ayatollah Khomeini. *Allahu Akbar. God is great. Death to the Shah. Death to America. God is Great.*

"I am not the hero of my life."

Arshan sighs. It is time. Time to remember, to confess. Time to repent.

★ ★ ★

Arshan is swimming upstream. He's fighting to ride the wave of people taking to the main boulevard. The chanting consumes him, like plasma he has to carve through with his limbs. Above the zombielike shuffling of the crowd, Arshan thinks he hears the boots of soldiers. And helicopters. There is a knot in his stomach the size of a pomegranate.

As the marchers coalesce onto the main street, Arshan pauses at the curb, holding on to a lamp post and stepping onto a car's bumper to get his bearings. He was right. Soldiers are advancing from the opposite direction. He has a front-row seat to see what happens when the two factions collide.

Arshan realizes he is holding his breath, which hisses from his lips at the first wave of gunfire. The front wave of people is picked off like soda cans. The rest of the thousands duck or scurry off to the sides, causing the car under Arshan's feet to sway and shake as if in an earthquake.

Arshan tries to maintain his position. He scans the faces that are streaming past like rats fleeing the sea.

When the soldiers fire another round, the screams unite into a collective shriek and the herd stampedes.

Arshan is shoved to the ground, landing atop a teenage boy. He grabs the kid by his jaw and peers into his face, hoping. But it's not his Reza. The boy's hands and face are bloody and as he returns Arshan's panicked look, he melts in Arshan's hands, from a strapping teenager into a terrified child. Arshan takes his collar and drags him out of the street. He hides behind the car and turns his attention back to the boulevard.

More and more people are mowed down by the soldiers. Men try to shield their comrades only to fall helplessly to the ground. Boys slip in the blood of their best friends. Even as they try to run away, men are shot in the back.

At Arshan's side, an old man clutches his clothes and sobs in disbelief.

Arshan still sees no sign of his son. He doesn't recognize anyone, any of Reza's friends or fellow students. Maybe he went home. Maybe his fear sent him home.

And then he sees it.

On the ground, beneath the horde of soldier's boots. A green jacket.

A strangled sound escapes Arshan's lips. The old man next to him seems to sense what's about to happen.

Arshan makes to dart into the street, but the old man grabs his shirt with surprising tenacity. The soldiers continue to advance, trampling triumphantly over the dead bodies in their path.

Arshan watches, frozen, as a soldier approaches Reza's body. He puts out his hands as he watches the soldier, not much more than a boy himself, raise his weapon.

The soldier fires into his son's chest, sending Reza's

body flailing like a narwhale harpooned on the deck of a ship.

Arshan turns and buries his face in the old man's breast. Now the father is the child, learning too late the dark side of fate.

44

NO ONE'S NOTICING THE SUNSET THIS TIME. The silence is broken by a flick of Jesse's lighter and the crackling of cigarette paper. She takes a deep puff and inhales slowly, almost as if she will speak. But there is nothing to say to a parent who has lost a child.

"Maliheh became somebody else. She buried inside of herself and whispered all her thoughts to gestating Mina. Maybe that's why Mina was born with all the wisdom of a woman. She absorbed the profundity of a mother's heart-break. My family intervened. They arranged our move to the United States through a cousin in Washington. Maliheh said she didn't care if we went to the bottom of the ocean. America would do."

Arshan sits forward, rests his elbows on his knees and scratches his beard with both hands. He sighs with utter exhaustion. "So that is how we came to America. My family gave us money until I found a job. When she was eight months' pregnant, Maliheh was in a highway car accident with my cousin. My cousin lived. Mina was born by emergency cesarean. But Maliheh died in the hospital before I could get there. They told me it was a miracle that my daughter survived. A gift from God."

Tears spring to Arshan's eyes. He swallows hard to keep them from falling. He's waited thirty years to confess this. No turning back now. "I hated her. My infant daughter. I didn't want her. I wanted Reza, and I wanted my wife. Not a screaming baby who reminded me every day of what I had lost. I got a nanny and a job at the university into which I disappeared. Mina grew and grew. I never told her anything about her mother, and she turned out exactly like her in every way. I thought it was a trick. I thought it was my punishment. It never occurred to me that she really was a gift. Mina was a gift and a chance at redemption. And I missed it. I turned away. All of you knew my daughter better than I did. If Maliheh had lived—Maliheh wanted Mina more than anybody has ever wanted a child. Days before she died, she made me promise to be happy. So that Mina could be happy. And instead I let her be raised by strangers—" Arshan turns his head away quickly so they won't see the tears slipping past his guard.

He's not looking for comfort. He wants them to hate

him. To condemn him finally for all his wrongs. The man who turned away from God. The man who could not save his son, or protect his wife, or love his daughter.

CHAPTER

45

"YOU WANT ME TO MAKE IT TO RAIN FOR you?"

Mina doesn't answer. She's hugging her knees with her chin nestled atop, her shiny black hair hiding her face.

"Do you want to be alone?"

Mina nods without looking at me. I put my fingers to my lips and place the kiss on the part of her hair where I think her cheek must be.

JESSE'S MOVED. SHE'S KNEELING CLOSE TO Arshan.

"She loved you anyway. Mina adored you. And she knew you loved her. That's what's got you scareder than a sinner in a cyclone, right? Arshan, that daughter of yours was so much smarter than any of us. She told me that you were brilliant, secretly charming, and wounded. She knew you. She knew us better than we know ourselves." Jesse wipes needlessly at her indelible eyeliner.

"Like Maliheh."

"It wasn't your fault." Jesse's voice is firm.

Arshan stares at the ocean, ignoring the statement.

"It wasn't your fault," Jesse repeats. "Your wife. Your

son. Your daughter. None of 'em was anybody's fault. You want to be blamed. Honey, I can tell. And Lord knows I understand."

Arshan's eyes are like glassy marbles.

"Well, I'm sorry, but we're not going to blame you, mister. Mina loved her life. Whatever you gave her, it was enough. So stop it. Stop blaming yourself and stop tryin' to forget them." Jesse gently takes hold of Arshan's jaw and turns his face to hers. "Make peace while there's still time."

A look washes over Arshan's face that I can't quite place. It's like a dawning of understanding. But the look is for Jesse, that much is certain. He's seeing Jesse anew, and wondering what happened to his faith in fate. Perhaps he'll always have his grievances with Allah, but the North Star of his youth was something he had called fate. And fate demands only that you trust and relish the present. He puts his hand on Jesse's wrist. His eyes crinkle with the echo of a smile. "Jesse, you're enough to make an old man believe in angels."

CHAPter

―――――

WITHOUT WARNING, ISABEL STANDS UP AND
walks away. I follow her down the beach, scanning the
sands warily as the others yell after her but let her go.
This is not a safe time or place for a stroll. Her feet drag
and stumble across the chilly sand. She hugs herself and
scratches at her shoulders. I can't make out her thoughts.
They're jumbled and muted, nonsensical. She's thinking
about Mina, Kendra and me, but in a repetitive fashion as
if she's banging her head against a wall.

I dance around her, as though I can stop her slow procession to the water. I'm in front of her, then behind, then
racing along the beach looking for help, then back at her

side. But of course I'm not there. Not in any way that can save my friend. It's like putting out your hands to stop a rainstorm. And I don't even have hands.

Isabel's mind finally settles on a memory, and grabs hold of it to steady her courage for her first steps into the water. The memory is beautiful—it's the dock, the lake house that summer we were eleven. It's the same as Mina's world, but complete and alive. The clouds cast shadows across the trees full of twittering birds, and the swaying grasses reveal scampering squirrels. I get swept up into it, too, lost in the details of a happier day.

Isabel remembers herself linking arms with Kendra to walk up to the house. She finds her mother on the porch laughing with Lynette, who pours them fresh glasses of pink lemonade. Isabel smiles, remembering how the ice sounded in the glasses; how the grass tickled her ankles as they walked back down the hill.

She sees Mina and me in the water in front of the dock, talking solemnly. Then Mina points and waves and Isabel feels the cold lemonade splash her toes when she waves back. Kendra scolds her, but they both laugh. Isabel is blissfully, simply, happy in a world that is whole and makes perfect sense.

At the instant Isabel's head dips beneath the surface, a set of waves rolls in fast, knocking her off her feet. She thrashes about, tossing and turning as if having a nightmare. But she doesn't have enough air in her lungs to keep up the fight.

In her mind's eye, Isabel continues to approach the

dock, but there is a shift, like a photograph catching fire. Suddenly it is just Mina on the dock, an adult Mina, standing in her yellow sundress.

I can hear Isabel whimpering aloud in the water. The water looks red, like blood filtering through an aquarium.

But it isn't Isabel that's whimpering.

chapter

41

SHIT. WHERE AM I?

"Samantha," I hear Mina say, "look."

I see Kendra sobbing in her sleep. She's curled up in a ball amongst the twisted sheets, grabbing her midsection. The whimpering was hers, but now they become the cries and groans of earthquake victims. Her face is contorted in pain, and sweat forms a dark halo on her pillow.

"What happened?" I ask Mina.

"The sheets. Look closer."

Kendra's legs are curled up tight, but now I see a foot peeking out of the bedclothes. It's sticky with blood.

Panicked, I try to pin down Kendra's thoughts. She's flashing through the horrors of the day in her mind.

She sees herself at work, held together by sheer will. She sees the wobble in her stilettos as she opens the clinic door. She hears the echoes of the counseling session. *Irreversible. Decision to live with. Emotional trauma. Risk of surgery.*

She remembers the cream tile of the ceiling, the nurse clutching her hand with latex gloves. The tense murmurs coming from the doctor. Kendra remembers how the numbness in her pelvis spread to her heart. She sees the blood on the doctor's gloves, remembers the flecks of hazel in the nurse's eyes above her mask.

Michael was there in the waiting room. He smiled when she came out and she wanted to stab him for it. He took her home in a cab, not even a town car. He'd brought his briefcase with him, work to do at Kendra's bedside presumably. Kendra didn't cry in the car; she's proud of herself for it. She molded her face like plaster of Paris and kept it dry all the way back to SoHo. She watched the dogged New York hustle outside the window and tried to find a metaphor in it that would give her strength. It worked.

When the doorman opened the cab door and saw Kendra's cracking plaster of Paris face, she gave him a tiny nod and he understood. He stepped back and Kendra got out and shut the cab door before Michael knew what was happening. The doorman strode forward and tapped on the window for the cab driver to drive away. Kendra bargained with her stilettos. *Just let me make it inside.*

She stumbled through the lobby and barely let the elevator doors shut before she sank to the carpet.

Kendra sees herself crawl into bed and pass out from the pain. She woke up several times to the disturbing feeling of warm blood pumping from between her legs, but she was too weak to move.

Kendra thinks she's going to bleed to death. Alone.

But now her thoughts turn a particular shade of indigo, and the roaring sound of waves rushes in the distance.

Kendra moans. She's whispering something on repeat: "Isabel."

And then I see it—Kendra's fever-fueled nightmare. She sees Isabel sinking in the water like a shiny penny in a vat of oil. The dark shadows of the sea are stealing her away, pulling at her hair, handcuffing her wrists and ankles.

Now Kendra's mind fills with a vision of Mina standing on a dock, her yellow sundress whipping in the wind, watching in terror at dark waters rising around her.

The worlds are colliding.

chapter

42

THE DOCK IS DRY AND HOT BENEATH MY
legs. I am sitting on the dock.

"What happened?" I ask frantically. "Go back! I have
to go back!"

Mina is staring at the sun, a sentinel presiding over her
placid world. The water is slack, the clouds inert again.
"They're in trouble, Sam. Should I bring them here?"

I suck in a breath and hear my heart jackhammering
in the sudden silence. The water at my feet is like impenetrable glass, my reflection a photograph frozen in time.

But we're not frozen. I'm not frozen. I remember my
epiphany on the dock about saving Mina, and a new un-

derstanding hits me like a kick to the chest. It's not just Mina I'm supposed to save.

I died for this moment. I died for my three best friends, for the chance to give them a future together. I've glimpsed the secret behind the curtain. In trying to find a way to stay connected to Mina, I stumbled upon a path to connect us all forever. I stumbled upon the path between life and death.

I'm going to save you all, I promise.

I stand up face to face with Mina. She is uncertain, waiting.

"An infinite ocean of possible worlds, Mina. We create our world, then mistake it for a script, indelible. We are so much more powerful than that. Miracles happen every day. What are they really? Instances where people believed in the impossible and saw it come true." We are stronger than death if we believe it. All that exists is belief and love.

The space between Mina and me begins to shimmer. The clouds fade to a blanket of white, the water brims with diamonds blotting together. The world is filling with light. Mina's face gleams like glitter let loose on a breeze. "Are you ready?" I ask her.

I put out my hands. Mina steps forward to take them and looks into my eyes with the same mischievous twinkle of a kindergartner I once knew.

I brace myself for what comes next. I have to believe. I have to believe that I can do it. That is the most important thing. My job. My responsibility. It wasn't a mistake, all the preparation for Mina's death. It wasn't a mistake that I had to die to find Mina in her strange world.

Everything was training, leading up to this moment. This moment in which we are all on the brink and we all need saving. The moment when everything would depend on me.

There is a sound like aquarium glass groaning. It will fracture at any moment and all will be lost to the depths of the sea.

It's time.

"What do you think we're supposed to do, Sammy?" Mina asks.

"JUMP."

Christmas Eve
Samantha

You're gone. You've really gone and left us alone in this big black hole.

I'm supposed to keep writing you, like we promised, but my broken heart doesn't know what to say.

By the time we got there today, you were pretty out of it. You asked me where all the "other worlds" are. Even though Kendra looked at me like I was a lunatic, I tried to explain where they could be hiding, in different dimensions millimeters away.

You asked me what world I would choose. If I would choose one with my mother.

I would choose you, Mina. You, Kendra, Isabel, and me. Every roll of the dice, I would choose a world with all of you.

ISABEL. ISABEL, ISABEL, ISABEL. SHE'S RUNNING past me in the grass, a flash of chestnut-colored hair and giggles. "This way, Sammy!" How old is she? Seven, maybe? She turns back and wags a little finger at me. "You're too slow, Sammy. Sloooowpoke Samantha." She pokes me and takes off running.

Kendra. Kendra. KendraKendra.

"Samantha, I can't. I have to study." Kendra has on those ridiculous horn-rimmed glasses. That means it's our sophomore year of high school.

"Those aren't even prescription glasses, you dork."

Kendra shoots me the look of an exasperated librarian before smiling.

★ ★ ★

Mina? Mina. Mina!

"Samantha, do you think we'll be okay without mothers?"

I remember that sleepover. I remember those unicorn pajamas.

I pat Mina on the shoulder. "Of course, silly. We have each other instead."

KendraMinaIsabel. IsabelKendraMina. Isabel. Kendra. Mina. The names swirl in the turquoise light all around me. No, it isn't light.

It's water. It's ocean water. I'm back in the raging sea, the day I went swimming with Isabel.

chapter

44

"SWIM, SAMANTHA," I HEAR MINA SAY.

But my body is a mangled bicycle, thudding against the ocean floor. I can't swim.

"Swim, Sammy. The world is waiting for you."

I try but I can't. The water is too strong. It's too deep. My heart's going to pop like a water balloon.

"Swim, Samantha. Ahari's coming for you."

I open my eyes and punch the sea in the face.

Then five dark fingers wrap around my wrist and my arm snaps out of view, yanked along under Ahari's shadow as if I'm grasping the tail of a black stallion. My

eyes clamp shut again against the sting, but make no mistake—my body is sailing upward, slicing through the sea.

Up. Up. Up to a waiting world.

chapter

45

"IS SHE ALIVE?"

Lynette's scream pierces my ears. Everything hurts. The sudden sensation of being alive slams into me. Saltwater scorches my throat. My eyelids grind together like mismatched gears. As my body is transferred from one set of arms into another, my feet plant in the slushy sand and water falls from me in sheets.

"Samantha?" Lynette cradles me in her grip. She kisses my forehead and pets my face with abrasive hands. My eyes blink open and the light is blinding. But this light has limits, and it turns to sky, a sky that holds Lynette's anguished face and Ahari's searing gaze. When my eyes catch his, his dark eyes narrow, but then he nods and leaves. I wish he would come back.

"Oh my God, oh my God. Hi baby. Hi sugar." Lynette crushes me against her chest. "Oh my God, Sammy, I thought—"

"Lynette, honey, let's get her out of here." That was Cornell. Cornell lifts me by my armpits and half drags, half carries me out of the ocean. My senses aren't working right. Everything swirls and echoes. Blue sky. The house in the distance. My feet stumbling over the sand.

But other images flash before me, too. The dock, Kendra's bloody foot, Isabel sinking in the dark water—slivers of visions slip through my fingers as if I'm scaling a mountain turned to sand. I can't get a grip on what's happening.

Isabel! Isabel's laid out on the ground, crying, with Arshan and Jesse huddled above her.

I did it. I'm here. Isabel is here. But—

The ocean roars in defeat at my back. I am crying, too, I realize. Deep, racking cries.

Time turned back. A second chance. For Isabel. For Kendra. For me.

But something went wrong.

46

THEY LIE ME ON THE SAND NEXT TO ISABEL, who immediately envelops me in her skinny arms. I feel the gritty warmth of her skin press against mine, the rapid beating of her heart and the frantic grip of her fingers. For a second, I let myself disappear in her overpowering gratitude to be alive. Just for a second.

"Where's Mina?" My voice doesn't sound like me. It is strangled and scratched, wind forced through a broken reed.

Isabel pulls back and cradles my cheek, her brow knotted in worry.

I sit up too fast. The world around me reels, tips off keel. I teeter to my feet anyway. *"Where is she?"*

Brimming with fury, I lurch back toward the ocean. My burning eyes make it painful to look at the bleached sand. An empty beach. Beyond the huddle around Isabel, I am alone on an empty beach before a mocking sea. What went wrong? What did I do wrong, Mina? I make it to the edge of the waves and my sobs pull me to the ground. I am flooded with failure, with emptiness, and remorse. Yes, I am alive. Miraculously, I am alive in a beautiful world. But it's a world without my best friend.

Featherlight fingertips touch my shoulder.

"Sam?"

I turn reluctantly to face Isabel. The others wait a few feet behind her, every face etched with worry. I'm scaring the hell out of them. Again. Isabel squeezes my shoulder to get my attention.

"She's gone. Mina's gone. But Sammy—we're alive!" Isabel looks over her shoulder at the others.

When she turns back, I get the sense she wants to say more, but she catches herself.

Lynette raises a hand to her lips and chokes back tears. Cornell pulls her to him. Jesse's mouth is open, in shock, watching me, unsure what to do. Arshan's frown says he's scared, too. I look at them and then back at Isabel. I need time to think. I need to be alone. I reach up and pat Isabel's hand. I stand up slowly and breathe in the salty air. With everybody staring expectantly, I turn to Lynette and Jesse.

"I'm starving!"

Everyone lets out a collective sigh of relief. Arshan grins. Lynette giggles, grateful, and Cornell hugs her tighter.

Jesse sidles over and slings her arms around my and Isabel's shoulders. "You heard the woman. Let's get these survivors somethin' to eat!"

chapter

47

KENDRA'S HEAD SPRINGS UP FROM HER BED like a punching clown. Her breath stabs the stuffy air in her bedroom, thundering over Michael's lazy snores. She's panting, gripping the sheets in fists on either side of her bent knees. Life courses through her body—pumping, sweating, rushing life—and she braces herself to take it all in.

Was it a dream? But she saw it. She could still see it, taste it, hear it—Isabel sinking through the midnight blue water. Sheets soaked in blood. The vision of the dock, Mina's hair whipping in the wind. Kendra remembers the expanse of endless light. And Mina's voice, like a song in a snowstorm: Take care of each other, she said. *I'll be watching.*

Kendra pounces out of bed and skitters barefoot to the living room. She has her cell phone in one hand and Mina's clover leaf in the other when she stops short.

She's listening to Michael's measured breathing. She looks at the date on her phone. Saturday. The Saturday morning Isabel and I drowned. Two days before her scheduled appointment.

How could—

The phone and clover leaf clatter to the floor.

Kendra puts both hands on her belly and sinks to her knees.

chapter

48

JESSE WON'T LET ISABEL OUT OF HER SIGHT. She steers her daughter into the kitchen to help with the cooking, finding every excuse to touch her, as if she's convincing herself her daughter's real. I watch them from the back of the room, while Lynette makes me lemonade and brings it to me with a look of concern and comfort. I take the glass and excuse myself to the palm grove.

"Let her go," Cornell says when he sees Isabel and Lynette about to protest.

I drag my hands along the rough bark of one trunk after another, feeling them scratch and tear the skin of my palm. My head is so full of conflicting thoughts and emotions, I can hardly pin any one down. I feel like life is speeding forward, carrying me along without my consent, the way a mother tugs at a toddler. I just want a second of clarity. I can't help but feel angry that life is moving forward without Mina so easily.

It's not their fault. For everyone else, Mina died six months ago. They know nothing of the dock. And it's not as if I'm not grateful to be alive. I am. The beauty of the world isn't escaping me. It surrounds and caresses me. The warmth, the swishing of the palms, the powdery sand between my toes—all so beautiful beyond words. But everything is tinged with failure. Because for me, Mina didn't die six months ago. She died just now, and this time it's worse. This time it's my fault.

What went wrong? Did I believe her somehow less alive than myself? Did I envision this world without her? I look at the light streaming through the palm fronds. *Well, I hate it, Mina, this world without you. Tell me how to go back and make it right.*

"Hey—Samantha!"

I must have jumped about ten feet at the sound of Arshan's voice. He's rushing through the palm trees toward me, brandishing something shiny in his hands. When he reaches me, I see what it is. Mina's journal. My heart starts to pound.

Arshan's out of breath. Now when he catches my eye, he looks embarrassed. "It's the strangest thing. I just found this in my bathroom. I—" He looks away. "I read some of it."

Mina wants him to read it. Is she watching? I glance around. "It's okay. We—I want you to read it." A thought comes to me. "I have some questions to ask you about physics."

"A lot of this stuff—" Arshan looks abashed again. "It's a little out of my realm."

I can't help but smile. "I think it's out of everybody's realm."

"But what I meant—well, when I lost my wife, I so desperately wanted to hold on to her. There were moments when I swore I could hear her—" He listens for a moment to the wind in the palms and then looks past me at the sea.

I think about the story of Mina's mother and brother. I would like to hear it again. And the others should hear it, too. "Maybe you can tell us the story of Maliheh one day."

Arshan startles at the sound of her name. He looks at me searchingly then down at the journal. He presses it to his chest with both hands and gives me a nod. His eyes fix on the house, but he is looking at the window of Jesse's room. When he turns to face me again, his eyes are smiling. "Yes, I think I could do that now. It's a very sad story. But it was such a long time ago." He squeezes the journal tighter. "I wish I had told Mina."

I put a hand on his shoulder. I don't know what to say. *What would he believe? What would make him happy?*

Arshan nods again and turns to leave. I watch him as he makes his way back to the house before resuming my walk to the beach. *What is Mina trying to tell me? Where is she? Why can't I hear her?*

I reach the gate and nearly trip over Ahari. He's obviously been watching me the whole time. He's smiling, which irritates me. But then I realize I haven't thanked him for swimming in to save me.

It's funny—the way the morning sun shines behind him, he looks like an angel in a chapel oil painting, like the light is pouring forth from *him*. He motions for me to follow him. I don't want to. My head is still reeling, combing the universe for answers about Mina, but I feel myself step into the warm sunlight and follow him along the fence until we reach a small garden. He kneels down beside a patch of citrus-colored flowers. He studies me as I kneel beside him. His skin is smooth and shiny. He looks much younger than I originally thought. A smile lights his face as if he heard me. He places a thumb on my forehead between my eyes and traces it down along the bridge of my nose. It occurs to me that I should find this strange, but it feels completely nonthreatening. It feels like the touch of a feather, like a blessing. I instinctively close my eyes. I feel him take my hand and place something light and ticklish in my palm. When I look, I see a tiny yellow blossom. I marvel at its perfection as if I've never seen a flower before. Like looking at it through a microscope, I suddenly see all its properties in perfect balance, an expression of fate and harmony and oneness. As I study it, the tiny flower turns from yellow to pink and then to orange, each change in hue the progression of a sunset. I gasp and Ahari's laugh echoes off the clouds.

"Ahari," he says.

I look up and his eyes are unblinking, clear. *Ahari.*

Suddenly I understand. "Your name means angel. Guarding angel." *A guardian angel.*

I look at the flower in my hand. I will it to change color. Purple. Purple. Purple. Purple, dammit.

Ahari laughs again and the flower turns as red as a rose on Valentine's Day. An angel with a mean sense of humor. Ahari lifts my chin with his fingers. He brings my eyes to his and I feel as if I am filling up with light. The sensation scares me, but, no, wait, it isn't light. It's thought. Or instructions. Or questions? He knows what I did somehow. He is *curious*, for lack of a better word. He seems to be screening me, listening.

Finally, he smiles with amusement and affection. It's so hauntingly familiar, it reminds me of—

He takes his hand away and the sensation of connection passes.

Suddenly I'm freezing cold in the absence of that feeling. My thoughts turn back to Mina and tears spring to my eyes helplessly. The beauty of the flower shrivels in my heart.

Ahari's face turns serious, as if he's listening to my thoughts again. Then his face fills with pity. He encircles my wrists with hands that are warm and smooth, as he rotates my palms to face the sky. Then he brushes a hand over my eyes to close them. A moment later, I sense his palms hovering just above mine. The buzz I feel is a vibration, the fuzzy hum of a generator.

When his palms make contact with mine, a jolt of lightning courses through me and I feel like I'm shooting into the sky faster than a rocket. I'm speeding through space with wind whipping along my face, my shoulders, down the length of my body. I want to open my eyes, but somehow I know not to. As I careen forward facefirst, I feel Ahari's palms pressed solidly into mine.

And then it stops. All motion stops and—

I open my eyes. We're back in the light. I look into Ahari's eyes and he looks back reassuringly, then nods over my shoulder.

When I turn around I see four girls holding hands in a circle. It's Isabel in a white dress, Kendra with a crown of braids, and me, all three of us with our eyes squeezed shut.

And Mina. Mina is standing in her sunflower dress smiling at me. But now a different look washes over Mina's face. A fleeting sadness, mixed with determination. She closes her eyes.

As I watch the four girls, the light around them shimmers and the strangest thing occurs. Suddenly we are little girls again, around the age we met. And as we hover in the light with our eyes shut, each one of us flashes through a million different incarnations in the span of an instant, too fast for me to make it out as more than a wild blur of jittery change.

But then I understand. Every moment of our lives is

washing over us. Wounds appear and heal, leaving scars on knees, elbows and cheeks. Our bodies shed a childish roundness as we grow taller and slimmer and then grow curves in puberty. I watch in awe as my childhood self morphs ever closer to adulthood. As I watch the years of teenage awkwardness fall away to the heydays of our twenties, I marvel and smile.

Then something happens. Mina stumbles. Or rather, she appears to freeze. She opens her eyes and stands perfectly still in her sunflower sundress.

But the rest of us are still changing. Kendra's belly swells and deflates. Isabel's hair is shorn and grows long again.

Mina watches as we flip from ball gowns to business suits and empire-waist dresses. I gasp when I see Kendra's belly swell again, this time in sync with mine. Not long after, Isabel's the one wearing a blur of maternity dresses. Then suddenly we're looking older. Kendra fills out around the hips and I look like I could use a little gym time myself.

As Mina watches in her pristine sundress, we speed away from her in time—our hair showing the first wisps of gray, our bodies flattening and rounding—until I see three old wrinkled women holding hands with beautiful, young Mina.

Kendra opens her eyes first, and Mina's ready for her. She lets go of Kendra's hand and puts a hand to her cheek. She whispers some words I can't hear and Kendra's eyes fill with tears. Mina continues to speak and caress Kendra's withered cheek. Finally, Kendra nods with the faintest trace of a smile. Then she fades away.

Mina steps into the gap Kendra leaves behind and stands watching Isabel intently. Isabel's shoulders stoop, her hair thins and then her still-piercing turquoise eyes open to meet Mina's. Mina repeats her actions with Kendra, consoling Isabel and saying her goodbyes. Isabel bites her lip. Mina wraps her arms around her until she is holding only empty light.

Now it is just Mina holding the hand of an old woman wearing a ridiculous green hat over dyed red hair. It's me, my eyes still squeezed shut. Mina chuckles and reaches out like she will touch my face. But she stops herself. She's apprehensive and proud, as if she's watching a toddler take her first steps. Finally, Mina takes up both my hands and kisses them with the softness of a flower blossom.

"Thank you, Sammy. For saving us all," she whispers as my timeworn self shimmers and fades into nothing.

Now Mina cries. Alone in the light, she wraps her arms around her bare shoulders and weeps the way one only weeps when there's no one to hear. I ache for her to see me. I shout her name, ready to give up anything to go back and stay with her on the dock.

But she doesn't hear me. She straightens up and drops her arms to her sides, smoothes down her sundress. She's no longer crying and she lifts her chin as if to prove it. She is waiting.

Then there is a shimmer of light and a woman walks toward Mina. For a moment, I mistake her for a child,

and not just because of her small stature. Her every movement speaks of joy, just like a youngster. I recognize her
now from Arshan's story, from the photo on top of his
piano. She is every bit as stunning as he remembers.

The woman puts a finger under Mina's chin so that
their eyes meet. Then she wraps her arms around her
daughter and rocks her back and forth in the light.

I'm falling down an elevator shaft. I squeeze shut my
eyes as the light dims to gray and I sink feetfirst as if to
the bottom of the ocean. Then I realize that I am sitting
in the sand next to a flower garden.

"Thank you," I say even before I open my eyes.

But Ahari is gone. In each of my upturned palms is a
purple flower. I look around. The ocean is all I hear. I can
feel the sun from the beach and nothing else.

"Goodbye, Mina," I say, and gently lay the purple
flowers on the sand.

December 25
Mina

This is it, Sam. I'm sorry it has to come so soon.

I have just one last thing to say, but I don't want you to
take it the wrong way. I understand everything we've said.
I get that there is no hope if we don't believe in our promises, in our pact. I believe in you like no one else on earth.
I know if there is a way, you will find it.

But I wouldn't be a good friend if I didn't tell you the truth. And the truth is the world will be fine without me.

I'm not saying to give up without one hell of a fight. But if ever there is a point where pain overshadows the joy in your life, you leave me be, Sammy. You hear me? You close your eyes and remember all our good times. But when you open them, you see the beauty around you, and all the good times to come.

You are going to have a long and happy life, Samantha Wheland. I will make sure of that, if it's the last thing I do.

chapter

49

WHEN I WALK BACK INTO THE HOUSE, JESSE and Lynette are setting out steaming plates of tortillas, eggs and beans. Jesse looks at me and smiles.

"You okay, kiddo?" She tucks her hair behind her ear and blows me a kiss. Lynette looks at me with the same face full of love and concern.

I nod. I must look awful. But they don't know. They don't know that everything's going to be okay. I try to give them my most reassuring smile.

Isabel comes barreling into the room. "You're back! Did they tell you?" She's brandishing her cell phone.

I look at their faces, now beaming with excitement. "What?"

Isabel grins. "Kendra's on her way."

"Really?"

Isabel presses the phone into my hands. I look at the text.

Tell Sam everything's going to be okay. Tell her I love her. Tell her thank you.

Jesse moves to snatch the phone from me. "I want to read—"

Isabel grabs it first and catches my eye. She shakes her head almost imperceptibly then flashes a smile at Jesse. When I fail to follow suit, she looks at me with questioning eyes. Lynette and Jesse eye us both suspiciously.

It hits me finally. Isabel and Kendra do know something. In the vision Ahari showed me, I kept my eyes shut, but they both opened theirs and spoke to Mina. I'm suddenly inundated with questions for them, but it'll have to wait. I settle for flashing Lynette and Jesse a megawatt grin.

The rest of the day passes in cozy anticipation. Jesse ropes me into a game of rummy. Arshan corners me with a pitch about the selling points of GW's graduate physics program. Lynette braids my hair the way she did when I was little, and tells me funny stories about her students. She delivers a perfunctory rant about how irrational it is for Kendra to come *now*. But everyone can tell she's thrilled. Cornell, too. He swept out our rooms and picked some of Ahari's flowers to fill the vase on our nightstand.

The whole day, anytime Isabel or I walk past, one of the parents reaches out and pats us or hugs us or smiles. Today is a celebration of life, a reminder of how fragile and fleeting and precious it is. But I wish I could tell them. I wish I could tell them about the secrets we uncovered, about how we are more powerful than we know. Maybe one day. One day, I will tell everyone.

chapter

50

AFTER DINNER, THE SIX OF US SIT ON THE patio and play cards. Kendra called. She hired a driver to bring her to the house. I'm not thrilled about that, but there's really no telling Kendra what to do. Or any of us, for that matter.

We're all a symphony of yawns by the time the van pulls up out front. Before I make it to the door, Kendra bursts through. Eight and a half hours of travel, and the girl looks fresh as spring grass in a green Versace dress. She hugs me and gives me a theatrically loud smack on the cheek. Then she leans in close, studying my face.

"I don't know *what* to believe, girl," she whispers.

I laugh as she hugs me again.

Kendra steps back, looks like she wants to say more, but the rest of the crew is gathering round.

"We'll talk," she whispers meaningfully.

Then the parents are upon us, all chattering to Kendra at once. How was her trip? How did she convince someone to drive her all the way out here? How's Michael? What was so important at work?

Isabel hangs back and watches everyone, then catches me doing the same thing. She smiles at me and I wink.

Nobody goes to bed for a long time. We walk down to the beach and the parents tell their version of the near drowning, how scared they were, how helpless they felt on the sand. They take turns telling Kendra about the car accident, the food poisoning, all the fun she missed. Kendra laughs and groans and gasps and squeezes my hand.

Finally, when it looks like the reunion is winding down, Kendra clears her throat and puts out her hand to shush Jesse from teasing Cornell about his argyle socks.

"I have news."

Jesse and Lynette go completely quiet and peer at her closely. Kendra looks radiant. Her hair is neatly combed back and her gold earrings sparkle in the light of the lanterns.

"Well, jeez, girl—" Jesses bursts out. "Spill it then! You've had us worried sick this whole trip."

"Michael and I broke up."

I look up in surprise.

Lynette reaches out a hand to her daughter. "Oh, sweetie, that's terrible, but I'm sure he'll—"

Kendra smiles. "No, it's fine. Really. That's not actually the news. That's the preamble. I'm—" She straightens up in the sand, looks at each of us in turn. "We're having a baby."

Isabel gasps and we both break out in big goofy auntie grins. I think of the swimming pool, of the pain on Kendra's face. I remember the horrible scene in her bedroom. I am so overcome, a tear dribbles onto my smile.

Lynette, though, raises a hand to her gaping mouth.

Kendra's eyes are on her mother. "Mom, are you okay?"

Jesse glares at Lynette as she slumps against Cornell's chest in response, a Scarlett O'Hara caricature of ruination. "Oh, hush, Lynette, don't you dare. I always knew that Michael was a jerk. And so did you." She grins at Kendra. "I'm sure you'll tell us the details when you're good and ready, but—God dog—you're glowing like a big ol' pile of uranium, gal. If you're happy, we're happy." She kicks Lynette with her foot. "That goes for all of us."

The beachgoers spring back into motion, with Cornell clapping his hands together and saying, "Lordy Lordy."

I can't help but think *the circle of life*. I look at Arshan and his sad smile tells me he is thinking the same thing. Jesse lets out a loud whoop but Lynette still looks shaken. She hasn't said anything or cracked a smile.

Jesse turns to her again. "Seriously, Lynette, think about it. This baby's gonna have more love and more *family* than it knows what to do with. Kendra, I think that you are one very brave woman." Jesse gives Kendra a wink.

"Takes one to know one, Mama." Isabel points a finger at Jesse.

Arshan gives Jesse a long, lingering look. Then he smiles and turns to Cornell. "Well, my man, I'd say—"

Arshan pauses to sweep his eyes over everyone in the group. He appears young and happy looking at all of us. I follow his gaze. Kendra has one arm linked in Isabel's and one hand on her belly. Isabel's twirling a piece of Jesse's hair. Cornell places a featherlight kiss on Lynette's ear. I think of all the stories I've heard this trip, all the mountains of love and loss we've experienced—these are the legends of my unlikely family.

"I'd say we are surrounded by some pretty amazing women."

When I finally open the door to the bedroom, Kendra and Isabel are huddled together, whispering like detectives in an alley.

"Finally," Kendra says. "Shut the door. Sit down. We've been dying to talk to you."

Isabel pokes Kendra at the word dying.

I rush to the bed opposite them. "Me, too."

Kendra straightens up, making this official. "Isabel and I— We had the same dream. At the same time. While you two were in the water, and I was asleep—"

"You died," Isabel finishes and her face crinkles like cellophane thrown in the fire.

Kendra takes Isabel's hand, but her eyes lock on mine. "You died and it was horrible. And I—" she averts her eyes "—I got rid of the baby. But something went wrong—so much blood—"

"I couldn't take it. I was shattered." Isabel's eyelashes glisten. "I went back into the ocean."

Kendra looks at Isabel. "Mina."

Isabel nods. "We both saw Mina."

Kendra and Isabel continue to stare at each other, and Isabel rubs at goosebumps along her forearms.

"On the dock?" I say and both turn to look at me like a ghost just flew in the window. I take a deep breath. "What if I told you it was real? That I did die? And I reunited with Mina, and we saved you both?"

The silence is like a blanket of snow. Or like the light in between worlds. I breathe out slowly. It's okay. I can wait. I have a lifetime now to make them understand.

Finally Kendra speaks. In a whisper. "But Sam, that's crazy—"

Isabel rubs at her arms again as if she feels the snow.

But Kendra stops short and exhales briskly, a familiar gesture of wresting control. "You were drowning," Kendra asserts, like she's listing the facts to an office assistant. "You were unconscious. You were dreaming—"

"The exact same dream." Isabel's face is a flip-book of human emotion—sadness then incredulity then awe.

I lean forward, intending to recount the vision from Ahari as proof, and I take both of their hands at once.

My mouth opens, but the words catch in my throat like a stone rolling atop a spring.

Because a surge is coursing through us, a river of electricity. I feel it flow into and out of me through my hands, joining us like a ring of fire. Instinctively, I close my eyes.

A flash. I see the four of us from above, like Ahari showed me. Four girls aging at the speed of racecars.

Kendra jerks her hand free and gasps, breaking the vision.

My eyes fling open to find them both staring at me, eyes like saucers.

"Sam, what the hell is going on?" Kendra whispers.

I look at their scared faces and I have to remind myself that they weren't there. They weren't part of the research project with Mina, and they weren't on the dock with us. They didn't die.

My whole life I've told them everything, down to the most banal preoccupations like bathing suits and traffic jams. I think it is this openness that wove the cloth that binds us, like quadruplets swaddled in a cradle. But now the world is bigger, my sense of it fractured. I need to find my own two feet, something Mina must have known when she sent me back alone. So, for now, the dock and the vision from Ahari must become like gifts from a secret lover, meant to be treasured and considered before shared.

"A second chance," I say and smile. "That's what's going on."

Kendra relaxes ever so slightly as she considers this.

Then she puts a hand on her stomach and nods. "A second chance."

Isabel takes my hand, perplexed. "She said she knew you'd succeed if you believed she'd be there. Does that make any sense?"

A whimper escapes my lips. Now, only now, after all that has happened on this long day, can I cry for Mina. She didn't choose her mother over me. She sacrificed herself for me, for all of us. Like she always has. I start to cry and it is the way I cried on the dock, my heart heaving as if the whole world's crying with me.

Because it is. Kendra and Isabel both wrap their arms tight around me and their tears are as indistinguishable from mine as streams flowing into a river. We cry like we did in the days after Mina's death. We cry because it is so unbearably unfair. Because we miss her. Because we know we will always miss her.

But at least we will bear it together. The only consolations in life, Mina said. Love and best friends.

chapter

51

PACKING TO LEAVE TAKES THE WHOLE morning. From the second Lynette opens our door and shoos us out of bed, she and Cornell hardly leave us alone for an instant. They sweep and laugh and clean and bark out orders. I've never seen anything like it, those two. It is only by the grace of their incredible organizational harmony that we are all packed by brunch time. I add my suitcases to the lineup by the door and head out to the porch to help Isabel set the table.

"Are you going to do the happy dance again?" I'm only half mocking. Consoled by the idea of a second chance, they've been positively giddy all morning.

Isabel smoothes down a napkin and looks at me. "Yep. Every day till we're a hundred years old."

Lynette comes out with a plate of sandwiches. "You girls still giggling like a pack of crazies out here? Three women about to turn thirty, one unemployed and one, *my* daughter, *eager* to be a single mother. Now what do you guys have to be so happy about, huh?" Lynette's fake frown reveals itself as a grin.

Isabel takes my hand. "Well, as it turns out, Lynette, a whole helluva lot."

Cornell appears with a fresh round of iced tea on a tray. "Honey, where'd Jesse and Arshan get to?"

Come to think of it, I haven't seen either of them all morning. "They're packing, I hope."

Suddenly we all jump at a loud thud. Isabel takes off running and I'm right behind her. We all pile up at the door to Jesse's room.

Please don't let anything bad happen. Please don't let anything bad happen. "Oh my God, I swear I can't handle—" I say as I raise my hand to knock.

"Well, me neither, missy," Lynette snaps as she pushes past me and swings open the door.

Nothing, not even coming back from the dead, could have prepared me for the sight before my eyes.

At my feet is an entire bookcase dumped clean of its contents.

And beyond the mound of seashells, romance novels and knickknacks are Jesse and Arshan doing it on the couch. A flash of crepe-paper skin, varicose veins, and— oh, Jesus—Jesse's five-inch heels.

Jesse tucks a long, sweaty shock of hair behind her ear and looks up at Arshan, who's turned to stone and pretending none of this is happening. "Great guns, y'all, march your sweet little butts outta here!"

Lynette shuts the door before any of us can blink, and we stand there rooted in place, the image seared onto our eyeballs like a nuclear explosion. I bite down on my knuckle and wait to follow Isabel's lead.

Cornell has no such tact. "Oh, you've got to be *shitting* me," he yells, slaps his hand to his forehead, and starts laughing so hard he punctuates the phrase the second time with barnyard snorts. "You've got—" snort "—to be—" snort "—*shitting* me!"

"Cornell!" Lynette makes an earnest attempt at consternation but takes another look at her husband and lets out a guffaw even louder than his.

I'm laughing so hard I think I just peed my pants. Isabel looks a little green around the edges but she's being a good sport. Kendra looks at me slyly and busts out with the happy dance. "Go Arshan! Go Jesse!"

And in some weird perfect moment in time, all five of us follow suit in a conga line back to the porch, laughing all the way.

While, I presume, Jesse and Arshan carry on about their business of falling in love. Finally.

HONDURAS IS STUNNING.

To be fair, we could be driving through a chicken coup after what we've been through and I'd think that was stunning, too. But Honduras does *got the goods,* as Jesse put it a few miles back. We've passed plantation homes next to aging military barracks, palm tree farms that stretch out like Iowa corn fields, vegetable gardens clear up the sides of mountains, and houses no bigger than a toolshed with eighteen people, a cow, and some chickens sitting out front. Kendra's got my camera pointed out the car window and I'm teaching her about drive-by shooting.

"Aim at something way ahead of you, then watch as it rushes in close, hold your breath, try to capture it one second sooner than you think you should, and then watch it fly away."

Click. Kendra takes the picture of a child balancing two yellow water jugs on a stick across her shoulders.

"If you get it right, the object of your desire appears crystal clear in a blur of swirling life. You get it right maybe one time out of a hundred."

"There's a poem in there somewhere."

"Me? Or out there?"

"All of it, Sam. Everything."

"I know what you mean," I say. "I know what you mean."

We're at the airport. Kendra's staying a day with me; everybody else is on the same return flight. The parents are off dealing with the roughed-up rental cars when I turn to Isabel. "Iz, you sure you don't want to change your ticket? Stay a day with Kendra?"

Isabel looks uncertain, then she smiles. "You two bond. I'm going to spend time with my mom. I've got a lot to think about." She gives me a hug. "Anyway, we've got plenty of time, right?"

Again, I desperately want to ask her about Ahari's vision. What did they see? "Iz—"

Jesse calls out to us, rushing over and tugging Arshan by the hand.

Isabel smiles at me again. "But, hey—no job and a severance package. Maybe I'll come back after your residency or you can meet me in Indonesia."

Kendra holds up her hand. "Whoa, there. If you need somewhere to go, missy, come to New York and help me figure out how the hell I'm going to do this by myself." She points at her midsection.

Jesse and Arshan butt in and give me a hug goodbye.

I take Arshan by the elbow. "Listen, I'm serious about the quantum physics chat. I'm going to call you."

"Astrophysics. Stars and planets. Not the spooky stuff. But I'll do my best." He narrows his eyes. "You staging a return to science, then?"

Before I can answer, Lynette comes up and kisses me on the cheek. Then she takes my face in her two hands, squeezing it like a vise. "Call your father. You hear me? You heard my story and Jesse's story. You might not have forever to set things right, kid. Okay?"

I gulp. I *do* want to talk to my father. I suddenly have a million questions about his life, about my mother. Why did I ever think it was too late to forgive someone who's been there since birth?

Cornell pries Lynette's hands from my face. He puts out his hand to shake, then scoops me up in a crushing hug. "Great trip, Samantha. Everybody survived. Good job."

I hear Isabel take a breath.

Jesse pulls me away and takes up my hand. "Time to go," she says, and kisses each of my fingers. "Samantha Anne Wheland. You gonna marry that man or not?"

My stomach flutters like a flight of fireflies on a summer's eve. I look around the circle at six peering faces that make up my entire world. *Breathe, Samantha.* "I'm not positive, but most likely I will. You all know I like to jump before I think about it too hard. Although I would prefer we chalk it up to my undying belief in love."

chapter

53

KENDRA AND I HOP INTO A CAB OUT FRONT of the airport. We fall into a comfortable silence. Our two faces stare out opposite cab windows, absorbed in our own worlds of thought, both knitting future scenes of our lives with new handfuls of thread.

So for me, the whole way back, past the stadium and the vegetable market, along the grimy alleyway streets with the broken windows and the corner bars, across bustling Boulevard Morazan with its parade of fast-food chains and electronics stores, and up the hill past the barb-wired police headquarters, I can think of nothing but Remy. My chest and toes hum and buzz and tingle with nervous energy. Outside the dusty cab window, I see flashes of life scenes to come.

Remy's hello when he answers the phone. His laughter turning to relief as I relate the vicissitudes of the trip. In three weeks, he picks me up at the Charles de Gaulle International Airport with roses and a waiting limo. He takes me by the waist and dips me like a movie star kiss in the middle of baggage claim. People clap. Old women cry.

The cab jerks to a stop outside of the apartment, jolting me out of my daydream. I look at Kendra and smile.

"Home sweet home, for a day," I say, and tug on the rusted handle of the cab door.

Kendra looks a little queasy. Is it morning sickness or the errant cow that just parked itself outside her cab door? I remind myself that Kendra isn't Isabel on the traveling front. She's a Green Zone traveler. Predictable five-star resorts with exotic letterhead.

"Come on, honey," I say, and tug her over to my side to exit, while I hand the cabbie some lempiras.

When Kendra comes out of the bathroom holding a washcloth to her forehead, I'm sitting on the balcony. I called Remy twice but got no answer. I left a positively ebullient message I'm now regretting. He knew I was getting home today and, what, he's not waiting by the phone? Kendra looks at me and then my phone and starts to ask questions I don't want to answer. I hand her a glass of iced tea and cheers her with my beer.

"So, Ana Maria—the girl's house we stayed at—she called, to see if we had a good time. And she invited us to a dinner party tonight."

Finally Kendra smiles. Dinner parties are a concept she can relate to.

I pat the seat next to me and Kendra sits down, putting her feet on the railing, an echo of the day Isabel arrived a week before. As I watch her look out over the city, I think of everything that has changed. Mina is gone. I know she was before, but now the absence is final in a very different way. Not sad, but in a way I would gingerly describe as freeing. It wasn't my fault. It isn't my fault that Mina is gone and can't return. The responsibility, the guilt—they've lifted. Mina gave me that. Now my choices are mine alone.

Kendra looks over like she heard me. "Are you really going to just marry him, Sam?"

"*Just* marry him?" I don't look over yet, but I can feel her eyes running over me, searching. Now I look. Hers aren't the judging eyes I was expecting. More like thoughtful concern. Who is this Kendra? Are we all changing then, so fast? "Not so long ago you were the one who would've been thrilled."

Kendra nods but rests both hands on her belly pointedly. "Yes, but things change, don't they?"

"Why did you break up with Michael?"

"Ah, now there's the question. I suppose I always knew what he was, who he was, but I was lazy. Lazy and in a hurry. A bad combination."

"I don't get it. You always seemed to adore him."

"I certainly adored giving that perception. On paper, he was perfect. But underneath, he was mean and lacking in integrity. Which is so painfully obvious now that I've had some time alone to think. Something I never took much time to do before."

It's true. Kendra surrounded herself with acquaintances and boyfriends in succession. She quantified her self-worth by her social network.

Kendra sees my answer and smiles sadly. "I think we choose people who mirror our own insecurities, either in contrast or collusion. My biggest fear was always that I was weak, that I wasn't a good person—"

I start to protest.

"Lemme finish," she says. "I play tough. But I've always suspected that I lack conviction, that when push came to shove I couldn't make the hard decisions you and Isabel make. That I wasn't quietly brave like Mina. And I knew I wasn't a woman who could be alone. I wanted to seal the deal on that one as soon as possible."

"But Kendra, you're not *pretending* to be strong. You—"

"Well, that's kind of the amazing thing. The worst, most humiliating thing that I could imagine was getting pregnant and having my theoretically soon-to-be fiancé insist on abortion. But it forced me to see my choices as my own, apart from anyone else in the world. Which is—well, scary, isn't it?"

Kendra looks at me and waits. Is she right? Will I be choosing Remy out of fear? Is he a mirror of my faults or a Band-Aid? What am I scared of? I'm scared of failing. I'm scared of being a nobody. I'm scared of living an ordinary life.

I sigh. I look out over the twisted city, the dusty chaos that doesn't scare me one bit. But in the fading light, it does seem distant and lonely. Being alone—is that the scariest thing?

"Come on, let's get ready for dinner."

chapter

54

IT ISN'T SAFE TO TAKE CABS AT NIGHT IN Honduras. It's an unwritten code, Ana Maria says. During the day, fine. But at night, theft is at their discretion. Now she tells me.

But that is how we come to be chauffeured by Ana Maria's personal driver, deposited gracefully in front of the restaurant. Kendra might have overdone it—she looks like she's going to a Manhattan gala. I look down at the trash in the street as she glides over it in her Manolos. But she doesn't seem to care. Actually, she seems elated. I realize now that I may *have* thought Kendra snobby and a bit, well, shallow. It's fascinating watching your best friends metamorphose. Or grow up? That's what it was. And I was changing, too, wasn't I?

The restaurant is a bustling oasis of light in the dark city. Salsa music greets us merrily in the street. Lanterns hang from the awning around the patio. People of all ages are bunched together in groups, laughing loudly.

It's not *exactly* like a record scratching to a stop when we enter, but pretty close. A gorgeous black woman and a freckled redheaded albino chick. We must look like an American TV commercial in 3D.

"Samantha! Over here!" Ana Maria gives me a big hug, and the room breathes a collective *aha,* the mystery solved.

Ana Maria was one of my roommates in college. It's fantastic to see her in her element. This is her friend's restaurant opening, and she is obviously the proud hostess.

If I had to guess, I would've thought it was a wedding. Everyone knows everybody, moving around the room like Cuban casino, a group version of salsa dancing. She sits Kendra down in a seat next to a handsome guy and then moves his equally attractive friend over so we're seated boy girl, boy girl. Kendra cocks an eyebrow at me and I laugh. Ana Maria winks and takes off to continue her duties, matchmaking apparently her specialty. Had I told her about Remy? That's odd if I hadn't mentioned him.

The attractive friend next to me pipes up. "Antonio. *¿Como te llamas, bella?*" His warm eyes dig into mine.

"Samantha, *Que—*" I catch sight of the panic in Ken-

dra's face. Her idea of a dinner party did not involve practicing her high school Spanish.

Antonio notices immediately. "And your friend here?"
he says in accented but clean English, turning to Kendra.
"Did you also go to school with Ana Maria?"

Of course—wealthy Honduran kids are sent to the
American school and then off to American universities.
Kendra beams in relief. "Kendra Jones. Nope, I'm just a
visitor. One night only, boys."

Antonio laughs along with his friend, whom he then
nudges and points at. "Armando," he says in introduction.

Kendra turns to Armando. "Hi there."

Antonio picks up a fancy shot glass next to my water
glass and pours a shot of expensive tequila. He raises his
own glass in toast.

Kendra again looks nervous.

"Kendra doesn't drink," I say, and throw mine back in
one gulp.

Two too many tequila shots later, and everybody at the
party is my long-lost old friend.

There's Señora Lopez, who is the aunt of Luisa, who is
one of the two owners of the restaurant. She makes the
best pupusas in town and I am having breakfast at her
house on Wednesday.

There's Charlie, whose real name is Marco Reuben
Ernesto Cesar Diaz, who is the cousin of the boyfriend
of Luisa's partner Mercedes. His father manufactures corn

chips, the equivalent of Doritos in the U.S. He's insisted we join them next weekend on his boat. Kendra is jealous.

José owns a restaurant around the corner. They have better soup, but the food tonight *is* divine, he admits.

Lorna thinks I dance better salsa than Mercedes.

Paco wants to take me shopping on Thursday.

Juan thinks Antonio and I make an adorable duo.

Ah, and Antonio.

Antonio is a breath of spring air. He is ice cream with whipped cream. He is s'mores over a campfire. He dotes on me all night. He isn't shy—he interjects jokes at all the right moments, he dances seductively, he laughs heartily. It's just that he watches me, appreciative. He presses for more stories. He thinks I live a beautiful, honorable, enviable life. In his eyes, I am powerful, brave and experienced. A feeling spreads through me warmer than the tequila, warmer than the crowded dance floor. The feeling is confidence. I hadn't even noticed that I'd lost it until tonight. I love my life. When did I start to judge it so unfairly?

It is well after three when we head out to the waiting car. Antonio walks with me. Kendra slips into the backseat, leaving me conspicuously alone with him.

"You are very surprising, Samantha. Will I see you soon?"

I look at his face in the soft glow of the lanterns. They are being blown out, one by one. I can still see his eyes, glinting in happiness. He is so young, meaning he is my age. But there is a confident maturity about him, very un-American in the best of ways. He is gentle, kind.

He raises an eyebrow, teasing me about the pause. I sigh and his face falters.

"I have—" I hesitate. I have no idea what I was going to say next. I have a fiancé? I have to think? I have a free day tomorrow?

"I have to go," I say, kiss him lightning-quick on the cheek and duck down into the car next to Kendra.

Kendra says nothing as we drive away.

"What?" I ask.

"Nothing. You're amazing."

Suspicious, I study her expression. She means it. Sincerely.

chapter

55

KENDRA WAKES ME EARLIER THAN MY tequila-laden brain would have preferred.

"What exactly is it that you have in mind?" I grumble.

"A hike. Sightseeing. You tell me. My plane doesn't leave till afternoon."

That is how I find myself hiking through a cloud forest.

Kendra is a bundle of glee. She hikes ahead of me, briskly, in awe of the landscape. "It is so green. It's like the world is trying to make up, in one day, for eight years of New York's infinity of concrete."

She stops to caress a tree trunk completely covered in green moss, decorated with twisting vines sprouting big, fat, moist leaves of green.

She's right. It's greener than pea soup, greener than Ireland. Actually, green is the *only* color. There isn't even much brown to speak of. The whole forest is like a unicorn fantasy movie, done up to perfection by a Hollywood set designer with a bucket of glittery green paint.

Kendra spins around. "God, I've really been missing the point, haven't I?"

I rub my throbbing head. At least there's no sun. The tops of the trees disappear into mist. "Of what?"

Kendra laughs. "Of everything!" From the ground, she picks up a palm frond larger than my head. "Maybe I should just quit my job and live your life."

I groan, remembering Isabel's similar statement. But the groan is a reflex. I'm swelling with some other feeling at Kendra's words. What is it? Pride? Trust is the closest thing I can think of. The feeling of calm that comes from simple trust in oneself. It feels like making the right decision, choosing the right path, returning to a remote location without a map. I take a deep breath, my headache burning off like fog at the beach.

Kendra tickles me with the palm frond. "You're fearless, girl. Teach me."

Poof, the calm is gone. "I'm not fearless."

Kendra drops the frond but continues to smile. "Oh yeah? What are *you* afraid of, Sam?"

We pushed it with the hike. I made the cab wait out front while we dashed inside to grab Kendra's suitcases and pack her muddy sneakers into plastic bags.

Now I'm watching her pay her exit taxes at the airport. It's hard to see Kendra go—disappear into customs with one last wave—forcing me into alone time with my thoughts.

Kendra was a perfect sieve, helping me filter and sort through my decision. But now—whew!—thoughts bounce around in my head like roiling soup molecules. It's like I spilled a puzzle on the floor, some pieces joined, some aching to combine, but my eyes can only flit over them, no clue where to start. And there's a timer ticking away. I'm sure I'll speak to Remy soon, presumably eager to spend the rest of my life with him.

Now my stomach's the one that's churning. What did Lynette tell me once? The right decision makes your heart race, but leaves your stomach out of it. Whatever. It's probably the hangover. And my heart *is* racing.

I turn finally to exit the airport, leaving the cool, clean building for the muck and the heat. I start sweating immediately but with the crawling sensation of a cold sweat, a fever.

In the cab I take out Mina's journal, tucked securely into my backpack. I flip through the pages, desperate for solace. At the end I notice all the blank pages. I can't help but find this sad—the missing pages of Mina's life with us—as I run my fingers over her final entries.

...a long and happy life, Samantha Wheland...if it's the last thing I do.

I put my fingers to my lips, chew on a fingernail, then sigh and fish a pen out of my backpack. *"Forced me to see my choices as my own,"* Kendra said. *"Apart from anyone else in the world."*

I make a list.

Pros
Successful
Wealthy
Handsome
Instant life

Cons
Controlling
Arrogant
Flirt
Makes me insecure

I bite my lip until it stings, considering the list. Every positive has its negative counterpart. A flip side of every coin. It's true of all people, I suppose. Boyfriends have always admired my conviction and bemoaned my stubbornness. "You don't get one without the other, m'dear," I've always told them. With passion comes rage; with intensity comes anxiety; with fire comes chaos. One particularly fiery relationship ended with me laundry-listing my complaints: his infidelity, gambling, temper.

He looked up at me and grinned. "You're no walk in the park, baby."

I look at the list again. Do these sound like good husband qualities to you? Isabel's voice rings out, the sound of the ocean behind it. I remember something else Kendra said. Lazy and in a hurry. A dangerous combination.

The cab screeches to a stop, knocking the journal to the dirty floor. I pay the cabbie three times what he asks for, and rescue the journal. I tuck it in my backpack and drag my other suitcase out the door as the guard opens the gate.

Oh my God!

Remy steps out from the shadows of my doorway. Remy in the middle of dusty hot Honduran concrete, in a tailored linen suit and shiny shoes.

"Finally," he says.

My suitcase smacks the concrete. It isn't a daydream. He's real! The list evaporates from my mind. I run and tackle him, jump into his arms and wrap my legs around his waist.

"How did you—" I want to ask, but he buries me in a hot scratchy kiss.

"I get what I want," he says, and squeezes my waist. He sets me down and puts a hand on my lower back to steer me toward the door.

I open the door with trembling fingers and Remy follows with my suitcase. The instant the door closes, he peels off my shirt. He takes my face in both his hands and brings my eyes to his. "You are impossible, Samantha Wheland. Making me follow you to this ridiculous place." He kisses me angrily. "I love you."

I inhale sharply.

Remy falls to his knees and buries his face in my navel. He kisses my belly button and either side of my hips. He runs his tongue down the middle of my stomach. He unzips my jeans and plants a kiss just above the rim of my panties. I'm melting to the floor as Remy undoes my bra. He positions me on his lap and I squeeze my legs around his hips again as Remy stands up and carries me into the bedroom. He flings me onto the bed, rips off my jeans and panties in one fell swoop, then steps back to study me.

"God, look at you, how you turn me on. You make me feel young."

And then he pounces on me, working his tongue over every inch of my skin, sucking in some places so hard there will be marks. The linen suit is sweaty and rough against my inflamed skin. I almost squeal when he bites down on my nipple, but in the same instant he cups his hand between my legs. He lowers his head to kiss each of my hipbones. And then my inner thighs. As his hot breath and soft lips take the place of his fingers on my pulsing skin, I hug my thighs around his head and hear myself groan, "I love you, I love you, I love you...."

chapter

56

IT'S DARK, AND REMY'S NOT IN BED. THERE'S
a TV on in the living room. I don't have a TV. I sit up
and grab a robe.

Remy is sitting in a plastic chair with his laptop, sipping
ice water and watching some old French movie. When I
tiptoe over and kiss the top of his head, he reaches around
and squeezes my ass. Then he points at the screen and
laughs. No subtitles.

"I'm starving!" I say. "Should we go have a nice dinner
to celebrate?"

Remy doesn't look up. He shakes his head and waves
a hand at me. "Where would we have a nice dinner in
this country, ma' chérie? Can you cook something? I saw

there is chicken in the congélateur." He puts a finger to his lips as if I were about to speak. He points at the movie again and laughs. "Hilare! And there is some, eh, garlic and pasta. You could cook this."

Yeah, or you could. Sigh. He did come to see me, after all. He came all this way, as a surprise. It's so romantic. Or arrogant, Isabel would say.

On my way to the kitchen, I see a bottle of vodka on the counter. I take a closer look at Remy's glass of water. Remy always orders vodka on the rocks. He will fill your life's bowl, a voice says in my head.

Seemingly sensing what is about to come out of my mouth, Remy says, "Come here, baby," and pats his lap. He sets down his drink so I can sit. Then he reaches into my robe and fondles my breast. I feel him get hard beneath my legs.

"Mmm," Remy growls, and finally he takes his eyes off the movie.

After another round of melting, pounding sex, I curl up next to him in bed. He shifts away.

"It's too hot, baby."

I forgot that he always says that.

"So, how long can you stay?" My head is piling up with activities we can do together. We can go hiking in the cloud forest, horseback ride on the beaches near La Ceiba. Maybe we can take a canoe into La Mosquitia. I still have a few days until the residency. Maybe I could even start a few days late.

"Just tonight, chérie. My work. I cannot be away from Paris now. We leave in the morning."

"You came all this way to woo me for one night?" Did he just say we?

"To woo you? You are too adorable, chérie. I came to rescue you, princesse. To take you back with me. I thought about it—you don't have to do this residency thing now. We'll get your work into all the galleries in France. My friends own them. And you'll have plenty of time to paint, or whatever you call it, at my house. It's not like you'll have to worry about money anymore, angel." He tweaks my chin. "You can have everything you want." He kisses my forehead and then my nose. I turn my head before he reaches my lips.

"You want me to leave with you tomorrow? To Paris? Have the wedding there and stay there?"

I try to imagine a fancy wedding in Paris, the girls in French couture, holding lilies. But for some reason, all I can think about is Cesar Guerra. Of course that makes me think about Jesse and now the image of Arshan's naked butt pops into my mind.

"Oh my God, I have to tell you," I say suddenly. I can't help myself, I have to share it. "This morning we caught Arshan and Jesse having sex!"

"Which one is Jesse?"

"Isabel's mom. Isn't that awesome? Gross, but awesome, right?"

Remy groans. "I think I would have to agree with gross."

I laugh and throw my arm across his chest. He nudges me away again. "It's five hundred degrees in this room without air-conditioning, baby."

For some reason, now his first comment annoys me more. "Wait? Don't you think that will be us in twenty years? Still madly in love and doing it in the afternoon?"

Remy laughs again and plants a soggy kiss on my cheek. "Your idealism is adorable."

Uh-oh, I'm hearing voices again. You will give him your youth, your idealism, and your capacity for hope.

Remy is looking at me, studying me like a Sunday buffet. He touches my hair, traces my freckles. He glides a finger between my breasts. He grabs my hair, pulls my head back and digs his teeth into my neck.

Electricity courses the length of my body, and I automatically give into the heat that threatens to burn me up. I try to imagine a happy life wrapped in that embrace. Instead, I feel a surge of panic and a premonition of regret.

"Remy."

"Mmm-hmm," Remy says, biting my shoulder.

"No, Remy, stop."

"Mmm, you don't tell me to stop." He growls and thrusts his fingers between my legs. The sensation is overpowering. Delicious and searing. Dangerous. Everything you could ever want. In a lover.

"Remy, stop!" I pull away, panting, and scoot to the corner of the bed.

Remy looks shocked. Then he smiles. The smile that melts me like Hershey's Kisses in the summer sun. The danger is gone, and there is safety enveloped in that smile and in those eyes. Eyes that have seen it all, seen a decade and a half more than mine.

I feel I'm going to scream. Shriek.

"I need—" I put my hands out instinctively, defending the buffer of space between us. "I need a minute. I don't feel well. I'm going to get some air. Just—" I inch away from him like a scuttling crab, claws hovering ridiculously between us "—stay."

The steamy air outside is flirting with cold. It feels heavenly. The chill scrubs my skin of the itchy heat from the bedroom. My heart stops thundering against my rib cage, and settles into a distant drumming. Just a second. I need a second to think. My brain's doing that spinning thing and there is the definite impression of bathwater being sucked down a drain. I wish I could roller-skate.

What is my problem? Just say yes. To all of it.

"Yes." I whisper it, trying it out on the city. She blinks, streetlights flickering, but doesn't answer.

Just say yes, Samantha, and everything will click into motion. There will be a wedding. And children. Every burden will be shared, some will simply vanish. There will be money and plans and routine. I will be legitimized. I will be successful. I will be loved. There will be sex and kissing and a succession of "good morning, honey" and "good night, baby." No more worrying or wondering if you'll find the one, because you'll be one of the ones that chose. Done. Just like that. Just accept and it will be done—the deciding—done and over.

So why am I crying?

The balcony railing heats up under the death grip of my fingers. I hang on tight but drop to my knees. I peer through the balcony bars, a comforting prison for my rushing thoughts. Mina left me. My mother left me. I have the vacation club, sure. But really, I take care of myself. It's a fact I've always prided myself on, but now the thought is exhausting. All these years, all these adventures. All the new decisions to be made, the arrangements, new people, new places—all of it alone. The weight of it—the weight of being responsible for my life story, my make or break success as an artist, my aging eggs, society's expectations—makes me feel like ostrich-ing out. Head in the sand. What if I can't do it? What if I end up a failure? What if I end up old, unsuccessful and unlovable?

I let go of the railing and lean my forehead against the bars, my eyes squeezed shut. Like Kendra said, we were going to have to start making decisions like this—all alone. This thought makes the air temperature feel another ten degrees colder. A breeze kicks up on the balcony and spits dirt across my bare legs, scratchy leaves scurrying across my thighs like mice, catching under my knees.

My eyes fly open. Caught under my left knee is a maple leaf. An orange and red and yellow maple leaf, a sunrise in the middle of the night. When I make to grab it, a breeze snatches it up and sends it over the edge of the balcony.

No! I shoot my hand out between the metal and glue my forehead to the bars, watching it flutter away.

A rustling tugs at my back. I turn to see the wind whipping up a minicyclone on the balcony. I gasp. A small tornado of maple leaves dances beside me. I watch them—yellow and orange and dazzling red—as they spin round and round together, seemingly laughing. Around they go, shifting with the breeze, colliding and rising. As I watch it my tears turn to laughter. The breeze is warm now and it encircles my shoulders like the familiar hug of a childhood best friend. The twister moves closer, a spinning top that pauses next to my knees. With a jitter, the leaves drop into my lap. I laugh aloud and shake my head. Then I look up at the stars above the city.

"Thanks, Em."

I pick out a red leaf and twirl it between my fingers, smiling.

The balcony door opens, making me jump.

Remy steps onto the patio with one hand behind his back. Without a word, he kneels down beside me. He holds out a green velvet box. I am transfixed. Remy seems to notice for the first time I'm not wearing the cheap ring he gave me. His confidence wobbles, but then he smiles. Still holding the leaf between my fingers, I watch him open the box to reveal an obscene yellow diamond glinting in the streetlight.

I'm an idiot. I'm a complete and utter idiot. But here it goes—"Remy, I want to marry you—"

Remy beams, slips the ring from its perch.

"For all the wrong reasons," I continue.

He frowns. I inhale. Steady does it.

"What you're offering me—" I can't look him in the eyes "—what an offer." I focus on the leaf, rubbing the smooth stem between my thumb and forefinger. "It's everything anybody should want. Security. A family. Fame and fortune." Tears. No. "And a lifetime of getting to say 'I'm married, I was chosen, I'm not alone.'"

Remy doesn't say anything right away. He watches the leaf, too. When he finally speaks, his voice is sad and haggard. "Those are very good reasons, Samantha. What other reasons are there?"

"Fear. If I married you, it would be because I'm afraid I'm running out of time. Because I'm afraid that I'm not enough on my own or that I can't achieve my dreams for myself."

Remy inches closer to me. "I have worked hard for many years for everything I have. Why not let me pull you up to that level?"

"It's not the same level without the work."

Remy smiles, but now his smile is cold. "You are too smart for your own good, you know that, princesse? Come here." He grabs me before I see it coming. He wraps me up in his arms and they are so warm. He whispers into my ear, "I love you, Samantha Wheland. I swear that I will do right by you and your dreams."

I freeze at those words, and feel the weight of sixty years bear down on me. I see Jesse's gray eyes meet Cesar Guerra's in a crowded nightclub, Lynette's red dress moving through a sea of screams. I see Arshan throw a rose on Maliheh's grave.

Now the tears come, hot and wet on my cheeks and spilling over onto Remy's shoulder. I know how cold it will feel outside his embrace. But for once I have clarity.

Kendra was wrong. I was wrong. We don't make decisions alone and apart from the world. I am more than my name and my individual lifetime. I am the daughter of a mother who left and a father who never forgave me for it. But I am a product of Jesse's laughter in the face of sorrow, of Lynette and Cornell's struggle to love against all odds. I will affect Arshan's battle with fate. I am indebted to the esteem Kendra holds me in. To the time that Isabel has invested in me. To the vows that Mina made me take.

We are all entangled like a field of grass, like water molecules in a cresting wave, like lines in a poem.

I am indebted to myself, to the gift of life that I won back. I will have to look at myself in the mirror of this world I chose. I am responsible now for the outcome. I will be worth only as much I believe I am.

"I'm so sorry, Remy." I kiss his forearm even as he stiffens and starts to edge away. "But I have to do right by myself." Remy drops his arms. I straighten up to face the chill.

Now it's time to stand up and walk to the door. Come on, Samantha. Get up. Get. Up.

I slide open the balcony door and see my cell phone inside on the chair. "And besides, after the residency, I'm moving to New York. Kendra, Isabel and I are going to have a baby."

★ ★ ★ ★ ★

QUESTIONS FOR DISCUSSION

1. The book opens by saying birth and death are uncontrollable. Does the book disprove this by the end? How literally did you take this notion? To what extent can we control our existence and shape our reality using our consciousness?

2. Do you think Samantha made the right decision about Remy and about her life path? How is her decision representative of the state of the modern woman? Women have more choices than ever in terms of their career and relationship roles. Do you think that is something exhilarating and liberating, as Jesse and Lynette might say, or do you think it's bound to be overwhelming, as Samantha feels it is for much of the book?

3. What did you make of Ahari? Is he a shaman? A protector? A spiritual being? Do you believe that there are people amongst us that can tap into a supernatural realm?

4. At one point, Samantha feels a sense of contentment about her unlikely family. How does the book define family? What family have you been a part of that wasn't related by blood, but no less important? If to raise a child means to nurture them, feed them, guide them and educate them—who "raised" you?

5. The vacationers have a tense discussion about the Garifuna as they drive through the villages. Which side did you find yourself taking? How else is the issue of race addressed in the novel? How would racial relations have changed or not changed in the time from Lynette's childhood to her daughter's childhood?

6. Kendra faces a heartbreaking decision when she discovers her pregnancy. What did you think of the way she made her ultimate decision? Do you agree with Kendra's assertion that ultimately we make decisions all alone or with Samantha's conclusion that the opposite is true—that our decisions are tied to the important people in our lives?

7. The book casts several major historical events—the Iran Revolution, U.S. Civil Rights, and political upheaval in Panama—through the lens of personal experience. We all experience history this way. What is the book's message about history? What, if any, is the difference between your elders' experience of historical events—Civil Rights, for example—and the experience of those younger than you of events in their lifetime, such as 9/11?

8. Religion is touched on only lightly in this book. What do you make of Samantha's metaphysical journey with Mina? Is there a way to make it fit with

classical notions of religion? Did that bother you in any way? Or do think there is a way to combine science and religion?

9. In Joseph Campbell's notion of the monomyth (also known as the hero's journey), the hero travels from his or her everyday world into an extraordinary realm, then must fight to return after having gained powers that he or she can then impart on others. In what ways does this apply to Samantha's journey?

10. The physics that Samantha references in the novel—the Copenhagen Theory, the Many Worlds Theory, etc.—are actual, well-known principles of quantum physics. Would you have been happy without any kind of scientific explanation about Samantha and Mina's reunion world? To what extent do you believe parallel universes and the power of consciousness can explain the mysteries of our world?

For further discussion and resources,
please visit the author's website at:
www.deborahcloyed.com

A little girl, all alone, with a note that reads 'Please look after me'. What would you do?

Four years ago, nineteen-year-old Travis Brown made a choice: to raise his newborn daughter on his own. So far he's kept her safe, but now he's lost his job, his home and the money in his wallet is all he has.

As things spiral out of control Travis is offered a lifeline. A one-time offer to commit a crime for his daughter's sake. Even if it means leaving her behind. Even if it means losing her.

What would a good father do?

www.mirabooks.co.uk

*'What was so extraordinary
about her? What did she
have that I'm so horribly
deficient in?'*

As your husband grieves his mistress,
you find yourself falling for the family she left behind,
but they don't really know you.

You can go back to the husband who loves you
second best or be content to live as a pale
imitation of another woman.

Two paths, two lies.
Which way would you turn?

www.mirabooks.co.uk

You have a choice—
But can you live with it?

Your best friend has suffered a devastating brain
injury. Alone and grieving, you turn to the
only person who understands the pain.

Her husband.

When Joelle discovers she's carrying Liam's baby,
she's torn between grief and unexpected joy.
How can she share her secret?

Tell him and face a lifetime of guilt or lie and
deny her unborn baby a father?

www.mirabooks.co.uk

One tragic secret
Four lives changed forever
Only you know
Can you keep a secret?

I don't know how to tell you what I did...

An unfinished letter was hidden amongst Tara and
Emerson's best friend's things after her suicide.

Noelle was the woman they entrusted to deliver their
precious babies into the world, a beloved friend.
Her suicide shocked them both. But the legacy
revealed in her letter could destroy them.

www.mirabooks.co.uk